MW01166979

The Garden Gnome

Theory of Magic - Book 1

By Jeff McIntyre

For Mike,
    Thanks for all the great
videos. Hope you enjoy my
Flight of fantasy.

Loki
Press

Copyright © 2022 by Jeff McIntyre

ISBN 979-8-9868177-0-5

jeff-mcintyre.com

Loki Press
lokipress.com

Cover design by 100covers.com

To my mother, for encouraging my love of reading

To Jacqueline and Jo, for helping me discover Sci-Fi and Fantasy

To Art, for being the best storyteller I've ever met

And lastly, to my incredible wife, for encouraging me to write and enjoying the ride.

Never boring...

Prologue

An old man trudged up the side of the mountain. His steps are slow, methodical. The steps of a man who understands the limitations of his own body. He didn't think of himself as old, but he certainly knew that this old body would betray him if he gave it a chance. So carefully he trod, avoiding broken bough and cracked stone.

A passerby might be confused at the sight of an old man clad in such finery ascending the peak of a fire mountain. His long gray robe, at first glance, seemed simple enough. On closer inspection, one could make out the faintest hints of subtle silver thread woven into the fabric in complex fantastical patterns. It was either a simple design entirely at random, or the most deliberate work imaginable. In either case, it would have taken someone skilled with thread and needle months of toil to produce. The trek up the mountain was taking its toll on the robe's hem. Its length spoke to being worn in some far more civilized venue and certainly not intended to be worn on a rugged hike.

The man paused, breathing heavily, and leaned on a gnarled wooden staff. The surface of the wood was coated and polished to the point it practically seemed to glow with the reflection of any ambient light. The red hue cast by the cauldron above gave the staff an eerie, menacing glint that pulsed in time with the roiling of the volcano.

The man himself looked haggard. Hard lines in his face made him seem stoic, almost statue-like. But laugh lines at the corners of his eyes and a mischievous twinkle in his deep blue eyes humanized him. Long gray hair bound with a leather tie swept past his shoulders, and an even longer, almost white beard, while neatly trimmed, was allowed to flow free.

With a grunt, he resumed walking, eventually reaching a boulder-strewn clearing that overlooked the heart of the volcano. His beard blew chaotically about his face as he crested the top of the mountain.

Smoke rose swiftly from the cauldron below. The massive pool of lava roiled and bubbled as though a great beast thrashed just beneath the surface. Smoke and ash swirled through the air obscuring his view of the far side.

The Garden Gnome

He sat down wearily on a boulder and sighed with deep relief. His mind drifted like the ash on the winds, contemplating endings and beginnings. He had journeyed far to reach this place. Despite all that he had seen, all the places he had been, he had never seen a fire mountain up close. This had been his longest and greatest adventure of them all. And yet a small part of him wished it would be the last. How could he possibly accomplish more than he had in this long lifetime? He doubted this would be the last; fate always seemed to have plans for him.

As he sat contemplating the misadventures of past and the vagaries of future, a shadow slithered across the ground behind him.

"What are you doing, you old fool?" a strong female voice yelled out from the darkness.

His shoulders slumped. "I had hoped you would not follow me. It is time my dear, this cycle is run, and I am worn out. I'm not used to growing old." he replied wearily.

"It is NOT time. I won't let you!" she roared. "You must not give up. Please don't leave me… I'm not ready." Her voice trailed off weakly.

The old man rose unsteadily to his feet with a strong wince of pain. "Would you have me rot away to nothingness in this old sack? Would you be that cruel?" His body shuddered with a sharp, heaving cough. His voice now a dry whisper, "My love, let me go. You know as well as I that the end is never the end, and I am tired. I deserve a rest, don't I?"

Heaving sobs came from the darkness, he longed to reach out to her, but lifetimes of experience told him that that would be the last thing she would want. His heart tore in two listening to her mourn him, but this time he wanted to end on his own terms. Fate had robbed him of his chance to say goodbye to her so many times he could no longer keep count.

"Go, if you must, but do not make me watch." she sobbed.

"I would not ask that of you. I'm not sure that I could bear it. Go now and leave me to it. I will return as I always do, and we will find one another."

The shadow retreated. "I love you," he called out to her. There was no response at first, but after a moment, as if from a great distance, he thought he faintly heard, "You'd better."

He chuckled quietly, slowly straightened to his full height, and turned to face the pool of lava. He breathed deeply, took two steps forward, and keeled into the cauldron without a sound.

Chapter 1

"Tony! Get your butt down here and eat your breakfast; you'll miss the bus!" Daniel Fitzroy yelled upstairs as he flipped a couple of dollar pancakes onto a waiting plate and poured a full glass of milk. He shooed Cleo off the counter. The orange tabby seemed unimpressed by his feeble attempt to remove her from her queendom of the moment and slowly moved to one of the stools and off the counter as if it was her intended destination all along. "Morning Dad, morning Cleo."

Tony piped as he avalanched down the stairs into the kitchen. Tony plowed into breakfast with all the vigor you would expect from a hungry ten-year-old. "HY MM," he mumbled around a mouthful of hotcake as a short, well-dressed woman with long dark hair walked into the kitchen, staring intently at her mobile phone.

"Don't speak with your mouth full, munchkin," Sophia tisked at him as she strolled by, pausing briefly to muss his hair and walked over to Daniel, set down her phone, and stretched up to give her tall husband a peck on the cheek. "SRE MM," Tony replied as he continued to shovel in breakfast with gusto.

"What excitement do you have lined up today, dears?" Sophia asked as she pulled a travel mug out of a cabinet and filled it with piping hot coffee.

Tony leaped off his chair, ran over to the secretary, and gently scooped up a colorful conglomeration of sticks and foam balls. "I get to show my solar system in science class!"

"Well, I get to sit through a bunch of undecided undergrads presenting their mid-term masterpieces on Mesopotamian cultures." Daniel's eyes glazed over, and then he visibly shuddered in mock horror. "Hopefully, no treatises on Conan this time."

Sophia grinned at her husband and son. Her son's boundless energy and her husband's witty yet endearing sarcasm energized her. She contemplated the two men in her life as she slowly sipped her coffee. Daniel was tall, devastatingly handsome (to her mind, at least) in a midwestern farm-boy kind of way. Sandy brown hair, ice blue Scandinavian eyes above a decidedly average nose framed by a spattering of freckles. He had an angular jaw leading to a narrow chin that she absolutely adored. In college, he had been almost unhealthily skinny, but thanks to her cooking, he had the slightest hint of a belly. Her son was a half-sized version of her husband with the cherubic cheeks of youth. "Well, I get to enjoy the company of the CEO today for our monthly skip level."

Daniel grinned at her "Teacher's pet. Say hi to Rebecca for me."

Sophia gave him an exaggerated dirty look. "Rebecca obviously sees what a valuable asset I am. Honestly, I think it's lonely at the top, and she just enjoys talking to me. We spend half the time talking about important things and the other half chatting. It's refreshing to see that the woman in charge is a human and not a machine."

A loud screech of well-worn brakes on a large yellow tube filled with screaming kids could be heard coming to a halt in front of the house. Tony leaped from his chair and bolted towards the door. "Crap! Ms. Kendall will leave without me!"

Daniel took three long strides and scooped up a Millennium Falcon shaped backpack off the floor and the foam solar system off the counter and followed Tony out the front door. "Tony, are we forgetting something?"

Tony performed a high-speed about-face and came hurtling back, snagging the bag, and gingerly taking the sculpture from his father's outstretched hands. Daniel snatched Tony in a quick hug and then pushed him back on his way. As Tony ran towards the school bus, Daniel yelled at his retreating back, "Have a good day. I'll be picking you up after school."

Jeff McIntyre

He waved at Ms. Kendall, who smiled and waved back. She glared at Tony and shook a disapproving finger at him as he leaped onto the bus. With the sound of grinding gears and screaming children, the bus lurched off down the road, headed for its next passenger. Daniel smiled at the careening bus and then headed back into the house.

Sophia intercepted him in the entryway with coffee in one hand and phone in the other. She smiled at her husband, waiting expectantly. Daniel grabbed her around the waist and leaned in for a long passionate kiss. After they both came up for breath, he smiled at her as he let her go. "Have a nice day, dear." Sophia smiled back at him, side-stepped around him, and replied over her shoulder, "You too, babe." She suddenly backstepped and smacked him in the right butt cheek with the heel of her foot. She hummed cheerily to herself as she sauntered out the front door.

Chapter 2

Leo Schafer stood at the bathroom mirror, carefully trimming around his mustache and beard. His lean cheeks and the tendons in his neck sometimes made it a little challenging to get a clean shave. The nearly black trimmings fell into the sink as the electric razor hummed. He turned his head from side to side, looking for any strays he might have missed.

Content, he set the razor on the charger and took stock of his appearance. While his facial hair was just as dark as it had always been, he could make out a few stray grays working their way into the hair on his head. He stepped back from the mirror a few feet trying to make out the gray and failed. No need to start coloring his hair, at least not yet.

He patted the tight muscles of his stomach, quite proud of his six-pack. Although these days, it was looking more like a four-pack. He pinched some of the excess skin and made a promise to himself to get back up to his regular workout routine.

Jeff McIntyre

He walked out of the bathroom and into the closet to pick out some clothes. He pulled on an undershirt and a light blue long-sleeved button-down that he was particularly fond of. He grabbed a pair of khakis, but his day started with a teleconference, so there was no need to start the day with pants. That could wait until he headed into the office.

As he headed down the hall toward the kitchen. He kissed his fingers and then passed the kiss to a black and white picture of a woman in a classic burlesque outfit posing for the camera. His little morning ritual for Granny Tina completed; he strolled into the kitchen and started the coffee maker. He fired up his laptop on the kitchen table while he waited for the burbling to stop. Normally he'd take a call like this from work, but it was early, and he had in-person appointments after this before heading into the office.

He filled a large travel mug with the steaming brew from the pot and added a generous helping of flavored creamer. It was not his typical mocha latte, but it would have to do. He sipped the coffee and skimmed through his notes as he waited for the video conference to begin.

As much as he enjoyed his job covering technology news, he didn't enjoy dealing with pure scientists. They were frequently arrogant, evasive, introverted, self-conscious, awkward, or some bizarre combination of all five.

He much preferred technologists and entrepreneurs. They were idiosyncratic in their own way but far more fun and engaging to deal with. Plus, they usually had fantastic expense accounts to entertain the press with. Today's call will undoubtedly be dry as hell. Filled with facts about the particle accelerator, the staff, and their accomplishments, but no matter how much he prods, they will not speculate or exaggerate. They will most likely only offer information that they have pre-scripted, and he'll have to fast talk them into revealing anything truly useful.

This was mostly a pointless exercise; Leo was a good journalist; he had done the research on all the technical details related to their upcoming test. This was mostly just going through the motions. He was far more interested in the drama and speculation surrounding the lab than in the actual test.

The science was way beyond his ability to understand, but he knew the talking points. Over a decade ago, Fermilab had shuttered their long-running particle accelerator experiment called the Tevatron. For many years it had been the premier accelerator in the world, but as technology advanced, it was no longer feasible to financially support it, so it had been shut down.

In the past few years, Fermilab had quietly upgraded the Tevatron using recent advances in materials science as well as some lessons learned from CERN's Large Hadron Collider (LHC). Then a few months ago, they had announced that HERBERT was nearing completion of its preliminary testing and that they would soon begin power up in preparation for full power collisions.

The High Energy Reverse Bose Einstein Relativity Test (HERBERT) acronym was a bit of a stretch; he suspected that the author of the foundational paper that spawned the experiment was a bit of a Dune fan. To the layman, this seemed like just another particle accelerator test. Leo knew enough to understand that HERBERT had every possibility of eclipsing the LHC.

The particle physics community always tried to drum up excitement for whatever new experiment they had cooking in an attempt to get the public at large interested in what they were doing, but since how many new exotic particles were discovered didn't typically affect stock prices or provide any technological advancements in consumer electronics most people had gotten quite bored with these types of announcements.

This one, however, had drawn the attention of a small but well-funded and influential organization called Nadir. Until the public announcement of this test, Leo had never heard of them, but he had seen their influence.

He wanted desperately to dig into them and their objections to HERBERT, but his editor was adamant that he not give this group the publicity they were obviously seeking. Nadir smelled like a religious organization, but near as he could tell, their membership consisted of people from a wide variety of races, backgrounds, and ethos. Their one unifying belief seemed to be a fear that laboratories conducting high-energy particle physics research were dabbling in things they didn't understand and that their research was endangering the public on a scale equal to the nuclear testing done in the south pacific in the fifties.

This same type of organization cropped up when CERN first fired up the LHC and proved to be unfounded. Groups came out of the woodwork to claim that these tests would open miniature black holes that would destroy the earth. If it were true, that would be a legitimate concern, but the scientific community scoffed at these claims, and as it turned out, the scientists were right.

Leo's musing was interrupted by the sound of the video conference connecting. A small conference room popped into view with two stereotypical scientists, complete with white lab coats, name tags, and instrument-filled breast pockets. Leo recognized the head of the project, Dr. Henry "Hank" Lee sitting on the left and one of his department heads, Inez something or other, sitting on the right.

"Hello, I am Leo Schafer. I'm a science and technology writer for the Chicago Tribune. I really appreciate you taking the time to talk to me about your upcoming experiment."

Hank nodded at the introduction and then gestured to himself. "A pleasure to meet you, Mr. Schafer. I am Dr. Henry Lee, and this is my colleague Dr. Inez Ramirez." A tan-skinned woman with short black hair was seated to his right. She blinked nervously and then gave a quick nod in acknowledgment.

Leo smiled warmly at the screen. "So. Tell me why you're so excited about HERBERT."

Hank began to earnestly describe the full details of the experiment's history, its current status, and the importance of the project to particle physics research. As Leo suspected, there was little in his overview that Leo wasn't already aware of. He threw a couple of softball questions in their direction, hoping they would relax.

Inez kept quiet, periodically reinforcing what her boss was saying. Leo turned up the pressure and asked some more pointed technical questions so they would know that he understood at a high level what they were talking about and that he was paying attention. This tactic had the desired result; they both became livelier in their answers. They were still pretty straightforward answers, but they began to elaborate a little more, especially when he asked follow-up questions.

Leo looked at his watch. He only had about ten minutes left in the time allotted by the lab for this interview. Time for the hardball, and he aimed it squarely at Inez.

"This is all very fascinating; I can absolutely see the importance of this research, and I look forward to reporting on the results of the experiment. Dr. Ramirez, I was wondering if you could tell me. Have you had to adjust the facility's security protocols in response to the protests and threats from Nadir?"

Inez's eyes grew wide, and she babbled, "I'm... sorry, but I CAN'T talk about the heightened security levels here."

Hank's demeanor changed instantly. "Mr. Schafer, I thought we were having a serious discussion about physics and the importance of our research. It's obvious now that you've come on a fishing expedition."

Leo shook his head fiercely. "Doctor, considering the energies involved in all particle accelerator experiments and the fact that a fringe organization with deep pockets has been protesting outside your facility for the last three months. And that some of those protesters have been making inflammatory, if not threatening, statements to the press. I think you owe it to the public to tell us how you are going to handle this situation."

Hank leaned back in his chair; a deep frown lined his face. He began tapping the conference room table quickly with his thumb as he contemplated the situation. Leo knew he had backed him into a corner and had not made any friends today, but he also knew it was the only way he would get any real information out of them. Finally, Hank seemed to come to a decision and leaned forward. "Mr. Schafer, rest assured that every precaution is being taken. We have always had robust physical access security, and in light of the protests, we have taken additional measures to ensure the safety of our facility as well as all members of our team. We are also cooperating with an ongoing investigation on whether some of these so-called threats are worthy of additional attention."

Leo's reporter senses began to tingle, "the Feds are involved? Homeland Security or FBI?"

Dr. Lee rolled his eyes in disgust. "I am not at liberty to discuss this any further. I believe we're done. Good day, Mr. Schafer." The conference room disappeared from Leo's screen.

He leaned back, scratched his chin absentmindedly, then picked up his phone and swiped through his contacts until he found the one he was looking for. A quick text message, 'Let me buy you a drink. Ruptured Duck at 6?' Thirty seconds later, a thumbs-up emoji appeared on the screen.

As the web conference closed, Hank leaned back and sighed heavily. "Well, that could have gone better," he said to the air. Inez fidgeted, nervously waiting for her boss to continue. "I'm sorry, Inez; I should have expected something like that. We both could have been better prepared for that type of question."

Inez relaxed a little "It's ok, Hank; I'm sorry I blurted that out. Up til that point, he had seemed truly interested in HERBERT, and he just caught me off guard. What do you think will happen?"

Hank sighed, "I don't know. I suspect that we're in for a very unflattering article, and that will not make our benefactors very happy. They don't want any negative attention on the project, and this whole business with Nadir isn't making them happy."

Inez stared at the back wall in thought as she spoke. "You know all this pressure on us to perform the first firing is not helping. I don't understand why they want us to rush the process."

Hank slowly shook his head. "They're not exactly pressuring us; they understand that science takes time. And it will take many, many collisions and years of observation for us to get the data we need. They've just set some expectations on when we will achieve the first full-strength test. They've been extraordinarily generous, and I don't fault them for wanting to see the fruits of their funding in a reasonable timeframe. We agreed to the timeline after all."

Inez looked at her boss sadly, "I know, but you'd think with all this negative attention and some of the incidents that have happened, they would at least give us a bit more time." She stood up and, as she walked out of the conference room, turned back, "I just hope this doesn't bite us in the ass. For all our sakes," and then turned and walked away.

A full minute after she left the room, Hank smashed his fist on the conference room table.

Chapter 3

"Morning, Chief," Sophia said cheerily as she strolled into the CEO's office. Rebecca Drake looked up from her laptop and smiled.

"Good morning, Sophia. I've been looking forward to this meeting all week. I'll be with you in a minute." Rebecca replied.

Sophia sat down at the small meeting table and took her time admiring the decor of Rebecca's office while she waited. The walls were covered in dark wood paneling with elegant white frosted glass and brass sconces at regular intervals. The carpet was a dark green low pile with an extravagantly thick pad that made it feel like you were walking on grass. Several credenzas lined the walls. The one behind Rebecca was a well-stocked mini bar. The walls to the left and right of Rebecca's desk each contained two, and their primary purpose was to display intriguing artifacts from antiquity.

Amongst the many items on display was a large undecorated bowl made from reddish clay, its bottom blackened from years of use over open fires. It sat next to a small handleless knife blade made of chipped obsidian. A carved stone slab with some sort of pictograms engraved on its surface sat next to a crude bronze sculpture of a naked woman cradling an infant.

Her reverie was interrupted when Rebecca pushed back from her desk and joined her at the table. "Let's get down to business, and then we can talk about the important stuff."

Sophia proceeded to give updates on several key initiatives that she was managing. Rebecca seemed to appreciate the scope of the updates, asked a few pointed questions for clarification, and seemed content with her answers.

She was continually awed by her boss. Rebecca Drake's background was impressive. She was an orphaned teenager living on the streets when she walked into Harvard to hand deliver her application and refused to leave until she was granted an interview with the Dean of Admissions. The Dean was supposedly so impressed that he shepherded her through the rest of the admissions process. Years later, she was asked in an interview why she had chosen Harvard. Her response? "Because it's the toughest school to get into, and I wanted a challenge."

After earning degrees in Economics and Applied Mathematics, she took up an internship with

Jeff McIntyre

a Washington DC based think-tank specializing in finance. While working there, she earned her MBA at Georgetown. She either impressed some very powerful people or was simply incredible at her job because her first position after the internship was as a Vice President for a small but very influential hedge fund. Within five years, she was the CEO of her own private equity firm. In the twenty years since, she has grown Infinity Financial International into not the largest, but certainly one of the most influential, financial services corporations in the world. Where and how IFI invests money was tracked by every financial analyst across the globe.

Sophia was a relatively small cog in the machine. She was a product manager in a division of the company focused on short-term investments for large corporations that needed flexibility with their cash reserves. She joked that it was like an interest-bearing checking account for the Fortune 500. It was a relatively new offering for the company, so there needed to be a lot of hand-holding between several different departments.

As Sophia wrapped up her updates, Rebecca stopped taking notes and sent an instant message to her assistant. A few minutes later, her assistant Jason walked in with a couple of large chai teas from the company coffee bar.

Maybe there was something between Jason and Rebecca. His eyes lingered on her as he turned to leave. It might just be wishful thinking on his part because Sophia was certain there was no time in

Rebecca's life for that kind of romantic dalliance. Still, she wouldn't fault Rebecca. Jason looked like he fell out of a fashion magazine. Chiseled jaw, ice blue eyes, and a physique that was so sculpted, even his business attire couldn't hide it. She pulled her eyes away from Jason's retreating backside and returned her focus to Rebecca.

On top of her many accomplishments, intelligence, and personality, Rebecca was one of the most handsome women she had ever met. It was difficult to call her beautiful in a classic Hollywood kind of way. Her skin was pale olive, and her eyes were slightly slanted, which implied at least some middle eastern heritage, but she had a long, strong nose and sharp jawline, which lent a certain hardness to her face. Sophia could tell that Rebecca used her makeup to enhance that hardness. She knew full well the pitfalls of a woman found to be 'too attractive' in the business world. But when Rebecca laughed, she could light up a room, and she had wit and charm for days.

Rebecca took a sip of tea, then set the cup down and leaned forward conspiratorially. "So, how are the men in your life Sophia?"

Sophia snickered at how the high and mighty CEO of IFI started the 'important' part of their meeting. "Daniel is... Daniel. He's got mid-term papers due today, which will keep him busy as a beaver for the next week."

"Oh? What's the subject this time? Rebecca inquired.

"Mesopotamian culture. It was part of his doctoral thesis, so having to read through a bunch of undergrads who thought his class would be easy, butcher their way through one of his favorite subjects is always painful for him."

Rebecca nodded sympathetically, "I can relate. Every time someone tries to give me financial advice, which seems like all the time, even if they know who I am! I'm all for a spirited discussion on Post-Modern Portfolio Theory but don't try to explain your take on investments and financial strategy and act like you're giving me some bit of sage wisdom. I'll make my own decisions. I have a bit of experience with this kind of thing." her voice dripped with exaggerated sarcasm at the end. Rebecca took a sip of her tea and then grinned wickedly over the top of her cup. "How are Antony and Cleopatra?"

Sophia rolled her eyes. When Tony was born, her historian husband had wanted to name him Antony. Sophia had refused. How on earth could you saddle a baby with the name of a man who committed suicide because he thought his lover was dead? That is way too much baggage for a child. She had compromised on Anthony, which was fine, but when they adopted a cat, she had agreed to let Tony name her. Little did she know, Daniel had already convinced him to name her Cleopatra. Rebecca knew the whole story and loved to needle her about it because she thought the story was adorable and knew it got under her skin.

The Garden Gnome

"The CAT is fine! Tony is doing… ok. He's struggling a bit with the new school. I think there are some bigger boys that pick on him a little but not enough to get into trouble. He loves his teachers, but he seems a little down sometimes. But he worked all weekend long on a foam ball and stick representation of the solar system. He gets to present it in class today, and he was really excited."

Rebecca smiled quietly as she listened to Sophia and nodded with interest. "You know I have no experience with children, but I can tell you change is always difficult no matter what your age. I've often found that doing something fun and spontaneous can take your mind off the stress of change. If you'd like, you can use my lake house this weekend. It just had its spring refresh and is ready for use, but I'm traveling out of town Saturday, so I won't be able to use it."

Sophia was a little stunned. She liked to think she was on good terms with Rebecca, and they both enjoyed these monthly meetings/social calls, but this was incredibly generous. "Rebecca, I don't know what to say."

She scoffed, "That's easy; you say thank you, and I say you're welcome. It's too cold for any swimming yet, but there's plenty of things to keep a young mind distracted from the trials and tribulations of a new school. I'll let them know you're coming, and you can expect a call from Joe, my pilot, so he can coordinate when to depart. I'll call you next week to see how things went. Deal?"

Sophia could only nod in stunned agreement and smile.

"Fine. It's settled. Unfortunately, I'm out of time today."

They both stood, and Sophia reached out and gently squeezed Rebecca's forearm with a look of quiet thankfulness. Rebecca smiled and patted her hand, and then returned to her desk. Sophia paused as if she wanted to say more, but then picked up her tea and quietly walked out of the office.

Chapter 4

Daniel sat in his car, waiting patiently for the daily explosion of school children. The radio was turned low, but he could make out Elvis Costello ominously singing 'Broken.'

He switched off the radio. It wasn't that he didn't like the song, but it wasn't going to help his mood at the moment. He had spent most of the afternoon trying not to take personally the enormous garbage pile of term papers that had been turned in. He found history and the stories it contained to be fascinating, but none so fascinating as the histories of the lands of ancient Mesopotamia. So, every year, he made Freshmen that took Topics in World History write a paper on the fertile crescent.

It was a little mean, but it helped him figure out which students might be interested in ancient versus modern history. The students who enjoyed this assignment tended to return for his other courses to fulfill their history requirements. He shouldn't be upset, but it would be nice if at least one of his students put in half an effort to write something interesting. That apparently was too much to expect from first years. He hadn't read them all, but he wasn't optimistic that there were any History majors among this year's crop of undecideds. Sorry Elvis, but I don't need any help being in a somber mood.

He heard a distant clanging from inside the school. Children of all shapes and sizes began to disgorge from every available exit of the school as they streamed toward waiting cars and buses. Daniel's mood didn't improve when he caught sight of Tony. He was trudging across the grass, dragging his backpack. Protruding from the top was a tangled mess of sticks and bits of Styrofoam. Daniel stomped on his temper. He was already in a bad mood, and jumping to conclusions would only make things worse. He could tell that Tony hadn't had a good day, so he steeled himself to try and be the dad he would need right now. Tony opened the door, chucked his backpack in the back seat, and clambered in.

"How was your day, chief?" Tony slowly fastened his seat belt but didn't immediately respond. Daniel sighed, put the car in gear, and slowly eased through the throngs of children and traffic jam of cars. "That bad, eh?" Daniel began gently poking his son in the ribs.

Tony squirmed sullenly but then began giggling, "DAD! Stop it!" He said breathlessly around his giggles.

Daniel eased up briefly, "Only if you TELL me how your DAY went," he said imperiously.

Tony held up his hands "fine, FINE!" Daniel smiled and waited patiently. Tony paused, biting his lip. "Dad? Why do big boys have to be mean to little boys?"

Daniel nodded his head; he had suspected this was coming. "Tony, the world is filled with people from all kinds of homes. Some of them are happy, but a lot of them are not. When a person is unhappy at home, they tend to bring that unhappiness with them wherever they go. They want other people to be as unhappy as they are, so they won't feel alone."

Tony nodded sadly.

"I wish I could tell you what to do, buddy, but there's no perfect answer. You can try making friends with them, or you can try ignoring them. If things get too bad, we can get teachers involved or talk to their parents, but getting them in trouble isn't always the best option. Whatever you want to do, I'll back you up, and I'm always here for you." Daniel couldn't help but think about his experiences with bullies. Nearly thirty years had passed, and he could still remember, if not the details, the emotional weight those events carried.

The traffic flowing by them reminded him of school hallways from long ago. Students merging with traffic as they exited their classrooms. The structured chaos of youth. Teachers and hall monitors acted as traffic signals, breaking up the inevitable jams created by excited cliques trying to cram as much face time into the brief interlude between periods. Occasionally turning into patrol officers when an argument turned into a fight or when there was an outbreak of obscenity or vandalism. The vice principals and guidance counselors were the traffic court, where the victims were frequently punished side by side with the guilty.

Swirlies, hidden punches, trips in the halls, verbal assaults, petty vandalism. These were all weapons of the bully. Laughter, however, was perhaps the cruelest. What should be shared with friends could be the cruelest barb from petty antagonists.

As they pulled into the driveway, Tony perked up a bit. "Is it ok if I play in the back yard with Bob for a while?"

Daniel grinned at his son and stopped the car. "Go for it. I'll be in the house reading papers if you need anything."

Tony hopped out and ran around the side of the garage, headed for the backyard gate as Daniel pulled into the garage. Daniel turned off the car, hung his head, and sighed.

Chapter 5

Leo threw his phone and satchel on his desk as he plopped down in his cube. Smack dab in the center of his monitor, one of his co-workers had creatively put four sticky notes together and used a sharpie to write "MARCUS WANTS TO SEE YOU" in large bold letters.

Teddy Lakefield, one of his compatriots at the science and technology desk, popped his head up from his adjacent cube and said, "Hey Leo, Marcus is looking for you," in an annoyingly cheerful way.

This duplication of communication did nothing for Leo's mood. He had, in fact, been ignoring texts and calls from Marcus for most of the morning. "All right, better get this over with." He said to no one in particular.

He stood up and walked with deliberate slowness toward his editor's office. He felt like he had been called to the principal's office. In fairness, he

Jeff McIntyre

knew exactly why he had been summoned to
Marcus's office. He had been told to deliver his article
on the experiment by today's deadline, and he had
failed.

Marcus Werner was a demanding but fair
boss. Deadlines were deadlines. Missing them meant
more work for everyone. He paused for a second,
girded himself for the ass chewing he was about to
get, and knocked on the office door.

"Get in here, Schafer," Marcus barked at him
through the door. Leo opened the door with
exaggerated gentleness; he delicately closed the
door, then tip-toed over to the chair opposite his boss
and gingerly sat down.

"Hey boss, what's cooking?" he said cheerily
in complete contrast to his body language.

Marcus looked at his computer screen and
spoke as if he were only half paying attention to Leo.
"Schafer, you're an 'ok' reporter. Your writing style is
relatable, you do a good job of dumbing down the
jargon, and you're usually on the button with
deadlines."

Leo interjected, "OK? I thought I was better
than just OK. Words hurt."

Marcus turned and glared at him. "I was
relying on you. We got caught with our pants around
our ankles. You missed your deadline, and
Lakefield's air aluminum battery article had to be held
up until we could get permission cleared up with the
patent holder. This was bad timing for you to turn
flake on me. We printed two absolute pieces of

garbage to fill the gap, and I'm going to get nailed by the publisher for this."

Leo leaned forward and looked his boss in the eye, "Look, Marcus, let me apologize. At the very least, I should have given you a heads-up that I was running behind on this article. I pulled on a string, and something interesting fell out. I've been spending all day doing leg work for another article that is related but way juicier than the actual experiment."

Marcus's eyes narrowed, "You aren't chasing after that Nadir bullshit, are you?" Leo held up a finger and opened his mouth to respond, but Marcus cut him off. "I told you. I wanted the experiment and nothing else. Let the Local desk handle that story. That's what they're there for."

Leo tossed a memory stick onto Marcus's desk. "Here. That's the fluff piece for the experiment. I was overly flattering as a way of an apology, as I'm sure I ruffled some feathers this morning. I know it's too late for today, but you can run it tomorrow. There's also two more pieces on there. One is a profile of the lead scientists and another on the non-profits funding the project. You can run it as a series. Just let me have some time to chase down the Nadir angle. The Local boys, I'm sure, are doing their level best to have an article ready three days after anyone gives a shit. I've got this by the tail, and I think I can make a killer story out of it. Marcus, the feds are looking into Nadir."

Marcus took the memory stick in his fingers and fiddled with it while side-eyeing Leo. "A series,

Jeff McIntyre

eh? All right, I'll give you until the end of next week to present your first draft to me. If I don't like what I see, you toss what you've got to the Local desk and walk away." Leo smiled and stood up. "And you still owe me a piece on that cybernetic prosthesis startup by Wednesday."

Leo's smile turned to a grimace. "Thanks, boss, you won't regret it."

Chapter 6

As she transitioned from shoulder press to firefly, Debra Kazdin re-focused her attention on her core and breathing. Firefly back to shoulder press. Shoulder press to downward dog. In through the nose, out through the mouth. Downward dog to crow. Crow to headstand. In through the nose, out through the mouth. Headstand back to crow. Crow to downward dog. In through the nose, out through the mouth. Time stood still for her in these moments. She could hear her heart beating. At last, she settled into child's pose and allowed her heart and breathing to slow. A sheen of sweat covered her skin.

Hard-soled footsteps destroyed her peace as a nameless pair of shoes walked up beside her mat. "Agent Kazdin, report to Agent Reynolds at 8 am. You're getting re-tasked." Without lifting her head, she raised the thumb of her right hand in acknowledgment. In through the nose, out through the mouth. The shoes turned and walked back out of the room.

Deb slowly raised herself upright and, with precision, looked at her watch. She still had seventeen minutes allotted for her workout but called it early. She would need the additional time to be early to Reynolds's desk and make a good impression. She stood up, carefully gathered her over-clothes from where she had neatly folded them, and picked up her shoes from their location to the left of her gym bag. She efficiently rolled up her mat, tucked it into a holder in the bag, and then turned towards the showers.

At 7:50, Deb walked up to Supervisory Special Agent Mike Reynolds's office. Early, but not too early. The office was currently empty. She looked up and down the hall and saw no sign of Reynolds, so she walked in, sat in one of the guest chairs, and began studying the office. Reynolds was an efficient and effective agent, but his office was a little cluttered for her liking. There were several awards on the wall. There was an untidy stack of papers on his desk, but the desk was organized. She resisted the urge to straighten the nameplate on his desk. It was slightly off parallel to the edge of the desk. There were no random objects strewn across his desk or office, no toys to distract him from his job, and no crumbs from

hurried meals in sight. The decor spoke of an FBI veteran and nothing more.

She had never worked with him, but his reputation preceded him. He'd been at the game for a long time and earned all those awards the hard way. There were no participation prizes on the wall and no years of service awards, even though she knew he had at least twenty years in. She was intrigued by the thought of being assigned under him. It was unlikely this had happened by chance.

She heard footsteps behind her as Agent Reynolds walked through the door. She hurriedly stood up to greet him.

He motioned her back, "You can stay seated; it's just the two of us." She slowly sat back down.

Mike Reynolds carefully considered the young woman seated across from him. She was barely thirty, although her hairstyle and makeup made her seem older, a common trait among young female agents who want to be taken seriously.

After reviewing her file, he had interviewed several of her peers. Most of them didn't like her; too anal was the general theme. A few tolerated her because she was good at her job. Most respected her ability, but at the same time, didn't enjoy working with her. As a result, she was frequently given solo assignments and had done very well for herself. She had studied engineering physics at Stanford, graduated, and earned her Master's in only four years. From there, she worked for a DC think tank that specialized in dreaming up infrastructure projects.

One of the DC field agents had worked with her on a case and been impressed with her attention to detail and had started the recruiting process without understanding Kazdin's shortcomings. She had blasted through all the early testing but got held up during the lengthy psychological evaluation.

The staff shrinks discovered that in her early teens, she had suffered from a nearly debilitating case of Obsessive Compulsive Disorder. She had undergone various forms of therapy and managed to reach a 'high functioning' state. They decided not to disqualify her. Other than some unique personality traits, especially when she was alone, they had no reason to believe she wouldn't make an excellent agent.

Teri Nielsen was one of her instructors at Quantico and had seen something in her. She helped Deb overcome the last bits of her OCD, especially when it came to doing her job. She knew how to push Kazdin's buttons and made sure the other instructors did too. In doing so, she made sure that no one could question why Agent Trainee Debra Kazdin had been allowed to graduate and become an agent.

Her early career with the agency had kept her on the east coast, close enough to keep an eye on. But after three years of excellence, they had let her off the leash. When an opening in the Chicago office for a forensics specialist opened up, she applied. She'd been there for about three months. Her boss loved her, and her co-workers hated her. She was quick to point out their mistakes and was merciless with her criticism, but they couldn't fault her results.

"Kazdin, as you know, I'm in charge of counterterrorism for this office. It's not your specialty, but what I need IS your specialty. None of my current agents are particularly familiar with advanced technology and research. We've got a situation involving Fermilab and potential threats from members of an organization called Nadir."

Deb nodded, "I'm familiar with Fermilab, and I can only assume this has to do with their latest high-profile experiment HERBERT. I'm afraid I'm not too familiar with Nadir."

He picked up a file and handed it across the desk. "Not too many people are. They're very new. Not at all what I would expect of an extremist organization, but there have been some incidents. Public and not-so-public members of this group have made threats. We've got analysts working on background files for the founder and any high-profile members, but for the time being, this is all we've got. I need you to familiarize yourself with Nadir, but I've got other agents chasing that angle. I want you to interview the staff at Fermilab that have reported incidents. Some of them were on Fermilab grounds, so if their security can provide video, all the better. I want details on every incident. I also want you to get to know them, their experiment, and the facility like the back of your hand. If we have to support their security, I want a report our operations people can work with, so they know what they're getting themselves into."

Deb was already scanning through the file as he continued. "This seems like a good fit for you, but I want your opinion. Like I said, counterterrorism isn't what you were trained for, but I could use your expertise with the science and the scientists."

She neatly closed the file and set it on her lap. "Thank you for the opportunity. I'd love to sink my teeth into this. I'm assuming this is already cleared with my boss?"

He nodded and smiled, "I don't snipe other departments without at least a phone call first."

Deb grinned. "Glad to be aboard. I'd better get busy."

Chapter 7

Brian Cooke studied the seven other people around the table. He knew all their names from the dossiers he had been provided, but he also knew a couple of them by reputation. The First Seat was occupied by Colonel Samuel Larkin. He was a large elderly black man with short cropped hair and a beard all gone to gray his deep wrinkles, and wire-rimmed glasses made him look like a kindly grandfather. An image that was helped by his big belly laugh and a broad smile. But he was also a veteran of three wars and a legend in the spec ops community.

Larkin was leaning over and chatting with Stephen Mercier, the Second Seat. Stephen was probably in his early fifties because Brian knew he had deployed to Desert Shield with the French Foreign Legion, but he only had a few wisps of gray. And while his hair said he could be in his forties, his skin and eyes made it seem like he was in his sixties. A French Canadian by birth, he had spent nearly twenty years in the Legion and retired with distinction as the equivalent of a Chief Warrant Officer before being recruited into the Knights. He could speak English, French, and German interchangeably and with little to no accent, but he tended to swear in French.

Clustered to Stephen's left in a small huddle were the Third, Fourth, and Fifth Seats in that order. Micah Krieg was about the same age as he was. He had a big bushy beard with a neatly trimmed gap caused by a distinctive scar that ran from below his left eye to his jawline. His light brown hair was slicked back, and he had piercing blue eyes. Brian knew that Micah had served briefly in the South African Army but had left and made a name for himself as team leader for various mercenary peacekeeping forces that operated all over sub-Saharan Africa. Micah kind of gave Brian the heebie jeebies. Maybe it was those blue eyes, but it always seemed like Micah was looking through whomever he was talking to.

The Fourth Seat belonged to Nathan Smith. Nathan was in his early sixties. His head was shaved, but the pure white hair in his mustache and goatee and a decent amount of wrinkles revealed his age. He was thin to the point of gauntness and wore simple black plastic framed glasses that looked like the kind the American military issued in the seventies. His dossier had revealed a twenty-year career at the Central Intelligence Agency. Some of the highlights from that career would make a decent Clancy series.

Katrin Lancaster occupied the fifth seat. Mid-forties, stocky, athletic build, short cropped blonde hair, no make-up. Katrin's dossier was short on details. It mainly consisted of a list of things she was considered an expert in. Hand-to-hand combat, explosives, and large caliber sniper rifles were prominent on that list.

Matz Schoeller, the Sixth seat, was a grandfatherly-looking gentleman with salt and pepper hair, bright blue eyes, and a wide smile. He was in charge of the Knight's lobbying arm, but Brian knew he had been an expert interrogator for the Stasi in East Germany right up until the fall of the Berlin Wall.

The Seventh seat was currently empty. Maya Abrams, the owner of that seat, was a twenty-year veteran of the Israeli Defense Force. She was currently meeting with the head of Palantir. She was trying to cut an under the table deal to license their identification software as an enhancement to the Knight's threat database.

Viktor Petrov was a lean, unimposing man in his mid-fifties, and he was most likely ex-KGB. It didn't specify that in the dossier that Brian had read, but based on the skill sets that were listed and the tally of accomplishments attributed to him, it seemed likely that the Eighth seat was from that organization. Maybe it meant he was still active in Russia's current secret police, the FSB.

Jeff McIntyre

He was the newest member and occupied the Ninth seat. It was recently vacated by the retirement of one of their longest-sitting members, who had been forced to retire due to the onset of dementia. He was being taken care of by a discrete group of caregivers that would see to all of his needs and, if necessary, keep all of his secrets.

Seats Ten, Eleven, and Twelve were also empty. Their occupants were on various remote assignments. His roundtable assessment was interrupted by Colonel Larkin rapping his knuckles on the table twice to grab attention from the various side conversations that were going on around the table. As the muttering tapered off, he coughed to clear his throat and began. "Let's get things started, shall we? Nathan, go ahead and begin."

Nathan nodded and began to read out notes from the previous meeting. "This gathering, the 18232nd of its kind, shall be brought to order by the Keeper of the Fourth Seat. The Knights of the Stone monthly moot is in session, and we have a quorum; eight of the twelve seats are in attendance. We have one tabled item from last month's session. If we can address it, then we can move on to new business. The disposition of various real-estate-based investments. Our financial advisors are recommending we liquidate one of our smaller holdings as an outside party has tendered an unsolicited offer of $40 million US. This would represent an approximately 30% return on our initial investment. Does anyone wish to discuss the subject further, or shall we put it to a vote?"

Viktor twirled his hand over the table impatiently and, in a mild Russian accent, spoke up, "Get on with it; we have more important things to discuss."

Nathan leaned forward and leveled a disapproving look down the table. "Viktor, I understand everyone's impatience to get to the new business, but we have procedures to follow. These procedures were put in place at the founding of this order and have helped maintain stability through dozens of crises."

Larkin interjected, "Nathan... the vote... if you please."

Nathan scowled but then returned to nominal professionalism, "All those in favor?" Each person seated around the table laid their right hand, palm down on the table. "All those opposed?"

Katrin reached out and laid her left hand, palm up on the table, and in a Welsh accent replied, "I believe I've already aired my objections, but I will reiterate. I do not think it wise to make a short-term financial decision about a long-term asset when we are on the verge of a Key Event."

Larkin nodded and smiled. "I understand your reservations, but this particular property holds no strategic importance, so the ayes have it. Nathan, make a note of the objection from the Fifth Seat so that Katrin can officially tell us she told us so."

Jeff McIntyre

Nathan began scribbling notes in a journal as Katrin flipped off Larkin and grinned. Nathan set down his journal and then paused a moment before proceeding.

"Before we hear reports from the various seats, I'd like to provide a status of the reliquary. Castor's Hummingbird is currently sitting at thirty degrees above ambient room temperature and climbing. No other artifacts are displaying signatures."

Katrin spoke, "So, it is coming; but we have time. That's up ten degrees from last month?"

Nathan nodded in confirmation. "Based on historical records, that gives us somewhere between twelve and eighteen months before we hit the critical threshold. Sometime in the next six months, we will begin to see activity in other relics that will help us narrow down the time frame."

Matz chimed in with a clipped German accent. "So, does this mean that the HERBERT project is no longer a priority? Our last estimate put them on track in six months."

Larkin shook his head, "I wish we had that luxury. So far, we haven't been able to determine how soon the first full-power test will occur. I think it's best if we keep Nadir in our pocket. That way, we can apply pressure to HERBERT if needed. The HERBERT experiment is still a likely candidate for a Key even; we just don't know if the timing matches up. But I think we can afford to slow roll for now. Continue to develop our assets and prepare. Better to have a plan with contingencies in case things heat up unexpectedly. In the meantime, I think we need to take another look at CERN and the LHC."

The meeting proceeded uneventfully. Each of the chairs present gave reports on their bailiwicks, and Nathan provided updates from those who were unable to attend. The meeting wrapped up, and the members began to file out of the room. Larkin intercepted Brian and motioned for him to follow him as he headed a different way that led to his office.

He gestured to a chair. "Have a seat."

Brian took the proffered seat and considered the man across from him.

"You are our newest member, and I know you've been told some of what this is all about. But now, one of the artifacts is responding, and that means a Key event is approaching. You need to be filled in on everything." He tossed a memory stick at Brian, who deftly snatched it out of the air. "On that stick is a file called 'The Deep End'; it is each new member's sink or swim moment. You have 72 hours to read it, at which point that memory stick will destroy the data it contains. You don't know enough of our operation to hurt us irretrievably. Yet. Once you read that, I'll need you to reaffirm your commitment to us. We wouldn't have recruited you if we weren't fairly certain of your resolve, but we can't reveal the critical parts of our operation until after you've read that and understand what's at stake."

Brian looked at the memory stick as if it contained the mysteries of the universe. "Sir, I've already given you my word and taken the oaths. When I joined the military, I pledged to protect my country against all enemies. From what you've told me, this is that same pledge, only with bigger stakes. I doubt I'll change my mind."

He nodded in approval, "I expected no less from you. All the same, you need to read that. Until you do, you won't fully understand and without understanding what The Knights stand for and why we are doing what we're doing. When the hard decisions have to be made, I want you to be prepared. Read it, and take a couple of days to absorb what you've read. Then come talk to me. There will be one last final oath to take, and it should not be taken lightly. Unlike most oaths, this one has very real consequences if you break it."

Brian looked at the memory stick now, like it might be about to bite him. He stood up, slowly nodded to Larkin, and walked out.

Chapter 8

Leo walked into the dimly lit interior of the Ruptured Duck. It wasn't actually dimly lit, but it was a fairly sunny day outside, so it took a moment for his eyes to adjust. The bar's walls were covered in vintage aviation memorabilia. A dust-covered propeller on one wall was surrounded by black and white photos of airplanes and pilots. A World War 2 bomber jacket was on prominent display. The back of the jacket had a hand-painted depiction of a uniformed duck with one of its wings in a sling.

He spotted a familiar back seated at the long mahogany bar that ran the length of the room. He waved to the bartender and sat down next to his friend. "Hey Jake, how's it hanging?"

The short, skinny, black man wore a fashion statement trench coat over his normal business attire. He paused, sipping his beer long enough to spout "A little to the left, thank you very much," and then pushed his wire-framed glasses back up his nose and resumed drinking.

Leo placed his drink order and then clapped his friend on the back. "How's Kitty?"

Jake winced, ran a finger through his lightly graying dark curly hair, and then sat his beer down. "Not... great... She's not real happy with me. I've been working a lot of hours lately, and I reFUSE to let her mother move in with us."

The bartender placed a frosty mug in front of Leo and walked away. He took a quick sip of the head before replying. "We could always build a mother-in-law suite in your basement. Daniel and I would be more than willing to help you do the framing and drywall; you just have to provide the beer."

Jake sighed, "Look, I love Kitty's mom, but there's just something weird about having sex with your wife when her mother is downstairs. I still enjoy having sex with my wife and would like to continue to do so without that in the back of my head."

He gestured to the bartender to bring them another round as he alternated between commiserating with and picking on his buddy from college, all the while plying him with more beer.

Jake, Leo, and Daniel had been buddies from literally their first five minutes in college. They'd been standing in one of the many long admissions lines waiting to fill out some piece of miscellaneous paperwork that nobody cared about except when you had to fill out other pieces of paperwork. They'd been bored and just started chatting. Standing in line together for an hour had led to a twenty-year friendship. Jake had been the mild alcoholic, Leo the flirt, and Daniel, the comedian. Jake always knew where the best parties were. Daniel could make people laugh, and he had a knack for spectacularly intricate pranks. Leo was the best gay wingman two college freshmen could want.

After two years watching his best friends try to play the field, he had taken pity on them and introduced them to his other two best friends, Sophia and Kitty. He might not have been all that lucky in love himself, but he was a pretty damn fine matchmaker. The Three Amigos became the Power Rangers. Leo had been content to be the fifth wheel in the double dates. He would occasionally bring his latest boyfriend along on their outings, but they came and went pretty frequently.

Their tight friendship had continued past graduation. He'd been the best man at both weddings. He'd been there for Tony's birth, and he'd been there for Kitty's miscarriages. He was there when Daniel got his Master's degree, he'd flown to Virginia for Jake's FBI graduation, and he'd been pallbearer for one parent and three grandparents.

Times had changed. After Quantico, Jake and Kitty had been moths to the FBI flame, flitting from duty station to duty station until Jake finally got the posting he'd wanted back home in Chi-town. Family life had taken its toll. Tony was a great kid, but Daniel and Sophia hadn't had as much time for the Power Rangers.

Jeff McIntyre

Jake and Kitty were still trying to have kids, although that clock was ticking hard now. Leo loved Kitty like a sister, and it saddened him to see her withdraw. He knew how desperately she wanted to be a mother, so he had ever so gently tried to nudge them towards adoption. There was a time when he would have had a blunt and open talk with her, but the years she had spent following Jake had subtly changed their relationship. She wasn't as open with any of them as she used to be.

On the other hand, he and Sophia were as close as they'd ever been. Daniel would have kicked his ass if he had thought for a second that Leo was hetero. Leo had been in the delivery room with Sophia when Tony came into the world, acting as stand-in dad until Daniel arrived. An accident on the expressway had kept him from getting there in time. Leo still had lunch with Sophia at least once a week, and they constantly texted one another.

Jake had gotten assigned to the Chicago field office about three years ago. The first few months had seemed like old times, but it rapidly became apparent that while Daniel, Leo, and Sophia had stayed close, in isolation, Jake and Kitty had formed their own pair bond. It's not like they didn't still get together, but it wasn't often, and it didn't have the same closeness that it used to.

Leo needed to get Jake home to his wife intact and only a little drunk, so he pulled out his wallet to pay the tab. He had summoned a ride share about fifteen minutes ago, and the app on his phone said it should be there shortly. "Jake, my man. I hate to be that guy but one, you need to get home to Kitty, or she'll kill us both. And two, I need to ask you a favor."

Jake grumbled, "Here we go."

He held up his hands defensively, "Hey, you know what I do for a living, and I have never asked you for help before. Besides, this is easy. I just need a name. What agent is handling the investigation into Nadir? I'll handle the introductions myself."

Jake grinned as he downed the last of his beer. "Hoo boy. That is easy for me and hard for you. The new girl, Deb Kazdin. She's a pain in the ass. When you talk to her, you don't know me. She could make my life a living hell if she wants. She can be pissed at me later... IF she ever figures out that I sent you her way."

He looked at his phone, "All right, my brother, our rides here. Thanks for the intel. Time to go, or you'll never have sex with Kitty again." and pushed Jake to the door.

Chapter 9

Daniel looked fondly at his son tightly tucked under the covers as he turned out the light. Tony had nodded off while he had been reading him his favorite bedtime story. They had been in an old used bookstore when Tony had run up to him with a book clutched to his chest. It was an old retelling of St. George and the dragon written for children, but it had one heck of a twist. Daniel was familiar with the story and wasn't sure Tony was ready for such dark themes. But after flipping through the book, he decided the tone was soft enough and bought it for him.

The story was a strange creation. It had been published in the thirties under a very obvious pseudonym. It told the story from the Dragon's perspective. In this telling, the villagers tormented the dragon and demanded it use its magic for their benefit. The greedy villagers had become accustomed to the wealth and prosperity the dragon's magic had brought to them and threatened to hire a knight to slay the dragon if it didn't do as they asked. One day the dragon became sick and was too weak to help the villagers when a great storm struck and damaged their homes.

Enraged, the villagers spun a story to a passing knight of the evil dragon that threatened their lives and destroyed their homes despite the great tributes they had offered it. Sir George, of course, took up their righteous cause and went out to slay the evil beast. He came across the dragon's lair and saw its sickly state and the terrible cave in which it dwelt. He saw no indication of the riches the villagers claimed they had given up as a sacrifice to the dragon. Rather than challenge the dragon, he chose to talk to it.

The dragon spun its tale of woe for George. Before long, the two became friends, and George spent many days in the dragon's company. George knew the villagers would never leave the dragon alone, so he gathered a bunch of the dragon's scales and sewed them together in the shape of the dragon's head. He helped the dragon find a new lair, then returned to the villagers, presented the stuffed head to the villagers, and convinced them that the dragon would never bother them again. The villagers were fooled, and much woe befell them once their benefactor was no longer there to protect them.

As a historian, he could appreciate the truth of a story being colored by the perspective of the storyteller, and he admired the subtext of being appreciative of those who help you and not taking them for granted. In truth, he loved the story as much as Tony did. He quietly closed the door and returned to the living room.

Sophia was sitting quietly on the couch with a glass of wine in one hand and a novel in the other. She sat both down as he walked over and sat down beside her. Daniel sighed and ran his fingers through his hair as Sophia leaned over and nestled into his chest, one arm draped across his stomach.

He wiggled a bit to get settled in. "So... Tony spent most of the afternoon playing with Bob."

Sophia tilted her head up with a worried look on her face. "He's spending more time with his imaginary friend than he is with any real friends."

At first, he didn't respond. His desire to protect her warred with his need to be honest with her. Honesty won out. "It gets worse; last week, he tracked in a bunch of sand and dirt from the back yard, and when I called him on it, he apologized for not cleaning up Bob's mess."

Sophia poked him in the ribs "you didn't tell me about that," she growled.

He winced and threw up his free hand in surrender. "I just didn't want you to worry any more than you already are. It's not uncommon for kids to act up in response to change, and this school is quite a culture shock for him. I'm worried about him, but at the same time, I know he'll get through this." Daniel recounted his conversation with Tony during the car ride home.

Sophia looked thoughtful for a moment. "Maybe I should turn down Rebecca's offer. She's giving us the use of her lake house this weekend if we want it, but maybe we should try and find a professional to talk with Tony instead."

He shook his head vigorously, "I don't think we're quite to that stage yet. I think a weekend retreat might be just what he needs. Let's enjoy your boss' generous offer and see how things go. If he's still down in the dumps and is still this focused on 'Bob' after the weekend, then we can talk about next steps. I think getting away and enjoying some time out at the lake could do us all some good. By the way, what made Rebecca offer her lake house?"

Sophia shrugged, "We were talking about this and that at the end of our meeting, and I mentioned that Tony was struggling in his new school. She said that her lake house had just been readied for use but that she had a previous engagement this weekend, and we may as well use it. It's incredibly generous of her; I've heard some stories about this place. It's supposedly massive."

"Be sure to thank her for me." He kissed the top of Sophia's head. "This could be just what Tony needs."

Chapter 10

Leo sipped at his beer as he began compiling his notes. Nadir was led by a man named Alvaro Esposito. Leo had watched or read every interview and article he could find about him but hadn't drawn any conclusions.

Alvaro was the son of Cuban refugees who settled in Florida. Like so many before them, they had little to their name except the clothes on their back when they arrived in Miami. Alvaro was born soon after, and his parents wanted to ensure he got a proper education so he would have every opportunity to live the American dream.

Despite their meager income as a landscaper and a hotel maid, they managed to send Alvaro to Embry-Riddle Aeronautical University, where he earned a Bachelor's in Aerospace Engineering and then worked his way through various NASA internships while continuing to study and eventually earned a Master's and then Ph.D. in Astrophysics.

While at NASA, despite his engineering background, he was quickly promoted to management. His charisma and drive helped him form incredible teams that excelled and got noticed. After nearly fifteen years at NASA, he abruptly quit. He was a mover and shaker on the fast track to being the face of NASA, and he abruptly disappeared without a trace.

Leo could find little about what he was up to for the five years that followed. He finally reappeared in the public eye only eighteen months ago as the head of the newly formed Nadir. An advocacy group that focused on bringing scientific research in line with the greater needs of humanity rather than deepening the pockets of big pharma or the military-industrial complex. They obviously didn't use those words, but that was essentially their dogma boiled to its essence.

Nadir has deep pockets. For every research program they protested, they funded two others. There was very little to indicate conflicts of interest either. While they protested HERBERT, they were funding other particle research experiments, but none were in direct competition for funding that HERBERT would be aiming for.

It was possible that this was coordinated anti-competition amongst competing research concerns. But if it was, the money was hidden exceptionally well. Hell, most of the funding for HERBERT had come from private donations. There were a few minor government matches, but mostly just private investors.

On the protest side of the house, the vast majority of their 'protesting' involved white papers and newspaper articles calling for moral and compassionate science. Mostly, they just seemed like a bunch of do-gooders interested in proper oversight of how research was done, which made their stance on HERBERT that much stranger.

It wasn't incredibly obvious because Nadir had arranged actual people on the ground protests at other facilities before. Usually, animal testing facilities, the occasional human drug trial, obviously some nuclear power research, and now Fermilab. What was strange is that the protests against HERBERT seemed to be escalating. Fermilab staff had reported confrontations off-site with people claiming to be from Nadir. There had also been some untimely accidents involving companies that provided logistical support to Fermilab. Then later, some anonymous claim is made to a random member of the press using verbiage that was part and parcel with Nadir's ideology.

This all made his reporter brain itch. Either Nadir was really involved in these incidents but was putting just enough plausible deniability on the table based on their pattern of behavior, or there was another player on the field doing everything in their power to sabotage HERBERT and lay the blame on Nadir.

The Garden Gnome

He finished off his beer and then compiled a nicely worded email to the press arm of Nadir, requesting an interview with Alvaro. He included a link to the as yet unpublished series on HERBERT and then fired it off.

He was about to close his laptop when he thought of something else he needed to do. A couple of searches later and he got as much public domain information as he could find on Special Agent Debra Kazdin.

There wasn't a lot to go on. She hadn't been involved in any high-profile cases, and her social media presence was practically non-existent. He did find three pictures of her so he could at least identify her. The first was a headshot that had been used as part of some symposium on forensics that the FBI had hosted for a regional law enforcement seminar. The third was older, taken from the internet cache of a DC think tank's website where she had worked prior to joining the FBI. The last was a group picture; she had been tagged in a post-graduation party when she completed her training at Quantico.

He could tell from the group shot that she was short, maybe five two, and athletic. The tank top she had worn to the bar that day revealed strong neck tendons, well-formed traps, and the upper arms of an athlete. Her hair was a dark chocolate brown cut short with seemingly natural curls. It was a simple, no-nonsense haircut that made her look ten years older than she actually was. Light freckles framed a small nose. She wore no necklaces or earrings, and her smile was disarming. In Leo's internal hetero categorization schema, she was attractive in what fell into the cute category.

Two of the pictures were very formal, the third very casual. The unnerving part was that in all three, she looked at the camera and smiled in the exact same way. The oldest picture was taken five years before the most recent. Same hairstyle, same smile, hell, even looked like the same suit in the two formal shots. It almost seemed like she was wearing a mask. This is going to be a challenge. He liked challenges.

Chapter 11

Daniel watched Tony and smiled. This was his first time in a plane, and he could practically see Tony's smile through the back of his head. The waters of Lake Michigan skimmed close below as the pilot descended for final approach. Daniel himself was a little nervous. He had never been in a plane this small before, and as Joe swung the plane around to line up for landing, he saw that it was a grass landing strip. He sat up straight and gripped the armrest fiercely.

Luckily, Tony and Sophia were so excited by the view they didn't notice his moment of weakness. With a surprisingly gentle flumph, the plane touched down, rapidly but smoothly slowed down, and then crept forward toward the end of the strip. A large golf cart was parked at the end of an asphalt path that trailed off into the trees. In the fading light, he could make out a shadowy shape standing next to the cart.

Jeff McIntyre

Before the plane had come to a complete stop, the shape had moved in and was unlatching the door to the aircraft and unfolding the ladder. The head of a large aging Asian man poked in through the open door and, with a light Japanese accent, said, "Welcome to Fantasy Island," and then broke into a huge smile. "I've always wanted to say that. We don't get many guests out here." Then the head withdrew, and the man began busily opening the external baggage compartment.

Joe finished shutting down the plane and then turned and saluted Tony as the three of them started to exit the aircraft. Tony cheerily saluted back and then clambered out onto the grass.

Sophia paused briefly, "Thank you, captain, that was an excellent flight and a beautiful landing."

Joe smiled, "My pleasure, ma'am. I'll be spending the weekend here as well unless Ms. Drake calls me. It'll take me a couple of hours to get this thing topped off and checked out tomorrow morning. After that, you two just let me know, and we can head back whenever you're ready. Just keep in mind the two-hour flight time if you need to get back to the city at any specific time."

Daniel gave him a thumbs up, "Thanks, Joe, it really was a smooth flight, and we'll try to give you a heads up when we're ready to head back."

As he followed Sophia out of the plane, Tony and the large man were already loading their bags into the back of the cart. As they approached, the man straightened up and bowed, then less formally, he smiled and extended a hand to Sophia. "I am Murakami Takashi. Since you are personal guests of Mistress Drake, you may call me Takashi. Welcome to the Little Spring Island Fitzroy family. It is my pleasure to be your host. It has been some time since we've had guests to the island."

He suddenly realized that not only was he large, he might have been the largest Japanese man he had ever seen. He had to be close to seven feet tall. He was barrel-chested with thick arms and massive hands that Sophia's small hand disappeared into as he gently shook hers.

Sophia seemed smitten with him as she laughingly responded. "Well, Takashi, you are quite the welcome wagon. I'd heard about you from Rebecca, but she really didn't paint a very good picture of you. I can't wait to enjoy your hospitality. I see you've already met my son Tony, I'm Sophia, and this is my husband, Daniel."

Takashi repeated the bow and handshake to Daniel, only this time the handshake was firmer, although not uncomfortably so. "Come, it's a bit of a ride up to the house, and we don't want dinner to get cold."

As the cart rolled down the path, he thought about the office gossip Sophia had shared with him about Rebecca's island retreat. Twelve bedrooms, fourteen bathrooms, bowling alley, ice cream parlor. There might be some nuggets of truth, but Sophia had been skeptical that Rebecca would have that kind of extravagance on her island getaway.

Jeff McIntyre

The cart rounded a bend and rolled into a clearing and what he saw was both more modest and more fantastic than he could have imagined. The central portion of the house was squat, only two stories, but made of a gray granite block stone. It was obviously intended to be a modern take on a medieval castle. There were even stylized buttresses and gargoyles. The height seemed to have been chosen so that it was shorter than the old-growth trees that surrounded it and thus would not be visible from the lake, with one exception.

Attached to the south end was a narrow spire that thrust far above the tree line. He remembered seeing it as they flew in and thought it was a lighthouse. But from this distance, it was apparent that it was only intended to look like a lighthouse. It was only wide enough to carry the spiral staircase that it undoubtedly contained, but the top had a much larger platform. The spire's top was well-lit, but it didn't have the tell-tale spinning beacon. It seemed little more than a place to enjoy what was probably a magnificent view of the entire island and Lake Michigan beyond.

On the opposite end of the house from the observation tower was a large, airy, glass and steel framework. The sun had gone down, and that wing's internal lighting highlighted a lush garden. He could make out a small waterfall that must tumble into some sort of large water feature or pool.

Framing the main house were several outbuildings. One looked like a small vehicle garage, one was probably a guest house, and another seemed likely to be a stable. He could only wonder at the purpose of the others.

Takashi pulled the cart to a stop at the entrance to the main house. He hopped out and opened the large oaken double doors. The doors had intricate carvings worked into them, but there wasn't time to make out the details. "Please, please, come inside. Dinner is waiting. Electra will be upset if the food gets cold. I will make sure your bags get to your room."

Daniel, Sophia, and Tony made a slow rubbernecking procession into the house. A grand entryway led into a marvel of modern construction. The entire first floor of the main house was one large open great room. Great care had been taken to ensure that the room flowed easily from one functional area to another. To the left of the entrance was a grand kitchen with a massive island for prep and casual seating. Adjacent to the kitchen but along the back wall was a formal dining area. There was a library to the right of the entrance and a living area with a large fireplace adjacent to it. It was easily three thousand square feet in one large room.

A rail-thin woman with a long silver ponytail that hung to her waist beckoned to them from the dining area. "Come, come; I have lamb stew and rhubarb pie." The smells drew the Fitzroy family to the dining table as much as the invitation did. There was much more to the meal than lamb and pie. There was a salad with blue cheese or Italian dressing. A simple but delicious potato salad and warm hard rolls. Their host introduced herself as Electra Katapodis. She sat at the table with them and began eating as soon as she was confident everyone had what they needed.

Before long, Joe joined them. He stopped long enough to give Electra a peck on the top of her head. She smiled and waved at him to sit. Soon Takashi approached the table from behind her.

Electra looked up and glared at him. "You've been out doing chores all evening. Go wash up before you sit at my table, you old fool." All eyes turned to Takashi. He smiled at her and bowed very deeply.

"Apologies. Of course." He practically darted to the kitchen, hurriedly washed his hands and face, then returned to the table and gingerly sat as far from Elektra as possible while still being adjacent to everyone else.

He studied Elektra as they ate and engaged in polite conversation. Elektra must have been a striking woman in her prime. Her ponytail was woven into a severely tight braid. She was rail thin with olive skin and eyes so lightly blue they seemed gray. Her accent, skin, and that prominent nose marked her as Greek even if her name hadn't given it away. Her face and hands were deeply lined from age and sun.

While she engaged in pleasant conversation with her guests and Joe, Elektra took a much more critical attitude with Takashi. He, on the other hand, was overly deferential and politely acknowledged her comments with patience and respect.

After they were all quite stuffed, Joe and Takashi cleared the table. Elektra smiled at Tony. "You look tired, young man. While there is plenty to do on the island at any time of day, I would suggest you all get a good night's sleep, and tomorrow after breakfast, we will show you all the activities that are available."

Tony tried to stifle a yawn and utterly failed. Daniel and Sophia both gave in to sympathy yawns. "Thank you so much for the delicious meal. Sleep sounds wonderful; it's been a long day." Sophia said.

Takashi gestured toward a doorway that seemed to lead toward the observation tower. "Let me show you to your rooms." The large man practically filled the hallway as he led them up a spiral staircase, exiting on the second floor even though the stairway continued up. Tony looked longingly up the tower before following.

Takashi led them to a set of darkly stained oaken French doors which led them into a small suite. It almost seemed purpose-built for a small family to visit. A decent-sized master bedroom and a smaller bedroom outfitted with a pair of single beds. Between the two rooms was a shared sitting room, and off the sitting room was a large and well-appointed bathroom. The furnishings were elegant but not extravagant, and there didn't seem to be much personalization. The whole place smelled like a guest suite. Still, it probably took up a third of the second floor.

As they explored, they discovered that their bags had already been deposited. Sophia and Daniel's in the master, and Tony's in the smaller bedroom all to himself.

Takashi backed into the hallway and said, "There is an old-fashioned phone here in the sitting room. If you find that you need anything at all, day or night, just dial one. I will see that all your needs are met." And then he closed the doors and left.

Chapter 12

Brian convulsed awake, his body flailing in terror. Soaked in sweat with the sounds of explosions and screaming still ringing in his ears and the smell of fire and burnt flesh in his nostrils, he dove off his bed, looking for cover. He clenched the bed frame, closed his eyes, and tried to will the sounds and smells from his mind. He forced himself to stop panting and concentrate on his breathing. His breathing and heartbeat began to slow as he ran through the mental exercises that helped him focus on the now.

It had been a long time since he'd had one this vivid. They almost always came at night now, when his control was down. But usually, it was just a nightmare; sometimes, he didn't even wake up. He slowly unclenched his muscles and stood up with a groan. There was no chance he was going back to sleep now. He turned on the coffee maker and hopped in the shower.

A cold shower helped clear his mind. He tossed on a loose t-shirt and some sweats and wrapped his towel around his shoulders. He paused at the doorway, looked back at the spot where he had been cowering twenty minutes earlier, then switched out the lights, hoping to banish the past from his mind. He crossed the sparse living room. He'd been here six months, and it still only had the stuffed leather chair his dad had given him when he'd gotten out of the military. It looked like it had been through a warzone, but it was still the most comfortable piece of furniture he'd ever sat in.

He grabbed a mug, filled it from the pot, and then sat down at the one chair he had for his thrift shop kitchen table. He sipped coffee while absentmindedly toweling his hair dry. It didn't surprise him that he'd had an episode. He'd spent the last day and a half reading through the documents that Larkin had given him. Not enough sleep, crappy meals, and a subject matter that seemed too fantastical to be real.

He scanned through portions again. There were only about four hours left before the data ate itself. They had given him the high notes when they'd recruited him, but a lot of what had drawn him in was the reputation of his recruiter, Colonel Samuel Larkin. The Colonel was long retired but was a legend in the special operations community. Hell, up until they'd approached him about joining the Knights, he'd thought Larkin was dead.

Arthur, Merlin, Gawain, Morgan; the whole Camelot thing was true. There were significant differences in this story from the ones in popular culture, but the gist was there.

Where things really diverged was the how and why the Knights of the Stone were formed. After Merlin's disappearance and Arthur's death, all of England and most of Europe plunged into the throes of the Dark Ages. Civilization began to crumble, and humanity as a whole suffered. Here's where things got wild. The Knights, specifically Gawain, who founded the order, believed that it was because magic had left the world. Historians believe it was caused by the decline of the Roman Empire and the lack of stability created by the power vacuum of their retreat. The Knights of the Stone laid the blame on Merlin.

Merlin disappeared a few years before Arthur's death at the hands of Mordred. With his disappearance, magic began to fade, and with it, the society that had become dependent on it. In the dark years after Arthur's death, Gawain and his fledgling society researched the ebb and flow of magic in the world. From conversations Gawain had with Merlin before he disappeared and from tracking down other users of magic of the time, they had discovered a cycle.

Magic would appear in the world, last for no more than thirty to forty years, and then mysteriously fade away. Then, after forty to fifty years, it would reappear; its arrival was as unexpected as its departure. Gawain began to believe that Merlin's disappearance was directly related to this fading of magic.

They found proof when they discovered Merlin's private sanctum and found his journals and artifacts. Merlin's journals revealed his many past lives. How in each life, magic would return, and he would try to use his mastery of magic to bring humanity forward. To provide the stability necessary for civilization to flourish. He had considered Camelot to be his crowning achievement.

Seeing the devastation wrought by the disappearance of magic, Gawain decided that he would do whatever was necessary to prevent Merlin, or whatever his true name was, from bringing the chaos of magic back.

The Knights of the Stone was an homage to Excalibur and the glory of Camelot. Most of the original members were knights of the round table that survived Camelot's fall. They discovered that every forty to fifty years, a boy would be born who had the potential to become Merlin.

They referred to him as The Lock. The boy was innocent until he achieved manhood, and some catastrophic event occurred. They called these Key Events. They usually took the form of some natural disaster. Meteor strike, hurricane, earthquake, volcanic eruption; all of them had been tied to Key Events. If a Key Event occurred in rough proximity to where The Lock was, Merlin's soul would be reborn in the man, and magic would begin to leak into the world. Not only was The Lock the access point by which magic entered the world, but he was also the most powerful wielder of magic.

For over fifteen hundred years, the Knights of the Stone had managed to keep magic from returning by using the items in the reliquary to track down the Lock. Some were from Merlin's sanctum, but others were much older than the time of Merlin. They were all keyed to him and his return. They had discovered ways to read the reliquary to determine when and where the Lock would appear.

Their methods were often ruthless, but they had used restraint if the situation allowed for it. There were pages and pages of documented Lock and Key Events. When it was required, they would eliminate the Lock. Always a young man in his early twenties. On at least five separate occasions, they killed him after he had awoken but before magic had returned to public awareness.

The most recent had been what they had used to recruit him. They'd shown him a video taken in April of 1980. Until that day, their records indicated only natural disasters could be Key Events. Artifacts from the reliquary had led them to a young man living in Portland. Mount St. Helens had been rumbling, which led them to believe that its eruption was imminent and represented the most likely Key Event. Standard operating procedure was to relocate the Lock until the event had passed or eliminate him if

73

necessary. Once the Key Event passed, the man was no longer a threat.

On April fourth, 1980, two Knights and a number of mercenaries kidnapped the Lock and relocated him to a safe house in Las Vegas. They were a thousand miles from the danger zone and waited for the volcano to erupt. Then on April 16, as part of Operation Tinderbox, the Pyramid Nuclear test was conducted just sixty-five miles northwest of Las Vegas. It was a relatively small test at only eighty-nine kilotons, but it was apparently large enough to be a key event.

Brian played the video for what seemed like the hundredth time. The screen flickered to life, and the grainy playback began. A young man is sitting in a chair in the corner of a large padded cell. He's surprisingly relaxed, considering he's being held captive. There's a large stack of magazines on a table, a large comfortable bed, the remains of a meal, and several empty beer bottles. Apparently, the Knights were taking good care of their charge.

Suddenly, a blinding flash emanates from the man. When the cameras recover from the flare, his body is convulsing in a seizure, and he collapses on the floor. He lays there for a good twenty minutes, not moving. It is apparent that no one is paying attention to the camera feed. Slowly he starts to move. He appears to be taking stock of his body, obviously in pain. He suddenly panics. He stands up, staggers to the door, and starts pounding on it.

The Garden Gnome

Eventually, the door opens, and four armed men charge in. Two of them grab him and pin him against a back wall. The third covers him, and the fourth stands in front, talking to him, trying to get him to calm down. His struggling increases, and suddenly the man in the covering position is violently thrown out of the camera angle. The Lock then appears to burst into flames, and the two men holding him do as well. They lurch backward and writhe in agony. The fourth man, untouched, quickly unholster his sidearm and begins firing rapidly into the head and chest of the Lock. The first few rounds are deflected by an invisible force, but the gunman keeps firing, and some of the bullets get through. The Lock collapses, his fire goes out, and his lifeless body slumps to the floor. The pistol bearer pauses briefly to ensure the Lock is down, then grabs a blanket off the bed and tries to put out one of the burning men. The video ends.

The after-action report included with this video went into great detail about the exact timing of the nuclear test and the flash in the Lock's cell.

Brian closed the laptop and slowly drained the rest of his coffee. He looked wistfully at the mug, wishing it had been scotch.

Chapter 13

Deb sat patiently in the Fermilab waiting room. She was roughly halfway through counting the floor tiles when security cleared her for entrance. She choked down the urge to finish, stood up, and smiled as they buzzed her past the security checkpoint.

The guard handed her a visitor's badge and led her down a long white hallway with identical doors differentiated only by their labels and multiple crossing hallways with signs indicating the paths to the cafeteria, loading dock, and other more esoteric destinations such as Lab 2A and Storage 23B.

The symmetry between Fermilab's hallways and half a dozen other government buildings' hallways was not lost on her. In the back of her mind, she was counting the steps. However, she did not shift her stride to avoid stepping on the seams of the tile. The sterile halls were slightly comforting to her.

The Garden Gnome

Her training had kicked in the moment she stepped through security as she mentally drew a floor plan of every area she could view as they passed. If her escort noticed her quickly peering down each hallway they passed, he didn't say anything.

At last, he stopped at a door labeled Conference Room 2D. He opened the door and gestured for her to enter. Inside sat two people. Hank Lee was a short, wiry older gentleman with thinning salt and pepper hair. Her file had told her he was a third-generation Korean American. His grandparents emigrated to the US like many others in the aftermath of the Korean war. He held multiple PHDs in a mixture of engineering and physics. He'd worked at Fermilab for over twenty years and was well respected in his field.

As he sat there, he fidgeted with some paperwork on the conference room table, which seemed to indicate nervousness, but his jaw was clenched in irritation. His eyes darted to the man to his left and just as quickly darted back to her. So, he didn't appreciate all the extra security precautions being taken. He was irritated at the other man's presence and nervous about her. Now to figure out why.

She extended her right hand. "It's a pleasure to meet you, Dr. Lee. I'm Special Agent Debra Kazdin. I found your paper on the Diffusion of Muons in Metallic Layers to be quite fascinating, but I have to say I'm eager to hear more about HERBERT."

Hank awkwardly stood up and grasped her hand. Despite his nervousness, he couldn't help but smile when she referenced a paper he had written nearly two decades ago. She knew it had had several co-authors, but it had been Hank's brainchild.

"Why thank you, Agent Kazdin, that's an oldy," he said warmly. "Please, sit." He motioned to the chair opposite him. He gestured to the man seated next to him. "This is Philip Baxter. He is in charge of the enhanced security contingent that has been put in place due to the recent undue attention focused on our facility."

Philip Baxter simply nodded. He was well dressed but not too well dressed. At first glance, he seemed to be a white male in his mid-fifties, pattern balding salt and pepper hair, medium height, medium build, a slightly crooked nose that implied it might have been broken once or twice, kind brown eyes, simple bifocals, and a half smile that seemed to indicate that he was amused by the situation. He could have been a neighborhood greengrocer, a country doctor, or an accountant.

Deb knew the truth of Mr. Baxter, and his presence here was a conundrum wrapped in a mystery. While securing a research facility against external threats was certainly within his capabilities, he was a very dangerous man, and security was not his regular gig. Military, CIA, Defense Contractor, in that order. Phil Baxter was a black bag operative for Titan Security Services, and TSS had contracts with the military and a number of three letter agencies, although, as far as she knew, nothing for the FBI. Worse, he usually supervised entire teams of black bag operatives. She was certain if Dr. Lee had the slightest inkling of who Mr. Baxter really was, he would be even less happy about the situation than he already was. Someone must have thrown a ridiculous amount of money and pulled some chain-sized strings to get Baxter here to babysit a particle physics experiment.

On the other hand, maybe he had gotten on someone's shit list, and this assignment was punishment. She entertained the possibility very briefly, then mentally crossed it out. She couldn't get that lucky.

Deb returned her attention to Dr. Lee. Externally she smiled and nodded at the appropriate times while he talked about the facilities, their timetables, his insistence that all of this hullabaloo was probably overkill, and that he really needed to get back to work.

"Dr. Lee, it's his job to ensure that you, your people, and this facility are properly safeguarded." She gestured to Baxter to reinforce her point. "I'm here to interview those amongst the staff who have had incidents involving people claiming to be from Nadir. I'll also be studying the facility and working with Mr. Baxter so that the FBI can create a response plan in the unlikely event you need our assistance."

She shrugged casually and softened her tone slightly in a way calculated to put him at ease. "Frankly, my goal is to get to the bottom of who is actually causing all this trouble. If it's Nadir, they will be held accountable. If it's someone just trying to put blame on Nadir, then we'll track them down and make them accountable. I just want you and your staff to get back to doing the science and not having to worry about people like Mr. Baxter or myself."

Hank seemed to consider her point. The smile on Baxter's face deepened briefly, and he rolled his eyes and nodded to him in a way only she could see. "Well, Ms. Kazdin. That does sound like the direction we want to head. Let me know if you need anything from me."

She shook her head gently, "I can do most of the coordination with Mr. Baxter. I'm sure he has most of the information I'll need. Just forewarn your people that I'll be doing short interviews with everyone who has reported incidents in the last four weeks."

"Thank you for your time, Dr. Lee." She stood up, extended her hand again as a physical way of excusing him, and handed him one of her cards. "Call me if you have any questions or if you have any additional comments you would like to make."

Hank shook her hand and pocketed the card. He turned and looked at Baxter, who nodded at the door, indicating that he was, in fact, free to go. He did not need any further encouragement and exited the conference room with haste.

The smile on Deb's face disappeared as her attention returned to Baxter.

"So, whose Wheaties did you piss in to get this assignment?" she asked.

He snorted, "I could ask you the same thing. Although you're new to the Chicago office, so it's always possible they just threw this at the new girl because no one else wanted it."

That comment gave Deb pause. She was the 'new girl,' and this wasn't a particularly glamorous assignment. The odds that Nadir was a domestic terror organization masquerading as a research oversight non-profit were very, very low. That meant whoever was behind these incidents was more than likely one or two radicals who were just trying to lay blame on Nadir because they had been vocal about the HERBERT experiment from the moment it went public.

"Look, I'll give you everything you need, but I don't need a little girl looking over my shoulder. I've already got a packet prepared; take it and tell your boss we've got this under control."

His patronizing tone hit her hard in the corner of her mind that housed all her teenage insecurities. She started counting out the digits of pi in her head. She was twenty-five digits in before she got herself under control and then allowed her training to kick in.

"Mister Baxter. Allow me to re-introduce myself in case you missed it. I'm FBI Special Agent Debra Kazdin. I don't care what you think you know about why I'm here, but a 'packet' prepared by you isn't going to cut it. I've got a job to do, and you can either help me do it or stay the hell out of my way."

Baxter sat motionless for a few seconds with that same half smile. Then the smile faded, and his face hardened. "Sorry about that, Agent Kazdin; I have a long tradition of busting the chops of any agents I haven't met before." There was no humor in his voice; if anything, he sounded even more patronizing.

Deb was quite familiar with the good ole boys club that permeated most federal agencies, and he had been part of one at one time. She didn't appreciate being tested, but she certainly wasn't surprised by it.

She placed her hands on the conference table and leaned towards him. In a soft, pleasant voice, she said, "Phil, if you ever call me a little girl again. I'll sauté your balls in a white wine sauce and feed them to you. Shall we start the tour?"

Baxter scowled, but he stood up and gestured to the door. "After you. Agent Kazdin."

Deb sat in her car reviewing the 'packet' of information that Baxter and his people had put together. She now understood why he had tried to blow her off. They had spent the entire day driving the grounds, touring building after building. Despite him being a first-class asshole, she had to admit they'd done a thorough and professional job.

First, it wasn't so much a campus as a small village. The Fermilab grounds would be impossible to secure. It was open for tours every day. To get on to the grounds, you had to provide a photo ID and a reason for your visit, but visiting hours were long, and a few buildings were open to the public without an escort.

The labs and support buildings were another story entirely. The security practices in place were standard, and they had been ramped up with all the undue attention on HERBERT. Baxter's people were enhancing the existing security staff, and they had already developed a good flow to who handled what. They were running drills on how to react to the most likely threat scenarios. This, of course, made the staff nervous, but it was necessary, and she approved.

Still, there were large portions of the ground that were unmonitored. She was pretty sure she had everything she needed from Baxter, and along with her own notes, she should have no problem developing some Tactical response plans. If they did have to intervene, it was going to be a nightmare.

The interviews had been relatively painless. Most of the staff were eager to provide their stories to a federal agent. She could sense relief in most of them that the events they had experienced were finally getting some attention.

It painted a disturbing picture, but at least so far, the incidents had been verbal, implied, or circumstantial. There had been at least a dozen verbal confrontations between lab staff and people claiming to be with Nadir. She had no doubt that most of those were legitimate incidents, but there were also several quasi-related reports. Slashed tires, anonymous notes, a fire set in a dumpster near someone's home. The staff was on heightened alert, making some of them paranoid.

She planned on doing a more thorough analysis of the incidents and would throw that in with her report on the facility and security procedures. For now, she just let everything she had learned today roam around in the back of her mind.

She tidied up her notes and then started the car. As she pulled out of the parking lot, she put the problem of Baxter at the forefront of her mind. If things went to shit here, she needed to know if he would be an asset or a liability. Sometimes the most well-trained professional lost their mind when someone with breasts started giving them orders. She decided she better put that problem to bed before things came to a head. She sighed at the thought of needing to do a research project on a misogynistic prick just so she could do her job. Maybe her boss Reynolds could give her some insight.

Chapter 14

Sophia rolled out of bed with a groan. She usually had a hard time sleeping in strange beds, but this enormous four-poster seemed to be made of clouds. She had quickly fallen asleep and had apparently been allowed to sleep in. She threw on a robe and explored the suite enough to know that her two boys were already absent. A quick shower washed away the sleepiness and travel funk at the same time. She threw on a fresh set of clothes, ran a brush through her still-damp hair, and headed towards the door.

As soon as she opened the French doors, she got a whiff of an amazing blend of coffee, fresh bread, and bacon. Her stomach instructed her feet to pick up the pace on the off chance that they might be close to running out of any of it. She needn't be concerned. As she came out of the stairwell and headed across the house to the kitchen, there were still mounds of food laid out on serving platters, and

Jeff McIntyre

Elektra was just pulling out another loaf of that amazing-smelling bread.

Sophia smiled at Elektra as she picked up a plate and began filling it with the vast array laid out on the kitchen's massive island. "Elektra, this seems like way too much food for even all six of us. Are there more people roaming around the island?"

Elektra scraped a fresh loaf of Tsoureki bread out onto a cooling rack and then turned to Sophia with a smile. "No, Mrs. Fitzroy, just your family and the three of us. Takashi and I enjoy leftovers. Technically, the bread was for lunch, but Joe loves warm slices of it with honey for breakfast."

Joe held up a butter and honey-smeared slice and nodded with an enthusiastic grunt of approval from the end of the counter. Daniel was wiping up runny eggs with a piece of toast in one hand and a large coffee in the other, and Tony had his legs crossed on a kitchen stool and was slowly spinning himself with one hand and munching on a piece of bacon in the other.

As Sophia started to dig into the delicious-smelling plate she had made for herself, Takashi walked in through the front doors. He had an armful of cut and split logs which he carefully deposited in a rack next to the fireplace. He beelined towards the kitchen, and got about two-thirds of the way there when Elektra's glare seemed to remind him of something. He turned back around, retrieved a small broom from next to the fireplace, and proceeded to efficiently clean up the bits of bark and branches that

86

had fallen from his load as he brought it in. Once that was complete, he smiled to himself, returned the broom to its place, and then made his way to the kitchen. Elektra studiously ignored his presence as he made a plate filled primarily with bacon and one very thick slice of bread.

Before long, all eating had paused, with only Daniel and Sophia nursing third and second cups of coffee, respectively. Takashi pushed back an empty plate with a sigh and addressed Tony. "So, now that our bellies are full let's talk about the things you can do on the island. The golf carts are suitable for the asphalt paths, but those really only lead out to the airstrip and down to the dock. We have a couple of side-by-side ATVs if you want to explore the various trails. It is a fun way to see the whole island in a short amount of time. There are, of course, the boats; we have a power boat and a sailboat. It's still pretty chilly out, so we would need to bundle up if you want to go out on the lake. There are several excellent fishing spots along the shore that I can share with you, or we can fish from one of the boats if you'd like. We also have horses; they are quite gentle and mild-tempered, and they are the best way to explore the island. The trails are also quite suitable for hiking. There are no signs, but I can provide you with a rough map of the trails. There is lots of wildlife on the island, but the one thing mistress Drake does not allow is hunting."

Takashi proceeded to point to the various features in the great room. "Inside the house, there is an extensive library. We also have a few board games, although most of them are classics like chess, checkers, and backgammon. There is also the grotto." He pointed to a doorway behind the kitchen that must lead to the garden that made up the North wing. "The pool is heated, so I would suggest it as a good end to a long day outside."

Daniel and Sophia both turned and peered significantly at Tony. Tony looked thoughtful and then blurted out, "Horses!"

Takashi smiled broadly, "Excellent choice," but then he pensively looked at Elektra.

The old woman glared at him with irritation, "Of course I will. Go get them saddled."

Takashi bowed and hurried from the room.

Sophia looked at Elektra with a curious expression, "What was that about?"

Elektra sniffed, "The big idiot is too large to ride the horses, but for some reason, he thinks I hate to ride, so is hesitant to ask me to accompany you. Gentle or not, if you're not experienced on horseback, you can get into trouble. Especially if you try to get the horses to go places they don't want to. I'll ride around the island with you just to make sure you don't get into trouble."

Daniel nodded but asked, "Do you? Hate to ride? We don't want to ask you to do something you don't want to."

Elektra looked at Sophia, "Your man is too gentle." and then looked back to Daniel severely. "Boy, no one makes me do what I don't want to. I usually don't ride the horses because there is no one to ride them with. With no one to keep me company, riding reminds me of days long gone." More gently, she continued. "I love riding horses; I do not love nostalgia. Keeping the three of you entertained and out of trouble should keep me from woolgathering." She smiled at all three of them, "I suggest you head upstairs and get dressed! Pajamas are not very suitable for horseback riding."

All three of the Fitzroys hopped off their stools and scampered for the stairs at the other end of the house.

Sophia tucked Tony into bed. It would take a category five hurricane to wake him now. He had been running at full throttle all day long. They had all gone horseback riding and rode the ATVs. Then he spent the evening swimming in the pool while Daniel and Sophia watched.

And what a pool it was. The south end of the house was truly miraculous. Rather than trying to emulate an island paradise or a secluded jungle pool, it instead was modeled after a desert oasis. A large rock formation was covered in succulents. Water flowed from the top of it through several small drops before cascading over a waterfall that hid a grotto. A large sandy beach ran the opposite length of the pool, and there were several date palms. There were no chairs. Instead, there were creatively carved boulders with hammock-like inserts strewn about in strategic locations. They couldn't be moved, but there were several to choose from.

Daniel was seated on the couch in the living area of their suite, reading a book as she quietly closed the door to Tony's room. "I don't know if this trip has helped Tony or not, but it certainly has done wonders for me," she said.

"Agreed, but I may need a vacation to recover from the vacation," Daniel said as he closed the book and tossed it on an end table. "I'm exhausted."

"Not too exhausted, I hope," Sophia said with a smile as she slinked into their bedroom.

Daniel hopped up and swiftly followed the love of his life. He quietly closed the door to their room, hoping Sophia's giggling wouldn't wake up Tony.

Chapter 15

Hank Lee was staring unhappily at his laptop when Inez Ramirez and Yuri Stepanov walked into his office.

"Big boss man, why so serious?" Yuri said in his deep Russian drawl. Hank looked up and sighed. "I have some new marching orders, and no one is going to like it."

Inez looked at her boss worriedly, "Please, please don't tell me we're pushing up the test."

Hank took off his glasses, pinched his nose briefly, then pulled out a cloth and began studiously cleaning the lenses without responding. Yuri gave Inez a questioning look, but she just shook her head and nodded at Hank. Finally satisfied that no particles obscured his view, he casually tossed the glasses on the desk and said, "Overtime is authorized."

Yuri guffawed, "Boss, we don't get paid overtime." Hank looked at Yuri without a trace of humor in his eyes. "I'm going to need both of you to work evenings and weekends. All three of us will be spending our evenings getting resources from the BABEL experiment up to speed, and then we will take turns supervising blended shifts between the two teams."

Yuri let out a 'Blyat' under his breath.

"We're expected to perform our first full power test by the end of the month." As he talked, his team leads had polar opposite reactions.

Inez looked down, her shoulders slumped, and she looked like she was about to cry. Yuri leaned forward, his mouth dropped open in astonishment, then closed in tight anger.

When Hank stopped, Yuri exploded. "This is grade A BULLshit. How in Stalin's bollocks did they get BABEL's resources? That project is just as high profile."

Hank shrugged, "I don't know. Does it really matter? Our patrons are exerting their influence. The expose from Mr. Shafer was actually quite flattering, and there was only a passing reference to the ongoing protests. However, he did his research well. He made a surprisingly accurate estimate on when HERBERT's power up will be, despite us being suitably vague during the interview. This has made our benefactors nervous. They called in some favors and pledged more money, but they are demanding that the first test be held by the end of the month."

Inez looked up; there were no tears but a deep sadness in her eyes. "Why are they doing this to us? What can it possibly accomplish, especially with all of the caveats we put on agreeing to the aggressive timetable in the first place? We can get to a full power collision, but none of the sensors will be in place. There's no science to be had from doing this, just working us all to death to meet some arbitrary deadline."

Hank nodded somberly, "I don't understand it either, but it's not the first time I've had to perform stupid scientist tricks for a high-profile donor. Although this is definitely the biggest donor dollar penis waving I've ever experienced." Hank quickly forwarded an email and then closed his laptop. "Ok, that was the stick. I've just sent you the carrot. Everyone understands that this is a huge pain in the ass, so there's a bonus involved if we do meet the date. It gets bigger if we can beat it. I've forwarded you the details. Go back to your offices and read it over. I want you to have meetings with your teams to break the news, good and bad, before the end of the day. The sooner we get rolling on this, the sooner we can put this all behind us and get on to the science. That's what we're here for, after all."

Yuri grumbled what were probably a few choice Russian expletives, but then he looked Hank in the eye and nodded fiercely. "Da boss. We'll make this work." He stood up, looked at Inez briefly, and then marched out of Hank's office.

Inez didn't move, "I don't think I can make this work, Hank. If this circus is starting immediately, there's no chance I can find someone to look after my kids on this short of notice."

Jeff McIntyre

Hank stood up, walked around his desk, and put his hand on her shoulder. "I was thinking about you and all of the other parents when this came down the pipeline. In addition to the bonuses, I demanded that we get in-house childcare, hire an activity director, as well as a dedicated bus driver to get all the kids out here. They didn't bat an eye at the additional costs, so I had them throw in catered meals for all of us while they were at it. It's still a massive imposition, but I need you on this, Inez, and I need you to try and be positive. The bonuses certainly won't hurt, but we need everyone's teams focused on succeeding and not focused on the bullshit. Can you do that for me?"

Inez nodded resignedly and then, with a sad smile, "No leftovers for a month; my kids will love that."

Chapter 16

Leo's fingers twiddled on the couch as he sat waiting. His eyes wandered to the large picture of Alvaro Esposito hanging on the opposite wall. He suspected that Mr. Esposito had a high opinion of himself, considering the size of the photograph and its prominent placement in the lobby of Nadir's home office. He was a handsome man with the dark caramel skin and dark hair of his Cuban heritage. He looked younger than his actual age, but a speckling of gray gave the slightest hint of his actual maturity. Worse, the gray only made him more attractive. His smile, even for a staged picture, was engaging, and it lit up his face. The man oozed charm.

Leo knew that if he had stumbled across Mr. Esposito in one of the bars he frequented, he would have flirted with him, maybe tried to take him home.

He waved at the receptionist and nodded at the picture. "That's quite a picture."

She smiled. "I know. He's very photogenic. He didn't want a picture of himself in the lobby, but the staff revolted, and we had it blown up and framed."

Well, so much for him being an egomaniac. Well, maybe he still was, but it didn't extend to self-advertisement in the lobby.

He quickly lost himself in some conversational scenarios he had planned for the interview as the receptionist answered the phone. She talked briefly, hung up, and motioned him towards the office door. "He's ready for you now."

Leo sprung up and nodded to the receptionist and let himself in. He didn't know what expectations he had, but he was remarkably underwhelmed. Despite the big picture outside, the office was small, reserved, filled with clean but not expensive furniture, and the carpet and walls were desperately in need of an update.

Alvaro Esposito stood up from his chair and extended his hand. Leo returned the gesture and was taken off guard by how tired he looked. Very, very tired.

Alvaro gestured to a seat, "Please, have a seat, Mr. Schafer. I must say I'm a little surprised by the request for an interview. Most of the press outlets have been handling us with kid gloves. Afraid to get in the way of an active investigation. Afraid to give a voice to an organization that may be a harbor for domestic terrorists." There was only a hint of frustration in his voice.

The Garden Gnome

Leo tried to guess how much heat must be coming down on Nadir. "Mr. Esposito, I'm here to report. I don't have an agenda; I just think your story deserves to be told. I've met with scientists from Fermilab, and my paper will be publishing an expose on the HERBERT experiment. You and your organization obviously have objections to what they are trying to do. I'm here to understand your organization and its position. I'll let the public make their own opinion after they've heard both sides of the story."

Alvaro considered Leo carefully, trying to decide whether he believed the dish he'd just been served. After a long pause, he seemed to come to a decision and nodded sharply, "Very well, Mr. Schafer. I'll give you the benefit of the doubt for now. We can begin the interview, but if I suspect you're aiming for a hatchet job, I'll end this. I'm not afraid of hard questions, but I'll not help you bury us while we still have a heartbeat."

Leo took out his phone and set it on the desk, "Please call me Leo. Mind if I record? I'll provide you a copy so you can rebut if you'd like."

Alvaro nodded affirmatively, "I appreciate that, and yes, please."

"All right, my first question. Why the name Nadir?"

Alvaro smiled, "It does seem like an odd name for an organization focused on transparency and responsibility in science, no? The bottom? In truth, I chose it because irresponsible scientists think they are unto God. They wish to ascend to the zenith of science with no thought of those they leave behind. The Nadir is the bottom to their top." He rolled his eyes ironically. "Besides, it's a word most people haven't heard which lends it a certain memorability."

Leo scribbled some notes, "So how come Nadir was virtually unheard of up until six months ago?"

Alvaro grimaced, "That's largely my fault. Nadir is not a very old organization. It took me a few years to form the concept, find the backers, and get things organized. To start, I wanted to keep things low-key. We quietly supported science we were in favor of and deserved support. For initiatives that we are critical of, we reached out directly to the organizations responsible and presented our concerns. Up until HERBERT, we were very successful and largely out of the limelight. When we approached Fermilab about our concerns, they were initially supportive, and I believed we were making progress with them. Then suddenly, things changed. They sped up; the more we pushed, the faster they went. Their recklessness has forced us to be more public in our activities."

"So, leaving HERBERT and Fermilab aside for now. Let's talk about your other initiatives, including the ones you're actively supporting."

As the interview progressed, it became apparent to Leo that Alvaro Esposito was very passionate about science. To him, pure research was the best approach to enhancing the lives of everyday people. Focused science had its place, but it was usually tied to greed or fear. Enriching corporations and their shareholders or enhancing a government's ability to suppress or kill people were not noble endeavors, and scientists who engaged in that type of research were little better than dogs. Very passionate.

"I hate to interrupt, but is that why you left NASA?"

Alvaro nodded grimly, "One of many reasons, but probably the primary driver. All those classified missions done on behalf of the Air Force, NSA, and CIA were not done for the betterment of mankind. I felt my beliefs were getting in the way of my job, and that wasn't good for NASA or my soul."

With genuine curiosity, he asked, "Do you consider yourself a spiritual man, Mr. Esposito?"

Alvaro turned and gestured to a picture on a table behind him of an older Hispanic woman, "If you ask her, I'm not." His voice went up an octave, his accent thickened, and he smiled, "Mi Chico, you must pray to the Lady. She will guide you." Leo couldn't help but smile. Alvaro's voice returned to normal, and he became wistful, "In truth, I am spiritual. I'm just not particularly religious. We, as intelligent, self-aware creatures, should use our abilities to improve this world and not destroy it. If there is a creator, regardless of whatever creed you cling to, I think that is what they want of us."

Jeff McIntyre

He paused to gather his thoughts. Alvaro was not what he expected. He was both more and less than that. He didn't pretend to be an expert lie detector, but he'd interviewed enough bullshitters in his life to be pretty good at it. Alvaro Esposito was either a world-class bullshitter, or he was exactly what he appeared to be. A passionate, rational man intent on making the world a better place. Unfortunately, passionate people sometimes do regrettable things in the name of their beliefs.

"Mr. Esposito, I want to transition to some more uncomfortable topics. First, let's start with the obvious. What exactly is Nadir's issue with Fermilab and the HERBERT experiment?"

"To the meat of things, eh? We have no issue with particle accelerator experiments in general. We have helped fund three other similar experiments. The science behind what they are suggesting for HERBERT could revolutionize how accelerators are built in the future. What concerns us is the, pardon the unintended pun, accelerated timetables. There is a lot of energy involved in experiments of this scale. Their public briefs suggest that this test may produce more power than the Large Hadron Collider at CERN with less complexity and lower costs. Such jumps in scientific development come rarely, and they need the proper oversight. And yet, their estimated timeline for the first full-power test keeps getting revised downward. They're rushing things, Mr. Schafer, and that is not good. It's not good for their staff, it's not good for the public, and it's not good science."

He tapped his pen reflexively on his notepad while he thought, "I'm not up to speed on the full timeline of how the project has progressed, but if what you're saying is true, you may have legitimate concerns. You said earlier that Fermilab reacted to Nadir's efforts to voice their concerns?"

"As a non-covert agency of the government, they are supposed to be fairly transparent about their operations. They were, in fact, the exact opposite of that. I have sources within the lab, Mr. Schafer. While the leadership of Fermilab was telling us that they were doing an internal review of our complaints and that our concerns were being addressed, they were actively bringing in more resources and accelerating their timeline." Alvaro sighed deeply. "This forced us to take an active role in bringing their activities out into the light. For our efforts, we've been investigated, sanctioned, and harassed by governmental agencies."

"Ok, I'll try to independently verify the timeline and their response. I have one more subject I want to discuss. I would like your response to claims that members of Nadir have been actively harassing Fermilab staff. There have been reports of disturbing incidents, although, to my knowledge, no one has gotten hurt."

"Leo, I'm going to give you the same answer I've given the police, but I'm also going to give you my no bullshit assessment. Nadir has not nor will it ever condone bullying, veiled threats, sabotage, or acts of violence under any circumstances. That is not

101

what we are about, and this is not how we choose to operate. Any of our associates found to be engaging in such acts will be ejected, and we will turn over any information we have to the authorities." He stood up and began to pace behind his desk. "That being said, we are all human beings. I'm not aware of any of our members being involved in anything like the incidents that are being reported. But we are all afraid of what Fermilab is doing with HERBERT, and fearful people do stupid things. Personally, I think it's a smear campaign, but I'm conducting my own internal investigation to try and find any 'bad apples,' so to speak."

He picked up his phone and stopped the recording app. "Mr. Esposito, we're out of time, and I appreciate you taking time out of your day to answer my questions. I'll send you a copy of this audio recording and an electronic copy of the article after it's been published." He gestured to the business card holder on Alvaro's desk. "Should I just send it to your contact on that?"

Alvaro shook his head and opened a desk drawer. He pulled out another card, one without the Nadir name or logo on it, and handed it across the desk. "Send it to this email address."

He took the card and glanced at it briefly. It had only Alvaro's name, email, and phone number on it. "Thanks. Lastly, did you have any questions for me?"

Alvaro extended his hand again. "No, I'm satisfied. I hope you will give Nadir a fair telling, Leo."

He shook Alvaro's hand and exited the office. As he entered the lobby, he saw a short, smartly dressed woman waiting in the lobby. She was studying the picture of Alvaro just as he had, but her attention shifted briefly to him. There was no recognition on her face, but he recognized her. Caught off guard, he fumbled in his pocket for one of his business cards as the receptionist addressed her. "You can go in now, Agent Kazdin." He walked up and interposed himself between Kazdin and Esposito's office.

"Agent Kazdin, I'm Leo Schafer, and I work for the Tribune. I don't want to hold you up, and I'm not looking for an inside scoop, but I would like to compare notes and share information I've gathered with you on the situation between Nadir and Fermilab. Feel free to give me a call when you have time to chat." He practically shoved his card in her hand and then quickly got out of her way and moved to leave without giving her a chance to respond.

Deb looked at the card and then at the back of Leo as he walked out of the lobby. She felt like she should say something, but he had moved so quickly that it sort of stunned her. Sometimes things just fall into your lap. Not often, but sometimes. She pocketed the card and then walked into the office, closing the door behind her.

Jeff McIntyre

Leo walked out of the building that Nadir's offices were in, then turned around and looked at the front door. He looked right along the facade of the buildings and then left and saw what he was looking for. With one last glance through the glass front door in case Agent Kazdin had followed him rather than go to her appointment with Alvaro, he headed left and veered down the darkened alleyway that was half a block down.

Chapter 17

Agent Deb Kazdin knocked on the closed door to Mike Reynolds' office and waited patiently for a response. His voice carried through the door, but she couldn't hear an answering voice, so he must be on the phone, and his door was usually open, so the call must be private. She turned her back to the door and casually observed the field of cubicles that Mike's office surveyed.

She knew that most of these agents reported to Reynolds, and although she at least temporarily reported to him, her cube was on another floor, so she didn't know many of them. There were heads bowed in concentration scattered randomly around the room. To her right at the end of the row, two people stood behind a seated agent, and they were conversing intensely about whatever was on the agent's monitors.

On the far side of the room, two agents with cups in hand were chatting in front of the windows. She was relatively sure it wasn't work-related based on how animated their body language was. It was a rare agent that could get that excited about a case. Considering the time of year, she suspected it was about this year's prospects for the Cubs or White Sox season.

Maurice, one of the staff from the mailroom, strolled by with a cart filled with packages and envelopes. He nodded at her without making eye contact. She didn't know much about Maurice, but she knew that he was on the autism spectrum. He took great pride in his job, but he didn't interact very well verbally and had a hard time dealing with criticism. Sensing his difficulties, she had opened up to him about her OCD, and while the two of them hadn't exactly become friends, she was one of the few people in the office that he actively acknowledged, and she tried to chat with him when they both had the time.

Reynolds' muffled voice came through his door. "You can come in now."

She gave a small wave to Maurice before she turned, opened the door, and walked in. She pulled the door closed behind her as she entered, which caused Reynolds to raise an eyebrow in curiosity.

"Sir, you'll have my preliminary ops report on your desk later tonight, but I have a couple of things I wanted to bring to your attention as soon as possible."

Reynolds gestured for her to sit down. "Well, that's very efficient of you. What's on your mind?"

"I'm not THAT efficient. I've spent some time with the security and staff at Fermilab. When I got there, they had a full dossier written up. It included a threat assessment as well as several response plans, including participation with outside law enforcement."

"Well, they did know you were coming. Nice of them to do all that prep work. Should make things a lot easier."

"The dossier was provided by Phil Baxter of Titan Security."

A low "shit" escaped from Reynolds before he had a chance to stop it.

"So, you've heard of him," she said, more comment than question.

"Yeah, I've heard of him. I've worked with the son of a bitch too." Reynolds tapped the top of his desk with his index finger. "What in the hell is Phil Baxter doing providing security consulting to Fermilab?"

"That was my question. I only know of him by reputation, but my first impression is that he's an arrogant misogynist. His reputation suggests he deserves to be arrogant, but this type of assignment seems way below his pay grade. He was certainly denigrating enough to the 'new girl' who had the audacity to demand she be allowed to do her job." She was proud that none of the heat she had felt during her encounter with Baxter crept into her voice.

Jeff McIntyre

Reynolds let out a long slow breath. "Well, I don't know what kind of hole you've just uncovered, but it's a lot deeper than I was expecting. I'll reach out to some of my contacts and see if I can find out how or why Titan is involved in this. For the time being, I want you to stay away from Baxter. This is going to be a little unprofessional but go around him if you need to arrange any further interviews or tours of the Fermilab facilities."

"Understood, sir. There's another subject I wanted to broach before I leave." She pulled out the business card that Leo had handed her at Nadir. "I had some free time, so I arranged and was allowed to briefly interview Alvaro Esposito. I crossed paths with this reporter." She handed the card to Reynolds. "He wants me to contact him to discuss the Fermilab/Nadir situation. He says he's not looking for an inside scoop; he just wants to share his notes with me."

Reynolds took the card and flipped it end over end in his hand as he thought. "I'm going to leave the handling of this up to you. You know what aspects of this situation are not for public consumption, and we can't give him any exclusivity. The press can be an asset or a hindrance. Consider the pros and cons, then decide on a plan of action. Do what you want with this reporter." He handed the card back to her.

She was a little taken aback. She was a very junior agent, and her supervisor was giving her an extraordinary amount of latitude. "Thank you for the vote of confidence in my ability to handle this, sir; I won't let you down.

"Don't let yourself down, Kazdin, and you won't let me down. Good luck."

Chapter 18

Sophia and Daniel strolled hand in hand along a wood chip-covered path that wound its way through the forested area of the island. It was still early spring, so the lake kept the air brisk, but it was warm enough that they couldn't see their breath. It was breezy, but the sun was shining, and the trees hadn't gotten enough foliage to cover them in shade. The hours had melted away along with their worries.

The morning had started with another fantastic breakfast from Elektra. When Takashi offered to take them fishing, Tony jumped at the chance. Sophia and Daniel had accompanied them for a while, but it seemed the two of them were having a grand time, and Takashi was so attentive they asked if he would mind keeping an eye on Tony while they went for a walk.

Takashi bowed deeply. "It would be my honor." He and Tony were becoming fast friends.

Tony had even helped Takashi with some of his chores that morning.

At their request, Joe would be ready to lift off at two, so they could get back into the city and home not too long after sunset.

Sophia reflected on the once-in-a-lifetime experience this weekend had been. It was as if they had been at an all-expense resort for three, and she wasn't eager for it to end. The trails, the pool, the incredible library, and the breathtaking view from the tower.

She and Daniel had climbed to the top of the tower as the sun rose. The night before, she had made him promise to get up early with her because they had been too tired to make the ascent last night and had missed the sunset.

The entire top of the tower was made of curved glass panels that gave a panoramic view of the whole island. The view was spectacular. There was one panel with a door that led out onto the balcony. A wide deck with railing encircled the central turret. Although most of the island was covered in trees except for the airstrip and the clearing around the house and outbuildings, the tower was a good twenty feet higher than the tallest trees, so the view of Lake Michigan was fantastic. If you stood on the East side of the tower, there was nothing to see but the lake. As they watched, the sun emerged from the waters and set the whole lake on fire.

Immediately below the tower but tucked in behind the house was a large circular clearing covered in white gravel. No trees encroached on the clearing, and no weeds poked up through the rock. Rebecca must like bonfires because the center of the clearing was a fire pit. The heat from whatever fires had burned there scorched the gravel a good ten feet from the edge of the pit.

She sighed deeply as Daniel looked at his watch and then showed her the time. Reality beckoned. She pulled Daniel to her and held him close. Listening to his heartbeat, feeling the warmth of his chest against her cheek. His arms enveloped her, and they embraced for a moment in time, relishing the solitude of this random path through the forest on a private island. For that moment, they had no cares, no worries, no responsibilities.

And then it passed. Daniel kissed the top of her head. She stepped back and smiled up at him, and they made their way back to the house.

As they approached, Tony and Takashi came from one of the other pathways with fishing gear in hand. True to his word, Takashi had kept him out of trouble and got him back to the house in time for lunch.

"Mom! Dad! I caught a salmon!" Sophia silently hoped they wouldn't have to fly back to Chicago with a dead fish in the plane. "It was only eleven inches, so we had to put it back, but it was HUGE!" Behind Tony, Takashi made a motion with his hands, suggesting the fish was at least three feet long. The smiles on both their faces were infectious.

Sophia and Daniel smiled and laughed with them all the way to the house.

Takashi handed Daniel a plastic bucket of mixed live fish to take to Elektra and then made a beeline for one of the outbuildings to put away the fishing gear. "I'll join you as soon as I have finished cleaning up." He turned and bowed to Tony, who returned the bow with surprising seriousness.

They entered the great room, and before Daniel took two steps, he asked loudly in the direction of the kitchen, "Where would you like the fish?"

Elektra's head popped up from where she had been peering into the oven. She took one look at the bucket in his hand and motioned him back out. "Just put it on the stoop out of the way of the doors. I'll deal with it later." and her head disappeared again. Slightly muffled because of the intervening island, came, "Go get cleaned up; lunch will be set in about ten minutes.

After they finished eating, Sophia and Daniel helped Elektra do the dishes. Takashi asked, "Are your bags ready to go? If so, I will bring them down and get them loaded in the cart."

Daniel nodded, "Yep, they're set. Would you like some help bringing them down?"

Takashi shook his head, "I already have assistance." He stood up and turned to Tony. "Entei? Will you assist me with the luggage?" Elektra's head whipped around, and she glared at Takashi, who seemed not to notice.

Tony smiled and said, "Hai!" as he jumped off his stool and followed Takashi to the stairs.

After they left, Sophia gently asked Elektra, "Did Takashi do something wrong?"

At first, the older woman seemed hesitant to answer. At last, she sighed, "Not really. We are servants here. We don't get many guests, but when we do, Ms. Drake expects us to act with a certain amount of decorum. That old fool giving your son a nickname only shows how much he's smitten with Tony. The three of you have felt more like family than guests. It has been a pleasure having you here."

Sophia's cheeks warmed. She knew enough about Elektra to understand that expressing affection wasn't exactly her strong suit. "We feel the same about the two of you. It has been a lovely weekend. Somehow, I'm going to have to figure out how we can weasel our way back out here again."

Elektra nodded and smiled, but there was a sadness in her eyes. It was unlikely that a return trip was in the cards, and they turned away from one another in unison and returned to the task at hand.

"What's Joe been up to? We haven't seen him except at meal times." Daniel asked.

Elektra rolled her eyes, "He has responsibilities related to the plane and island maintenance, but he spends almost every waking hour holed up in his room reading selections from Rebecca's library. I think he was reading one of her collections of Aristotle's works this time."

Daniel looked wistfully at the library in the corner. "Aristotle? That's some heavy reading. I wish I had had more time to look at her collection."

After much hugging and maybe a few tears, the Fitzroys rode in the golf cart with Takashi back out to the plane. Joe and their luggage were already loaded, and the engines sputtered to life when they came into view of the plane. Apparently, Joe was ready to get back.

Before they embarked, their arrival was played out in reverse. Takashi shook hands and bowed to each of them in turn. As Sophia and Tony climbed into the plane, Daniel paused and turned back to Takashi. "You called Tony 'Entei'. What does that mean?"

Takashi smiled sheepishly, "Dam. Because he can be as stubborn as one." He paused before continuing, "It is also a Pokémon."

Daniel burst out laughing. He gave Takashi one last bow before boarding the plane.

Takashi stepped back to the golf cart and waved at the plane as it turned, taxied past him, and then surged into the sky. Elektra appeared out of the tree line and walked up beside him as the plane disappeared into the distance. "I'll need you to fill me in on everything the boy talked to you about. She wants a full report by morning."

Jeff McIntyre

"Yes, my dear." He turned and helped her into the cart. "I really like them. It's a shame what they're about to go through"

"I do too, but this is necessary. For all our sakes. Now take me back to the house; I have fish to clean."

Chapter 19

Leo sat in a private booth at Big Lou's pizza. He liked conducting in-person interviews here because the deep dish was amazing, and the private booths were away from the hustle and bustle of the main restaurant. People seemed to loosen up when they'd had a beer and a slice of pie. His eyes wandered around the room from the black and white photos of prohibition-era Chicago to the vintage signage and the vaguely Italian paraphernalia hanging on the walls as he waited.

The minutes passed, and he tried to keep control of his patience. Their brief conversation on the phone had been vaguely positive, and she had agreed to meet him here to discuss in more detail. He hoped that she would be interested in any information regarding the Nadir situation and that her curiosity would convince her to come.

But as the minutes passed, his self-doubt kicked in, and he suspected that she might just blow him off. It was always tricky approaching federal agents or police, for that matter, about active investigations. He knew he would have to do this with his hands open and hopefully earn some quid pro quo with her.

Even though she wasn't even late, his nerves were starting to get the best of him when Agent Kazdin pushed through the privacy curtain letting in some of the bustling sounds of the main restaurant and a heady waft of garlic and cheese into the booth. He tried not to look relieved but was pretty sure he failed as he stood up and extended his hand across the table to her. "Thanks for coming. I understand how delicate the situation is for you."

"Mr. Schafer, I hope you're not wasting my time." Deb took a seat and gave him a stern look. "I have permission from my supervisor to discuss some aspects of the case with you. I make no promises about what details I share with you. If I think you can be of assistance, I may even share sensitive details, but I will be very clear about what is on and off the record. Are we clear?"

"Crystal." Leo sat down slowly and took a deep gulp of water. He was used to being a cheetah, slowly circling a grazing gazelle. Trying not to make it bolt across the plain and out of his grasp. The way Deb Kazdin looked at him, he knew how the gazelle felt. "First off, I'd like to share my interview recordings. They were not done in confidence, and nothing was off the record, so I can share them freely. I have a video conference with Hank Lee and Inez Ramirez from Fermilab, and I have an audio recording of my interview with Alvaro Esposito."

Deb leaned back with a disappointed look on her face. "While that's quasi-useful, at least to corroborate my own interviews, I doubt there's anything revolutionary in there. Is that all you've got?"

Leo shook his head, "No, of course not. I'm also going to give you all the background I've compiled on Esposito and Nadir and the dossier I've created on the HERBERT project, as well as all of the principal researchers." Leo could sense growing discontent as he spoke, so he forged forward without giving her a chance to respond. "I also have details from an insider about agitators that have been showing up at organized protests that don't seem to be associated with Nadir and the time and place of the next protest organization meeting."

She perked up at that little revelation. "That… could be useful. Why do they need to organize their protests?"

"Nadir is a new and fairly small organization. All of their protests are attended by members, but they hire extra bodies to flesh out the protests." Leo sipped his water, "It's not that uncommon of a practice, although I've seen it more commonly from lobbying organizations, not advocacy groups."

Deb got lost in her thoughts. Thankfully the silence was broken by the waiter arriving to take their order. A flamboyant young man with a thick Italian accent. "Ello, my name is Alfonse, and I'll be a serving you this EVening."

Half a large deep-dish sausage pizza and half a dozen beers between them later, Alfonse had just left to get a to-go box for the other half of the pizza. "I wonder if that accent is real or if he just does that for fun?" Leo pondered.

"For the tips. Locals come here for the pie, but tourists love the kitsch, and they tip better. Since he never knows who he's dealing with, he stays in character. Locals will ignore the silliness or call him out on it, at which point he laughs it off and drops the character."

"How did you come to *that* conclusion?" he asked.

She grinned over the top of her beer, "When I came in, I heard him dropping an order at the bar. His real accent is pure Wisconsin cheddar."

He snorted in amusement. "You're very observant, Agent Kazdin."

"It's Deb. Over beer and pizza, you can call me Deb." She drained the last of her glass and then spun it in a puddle of condensation where her glass had sat. "Why are you giving me this information, Mr. Schafer?"

"Just call me Leo. I don't personally think that Nadir is the cesspool of infamy that some in the press are making it out to be. But I'm pragmatic enough to believe that it's entirely possible. I don't have the resources or clout to get to the bottom of this. In fact, my editor will kick my ass if I spend too much time on this story." Leo began unconsciously tracing the pattern in the tablecloth as he stared at a picture of the Valentine's Day massacre that hung on the wall. "I'm not interested in sensationalizing the situation just to further my career. There's too much at stake. I could fan the flames, and people could easily get hurt. I don't think I could live with that."

Deb stared at him thoughtfully for a long moment. To Leo, it seemed like she was contemplating whether to eat him or not. At last, her gaze dropped to her now empty glass as if wishing more liquid courage was at hand. "What I'm about to tell you is off the record for the time being. I may let you publish it later, but for now, it has to stay silent. If you're serious about wanting to help, find out how Philip Baxter got brought on board at Fermilab as a security consultant."

"Philip Baxter? Should that name mean anything to me?"

"God, I hope not. He's a spook for Titan Security. Nothing he does is above board. My boss is exploring the government side of things, but I'd like to chase the civilian side of this in a way I can't. You see, he's not under investigation in any way. He's supposed to be providing additional security for Fermilab in case anything goes down there. But Phil Baxter being assigned as a 'security consultant' is like putting SEAL Team 6 on latrine duty."

Jeff McIntyre

He picked a piece of Italian sausage off one of the remaining pieces and popped it in his mouth. He thought he saw her eyes narrow ever so slightly. It might have been a trick of the light because her expression otherwise didn't change. He nervously wiped his hands off on his napkin and shoved his hand across the table at her. "Deal. I'll poke around and see if anything falls out regarding Titan."

Deb glanced wryly at his outstretched hand before extending her own. "The only thing I can do for you short term is make sure you're present for any press releases we make regarding this case. If I have the opportunity to release anything exclusively, I'll do it through you, but that level of decision is made above my head, so no guarantees."

He nodded thoughtfully, "I think that's all I can ask for. Hopefully, this will benefit both of us, and with luck, we can get the Nadir versus Fermilab feud de-escalated before anything truly unfortunate happens."

Deb stood up and pushed the curtain aside. As she left, she said, "Luck is the last hope of fools. You can have the rest of the leftovers, Leo."

Despite his promise to himself to eat better, Leo picked up another piece of deep-dish pie and nibbled on it. She was an old soul, but he thought he might have made a chink in her armor. He liked her already, but he also knew that one wrong step could destroy any chance of getting her to work with him.

Alfonse pushed in through the curtain and flipped and folded a piece of cardboard with a practiced flourish until a pizza box appeared. "May I box up your leftovers, signore?"

He smiled at the waiter, "Sure, but let me ask you. Why that ridiculous accent?"

The waiter grinned, and his accent disappeared, "For better tips. The tourists eat it up."

Chapter 20

The soil was a rich loam. He could tell it was not native but had been placed here to help the shrubs and grasses grow. The dichotomy of this and the habit of trimming the grasses before they had a chance to seed made him uneasy. Almost everything about this age made him uneasy.

He strained to hear worms and beetles and spiders and voles working their way through the soil. The sounds of water, gas, and humanity's waste flowing through pipes and the thrum of electricity in underground cables threatened to overwhelm him. He focused and allowed these unnatural sounds to pass through him and bleed away from his perception. At last, his senses brought nature to the forefront.

The cacophony of the minute calmed him. A slight breeze moved through, brushing the grass and causing the branches of the shrubs that surrounded him to rustle and scrape against each other, tickling his back and sides. It was comforting.

The Garden Gnome

He reached out, becoming one with the earth and air. Two squirrels chased each other through the branches of a young elm. A pair of magpies heckled each other from opposing branches of the great oak tree. A stray cat silently stalked toward him. It could hear his movement in the shrubs but had not yet spotted him. It must be stalking the young rabbit nestled up against his back. It was going to be in for quite a surprise.

As he patiently waited for the feline to realize the error of its ways, he contemplated the situation he found himself in. It was good to be awake and active again. It had been far too long since the last Dawning. So much had changed. He could not remember a gap this long between cycles.

Even so, something felt wrong this time. He could sense the approach of the dawning, but somehow it felt rushed. As if some great force was pushing it from behind. A Dawning event was not something that should be rushed. It filled him with foreboding, as so many things did these days.

The cat's stalking brought it right to the edge of the little hollow in the bushes he was resting in. Its eyes laser-focused on the baby bunny cowering beside him. In a low rumble, he said, "Boo." The poor cat did a vertical leap straight up and out of the bushes and tore off across the yard as fast as its furry legs could carry it.

He grumbled in satisfaction and returned to the task at hand. For he had been tasked, and he was not one who would fail to meet his obligations.

Jeff McIntyre

You could more easily move a mountain than make him break a vow. It was good that the family had moved here. More nature and more privacy. Their residence downtown had left him lurking from too far away for his own comfort.

He reached out again with his senses. Ahh, there it is. He could feel the contraption's weight upon the earth as it approached. He peered through the bushes as the large metal object rolled by with the boy and his father inside as they did on most 'school days.'

He waited patiently for the boy to come to him. Tremors in the ground told him of Tony's approach as he sprinted around to the back of the house. Although Tony ran with vigor, he could sense that the boy had not had a good day. He cautiously poked his head out of the bushes as Tony approached.

The boy's face suddenly lit up, and he said, "Hey, Bob!"

He nodded and returned the greeting, "Hello Tony, how was school?"

Daniel stepped out of the kitchen into the back yard and looked around for his son. The sounds of his son playing came from the playground. He was quite proud of the lumber, plastic, and steel amalgamation. It was mostly a kit, but Daniel had taken time to make some modifications so it would continue to entertain

The Garden Gnome

his growing boy. He knew how much Tony liked to climb and hang from things, and he'd rather Tony do that over the sandpit than try similar antics in the big oak tree, so he had built a climbing wall that led to a set of monkey bars that didn't come with the original kit.

Sure enough, as he stepped out into the yard, there was Tony hanging inverted from the bars. Cleo was sitting at the top of the slide, watching Tony with fascination, her tail flicking occasionally. He walked over and sat down in the grass at the edge of the sand. "Hey, big man, how's it going?"

Tony twisted and looked under his arm at him. "Hey, Dad. It's not time to come in yet, is it?"

Daniel shook his head. "Nope, I just wanted to talk to you a bit. Come over here for a minute."

Tony bent at the waist, reached up to grab the bars, then deftly flipped his knees off the bar and did a half flip to the sand. His dismount wasn't quite perfect, causing him to stagger and then drop to his knees in the sand with a giggle.

Daniel smiled and patted the grass next to him. Tony hopped back to his feet, strolled over, and plopped down next to him. He looked out into the woods behind their house for a moment before speaking. "Let's talk about Bob. You've been spending a lot of time with him lately, and I just want to make sure everything's ok." Tony's head sank, and he kicked listlessly at the sand at the edge of the pit. "I know things haven't been going well at school. I want to help you through this. Your mom and I are

127

worried that Bob is keeping you from dealing with your problems."

Tony shook his head. "I don't know what to do about the boys at school, I'm just lonely, and Bob is always here." Daniel pulled his son's chin gently up and around so he could look him in the eyes.

"Tony, how come your mom and I have never seen Bob? Where is he at now?"

Tony shrugged, then quickly scanned around the yard, leaning first forward and then back to see past Daniel. "I donna know, he was here a little while ago, but he always disappears when anyone other than me or Cleo is around. Gnomes are shy, I guess."

He started, "Gnomes? Bob is a gnome?" He couldn't help thinking about the large collection of ceramic garden gnomes that their neighbor Maria DeLuca had.

Tony nodded slowly. "Well yeah, that's what he told me."

Daniel rubbed the back of his head thoughtfully and chose not to press the issue. He swiftly stood up and did an exaggerated jump in front of Tony with his knees bent and his arms reaching for him to begin the long overdue tickling. Tony shrieked, rolled over, and tried to crawl away, but Daniel was faster.

From her perch at the top of the playground, Cleopatra the Great momentarily paused her grooming to stare in fascination at the ball of laughter coming from the sand pit. She determined that it was neither threat nor prey but that the noise would interrupt the nap she was about to take. So, she hopped off her perch and made her way through the cat door and into the house, leaving the noise behind.

Chapter 21

Samuel Larkin sat at his desk, hunched over his laptop as he scanned through the reports of the various companies that represented the visible arms of the Knights of the Stone. The financial reports were stamped with the Taula de canvi of Barcelona logo, and they looked to be in good order.

They had not yet started Key event spending as they didn't have a focus yet, but they'd built up a good war chest over the last forty years. They had spent hard in the 80s and 90s to facilitate nuclear talks, but they had rebounded and then some during the tech bubble at the turn of the millennium. They had seen the bubble coming and swung their portfolio to take advantage of it. For the last twenty or so years, they had focused on stable investments. They were in this for the long run and had vast resources. Better to build them slowly than risk the volatility of the stock markets.

The report from their lobbyist's arm, Volga Partners, was pretty typical. There were four reports stamped by the North American, Latin American, Europe Middle East and Africa, and Asia Pacific regional offices. Spread across the four reports were twenty major initiatives in play across six major powers and the status of another twelve proposals in the pipeline waiting for the appropriate timing and funding approvals. Most involved suppressing or defunding high energy and nuclear energy research, a few involved mandates or funding for volcanic and plate tectonics research initiatives, and a couple were trying to get funding for space threat tracking. All the planning in the world could be ruined by a decent-sized meteor strike.

Intelligence, counterintelligence, and operations were run through the military contracting arm of Guardian Defense LLC. It was remarkable how many of their operations they could mask through that company. It also had a large presence in the home security automation market as well as the emergency preparedness sector. Their report was quite thorough, and as usual, they seemed to have things under control.

Intelligence had asked for and received funding for a threat correlation database. Their current one was based on the first generation developed post cold-war. The new one was being acquired from and enhanced by the same software company that developed the European Union's database. The EU wasn't quite as paranoid about protecting their software as the US and Russia were, so this deal was slipping through the cracks.

Counterintelligence already had an internet and social media tracking and parrying system in place. Anytime a subject that could be even remotely linked to one of their initiatives started to gain traction, algorithms dumped counter posts that downplayed the sensitive topic and up played irrelevant adjacent data. In addition, five random inflammatory topics or news blurbs were chosen, and advanced software began reposting and commenting to drive those subjects' relevance up in newsfeeds, thus driving attention to their initiatives. The counter-intelligence IT department called it The Kraken because it had countless arms and could be unleashed upon their enemies, leaving devastation in its wake. He kind of liked the name.

The Operations team had filed an extensive report on their assets in and around CERN, ITER, and Fermilab. They kept an eye on all high-energy research initiatives, but most of those had been deemed low priority. They still didn't have a good handle on how much "energy" was needed to unlock the key, but their resources weren't unlimited. They had to make intelligent guesses on what the most likely sources would be and have resources and action plans in place to deal with them.

Nathan, the Second Seat, was filing a weekly report on the status of the objects in the reliquary. The activation of Castor's Hummingbird had started the countdown, and depending on how things progressed, the report cadence would increase. He had attached a copy of the reliquary playbook to his latest status reports so they would be able to follow the progress of events.

Over the centuries, the Knights had developed a methodology to understand when X event happens; then they are at Y in the timeline. Some of the artifacts reacted to the timing of the Key event and could be used to predict when it would occur, while others were inert until very shortly before the event but could be used to track down the Lock. He was perusing the playbook when there was a knock on the door frame of his office. He looked up and saw Brian, the Seventh Seat poking his head in. "Do you have time to talk?"

He closed his laptop and waved him in, "Yep, I was expecting you. Just reviewing reports while I waited. Have a seat."

Brian walked in and took the offered seat. He had the look on his face that he had come to expect with new recruits. A bit of, I can't believe what I've just learned, and a whole lot of, I have so many questions I don't know where to start.

He smiled at him and decided to help him get things rolling. "Yes, Arthur and the Knights of the Round Table were real, although most of the tales we've come to know are heavily distorted from what our records tell us. And yes, the fact that the tales of Camelot are at least somewhat real is a pale shadow compared to the fact that magic is real and is the greatest threat to humanity short of nuclear annihilation."

Brian nodded. "I've read everything you gave me, but I'm still trying to absorb it. There's lots of facts but not a lot of context. Why do the Knights believe that magic is such a threat? I mean, Gawain's original transcripts, if the translations are correct, paint him as a bit of a madman leading a bunch of fanatics."

"The context you're looking for is in the detailed accounts of Key events. What I gave you only has the highlights. Over the centuries, there have been a few times when we were too late. We had to come in after magic had returned and assassinate the Lock. Some of those were horrifying, knights and mercenaries fighting against monsters and magic. Thousands were murdered by the reincarnation of Merlin. Gawain may have been insane, but he wasn't wrong. Humanity, especially in the modern age, is not prepared for magic to return, and we take it as our solemn responsibility to ensure that it doesn't."

"So, magic has returned? Why aren't there any accounts of it?"

He turned somber. "We're very good at our job. It's never taken us more than six months from the Key event to deal with the Lock. Not only are we good at tracking him down, we're good at covering up the evidence. Still, over the centuries, there have been reports of strange phenomena that can't be explained. Superstition is our ally. In the modern day, we discount the historic tales of witches, fairies, and demons as superstitious hysteria. Because we've been able to keep Magic from lingering for any length of time, we color people's perceptions. The Knights of the Stone are the original social media influencers."

"Sir, what was so important about the 1982 Key event? I'm not getting the full picture." Brian asked.

He nodded, "Over its long history, the Knights realized that if you removed the Lock from the Key. If you could extricate him from the natural disaster before it occurred, he wouldn't be activated, and magic wouldn't return. So, in an attempt to be more humane, we tried kidnapping and relocation. Assassination was a last resort, and we were successful at that for about five cycles. Unfortunately, that nuclear blast proved that a man-made event could trigger it anyway. We now have to be more nimble and more ready to pull the trigger, so to speak."

Brian studied the palms of his hands. He could tell that whatever he was going to ask next was the key to whether Brian would remain in the Knights of the Stone or become another statistic. In the eyes of the world, Brian Cooke was already dead. He had been killed by an IED while doing security consulting in Iraq, and human remains with matching albeit falsified DNA had been buried in Arlington. Making him disappear if this conversation didn't turn out the way he hoped; well, that was an unfortunate side effect of the Knight's recruiting process.

At last, Brian looked up from his hands. "Why did you recruit me, sir? I'm just a grunt. What is it that the Knights need from me?"

This time when he spoke, he wasn't smiling. "You are anything but 'just a grunt.' If you were, you wouldn't be here. You are intelligent, driven, and, most of all, loyal. You understand that there is a greater good to be served. Almost all of our recruits are soldiers or law enforcement. We have been tested in combat, and we have been forced to make hard decisions. But the one thing all recruits have in common. We have been forced to sacrifice one life to save another." He gestured at the laptop. "If you've read the history, you should understand why. In our lifetime, we may be called upon to end the life of the Lock. A young man who has done nothing wrong but is a victim of fate. Chosen to be the vessel for Merlin's rebirth and the return of magic. That means cold-blooded murder in the name of a cause, and you must be able to do that without a moment's hesitation."

Brian nodded sadly. "You've chosen the right man."

"That's what I thought, but now you have to prove to me why you deserve to be here." Sam pulled the suppressed .45 pistol out from under his desk and pointed it at Brian. "I've explained to you what's at stake and, in broad strokes, why you were recruited. Tell me, why did we choose you?"

Brian stared at the open end of the pistol pointed at him. There was no fear in his eyes. The standard issue sidearm of the United States Army up to the early 90s had been refitted with a threaded barrel so that an aftermarket suppressor could be affixed to the end of it. It would change the sound of the pistol firing from a roar to a loud bark. Even with the door open, people in nearby offices might think that Larkin had dropped a book. Brian's eyes drifted up to meet Larkin's, and that seemed to get his brain back in gear.

"I'm assuming you're referring to the Louis Pelletier incident?" Samuel nodded and suggested with the pistol that he should elaborate. "Louis Pelletier was a French arms dealer. Mostly known for providing small arms to the Afghan warlords that were making our life a living hell. Our intelligence briefing indicated that he was trying to step up to the big leagues. He had acquired a sizable amount of Sarin gas. We didn't know who he had sold it to, but we wanted to find out before they had a chance to use it. Sarin is some nasty shit, and when the warlords aren't trying to kill us, they like to attack villages under the protection of rival warlords."

He disengaged the safety and pulled back the hammer on the pistol. "I know all of this, Brian. I've read the report. Tell me what's not in the report."

Brian stared down the pistol, but his eyes lost focus as he thought back to that day. "Pelletier was spotted in Kabul. We knew he was trying to get out of Afghanistan, but we didn't know how. There were several teams engaged in the search, but mine was the one that found him. Unfortunately, he had guards.

Jeff McIntyre

A running gun battle ensued. We managed to separate him from his retinue, but most of my team was incapacitated. Sergeant Reynolds and I were pursuing him on foot through a market. People were hunkered down because of all the gunfire. He reached an open street with us right behind him. Grabbed a woman and used her as a shield as he opened the door of a cab. He's trying to back into the cab, using the woman's body to protect him. Reynolds and I take up positions. I know if he gets into that cab, there's a good chance he'll get away. We have no eyes in the sky, and there's no sign that any of the other squads have reached our position. The woman is screaming, the cabbie is screaming, Pelletier is screaming at the cabbie. Reynolds isn't even watching Pelletier. He's terrified that the bodyguards will come up behind us."

Without realizing it, Brian's hands had come up like he was holding his M4 carbine. His left eye closes as he aims down the sight.

"I saw an opportunity. They wanted Pelletier alive. They needed to question him to find out where the Sarin had gone. Reynolds was trained as a medic, and the other teams were at least headed this way. I fired through the woman's lower abdomen and hit Pelletier in the leg. They both collapsed on the ground. Without a gun to his head, the cabbie took the opportunity to bolt into traffic." Brian dropped his hands and stood up. He walked over to Larkin's office fridge and pulled out a bottle of water. He took a long cleansing drink and then turned back to Larkin's.

138

"Did they live?" He asked as he de-cocked the pistol, re-engaged the safety, and then placed it on his desk.

"Pelletier ended up with a limp. He hadn't managed to make a sale, and they recovered the Sarin from a warehouse. None of the warlords he made contact with were crazy enough to buy it. They got the woman, Taara, to a hospital. But Afghani hospitals are not as well equipped as western hospitals. They're quite experienced at dealing with gunshot wounds, but I apparently nicked her intestine in three places, and they only found two. She got sepsis and died about a week later."

"And does this event still trouble you?" He asked. "You've had counseling for PTSD."

Brian shook his head. "Nah, that's under control. For the first couple of months after this, I would run through the scenario in my head and see if there was anything I could have done differently, but I came to the conclusion that I made the right call, and so did the investigators. I didn't even get chewed out. Over the course of the firefight with his guards, twelve people got shot, and three of them died. It just became a depressing statistic on the daily report that was offset by the fact that we had captured an arms dealer and recovered three hundred kilograms of Sarin."

He stood up and extended his hand. "I'm glad I didn't have to kill you. Your probation is over. Now is when things get interesting."

Chapter 22

Hunger, thirst, fear. Softpaws did not understand what drove her. She had not eaten in days. Every time she smelled prey, the voice in her head urged her to move on. She stayed close to the river, when possible, but it had been surrounded by dwellings of the two legs for many miles. So many strange noises, so many strange creatures. Her pack never came into the land of the two legs. Better to stick to the forests and fields. Even the straight rows created by the two legs were safer, more familiar. Every instinct cried to retreat, get away from the awful sounds and smells. But still, something called her. She could not ignore the whispers in her head.

Daniel sat at the kitchen table, grumbling as he read one of his first year's papers. It was supposed to be about what techniques may have been used to create the Lapis Blue reported to adorn the Tower of Babylon. It was a clever subject and could have earned high marks.

Unfortunately, the author had chosen to hand write it, despite explicit instructions to type it. Not only was his handwriting nearly illegible, but it also had an untold number of typos and punctuation issues. It was giving Daniel a headache just thinking about trying to slog through it. It was at least five thousand words of handwritten mess.

Tony came hopping down the stairs and made a beeline toward the back door. "Tony… shoes…" Tony's sock-clad feet slid to a halt. He spun around, windmilling his arms, and did a sock burnout as he accelerated into the living room. A few minutes later, he clomped his way through the kitchen, exaggerating his steps so that Daniel knew he was in compliance.

Daniel looked over his shoulder as Tony opened the door. "Hey sport, if you get in the sand, don't forget to shake out your socks and shoes before you come back in."

Tony gave a wild-armed salute as he pulled the door shut. He then leaped off the stairs and bolted out of sight in the direction of the sand pit. Daniel grinned and turned back to his papers with a sigh.

Jeff McIntyre

The urging guided Softpaws from safe space to safe space. Led her to places to rest and hide until the sun came down. But it kept her hungry, eager, desperate. Now, as she neared its unknown destination, the urge forced her to move in daylight. Flitting to and fro, avoiding the two legs, avoiding the foul-smelling beasts on the paths of black and gray. Always pulled back to the trail.

At last, she sensed that she was nearing the end. She could smell a two-leg and hear its noises beyond a row of trees and shrubs. A young one. Saliva dripped from Softpaws jaw. Hunger overcame her natural fear, and she crept through the shrubbery. The urging was uncontrollable, driving her forward. It was small, and there was no sign of a larger member of its pack to protect it. She slowly stalked across the grass toward her prey.

Daniel chucked the paper he had been reading across the table as if it had offended him in some way. He sighed and massaged his temples as he girded himself for the next literary masterpiece. As he reached down into his bag to grab the next paper, he caught a glimpse of movement out of the corner of his eye. He turned his head and looked out the back door, expecting to see Tony swooping around the back yard.

What he saw sent a chill up his spine. A large gray and brown mottled canine was slowly stalking across the yard. Its eyes fixed upon the corner of the yard where he knew Tony was playing. His mind raced as he hurtled toward the door. Is that a coyote? It's enormous. Maybe it's a wolf? What the hell would a wolf, or for that matter, a coyote, be doing this deep in Chicago? It's gotta be a coyote. All that drool hanging from its mouth, maybe it's rabid? Oh, shit oh shit oh shit. In his haste, his feet got tangled in his chair, and he lurched off balance and staggered toward the door.

The coyote accelerated and disappeared from view. He scrambled to open the door, but it took him precious seconds as his hand-eye coordination failed him. He yanked open the door and heard an inhuman yelp that chilled him to the bone. As he stumbled down the stairs, the coyote hurtled at top speed in the direction it had come from. Bolting past him as if he wasn't there.

A fist clenched his heart as he whipped his head to look for his son. Tony was twisted around as he sat in the sand pit, looking confusedly after the coyote. "Hey, dad."

Daniel ran over, grabbed Tony out of the sand, and began patting him in a panic, looking for signs of wounds or blood. "Are you hurt? Are you ok!?"

Tony looked confused as he tried to swat away Daniel's aggressive pat down., "Daaaad, I'm Okaaay. It was just a dog. Bob scared it off."

Daniel pulled Tony close to him and scanned the yard suspiciously, looking for more signs of trouble. He saw... something, but he didn't take the time to analyze it. He hustled Tony into the house while keeping an eye out for the coyote. Once Tony was safe inside, and he was satisfied that his son hadn't been hurt, he called animal control to report the coyote sighting.

The woman he talked to was polite but was obviously humoring him. They lived adjacent to the Big Woods Forest Preserve, and at least twice, she commented that there had never been coyotes sighted there in all the time she'd worked here. Daniel hung up the phone in disgust, but at least he had done his civic duty. Hopefully, that coyote didn't attack anyone else's kid.

Then he called Sophia and broke down what had happened. He had toyed with waiting until she got home so as not to disturb her workday but knew she would want to know as soon as possible. It took him fifteen minutes to convince her that Tony was fine and unhurt. He got her to hang up only after he promised to keep an eye on him in case his injuries weren't visible.

There was no need to promise; he wasn't letting Tony out of his sight. He just needed to take a look at one thing first. He sat Tony down at the kitchen table, handed him some fruit snacks and a glass of milk, and told him not to move. Tony nodded and promised, but it was evident he also was humoring his dad. He didn't seem to think anything unusual had happened.

Daniel stepped back out into the back yard, closing the kitchen door behind him. He quickly scanned for signs of the coyote again. Seeing nothing as he completed a circuit of the yard, he made his way over to the edge of the sand pit where Tony had been playing. A recent rain had made the ground soft and the grass slick. It wasn't muddy enough for him to find the tracks of the coyote, but he could now see more clearly what had caught his eye earlier.

There was a strip about a foot wide and ten feet long where the grass had been ripped clean off. It started at the tree line at a right angle from where the coyote had been stalking Tony. At the end of the strip, the grass was flattened for another three feet, and there were clods of mud and torn-up roots scattered all over the place.

He took out his phone, took several photos, and then walked back towards the house. He opened the back door, turned, and scanned the yard once more, his gaze lingering uneasily on the tear before finally closing the back door and turning his attention back to his son.

Daniel led Sophia into the back yard and showed her the tear in the grass. She walked around the damage; concern darkened her face. "Are you sure this wasn't here before? Maybe some teenagers came out of the woods and were looking to play a prank."

Daniel shook his head, "Nope, I came out here with Tony when he started playing to make sure it wasn't too muddy. Either I'm going blind and or insane, or this wasn't here until after the coyote attacked."

Sophia walked a complete circuit around the damage in the yard. "You don't think Tony did this do you?"

Daniel sighed and looked over his shoulder before answering. "I don't want to, but kids that are depressed do strange things. To make matters worse, Tony said that Bob scared off the coyote. I think we need to get him some help."

She looked back at the house as though she could see her son through the intervening walls. She longed to run to him, hold him, comfort him. Whatever was necessary to help him, she would do. "I feel like we've failed him." She rubbed the palms of her hands against her eyes, absorbing the tears before they could escape. Daniel was suddenly near her. He reached out and simply rested his hand on the small of her back. Somehow, it was all she needed. She scrubbed her eyes dry and simply responded, "Agreed."

Daniel grabbed Sophia's hand and led her back toward the house. "I know a couple of professors in the Psychology department. I'll ask them if they have any recommendations. Either next steps or maybe a referral to a doctor they trust. Don't worry; we'll get him through this."

Chapter 23

Leo leaned against his car while he created a list of boilerplate questions. Across the street, a dozen people were circling and chanting while waving handmade signs, the Fermilab sign looming behind them. The protest was orderly but having been here day after day for weeks; the protesters were neck-deep in boredom. Traffic was light, so the sign-waving and chanting was subdued. He was sure things would pick up once he presented his press credentials, but for now, he was quietly observing them to get a feel for the group.

He had already picked out the shift leader whom he had dubbed El Capitan. El Capitan was probably mid-30s, so the oldest of the group by far. There were eight true believers whom he had dubbed the Mob. They were young, fresh-faced, optimistic. The mob was from a broad group of ethnicities and evenly split between men and women. It was impossible to tell without talking to them, but Leo suspected there was a full spectrum of LGBTQ representation in there as well. A beautiful melting pot of humanity.

But there were three others that didn't seem to belong to The Mob. There was no optimism there. Two of them he called Dee and Dum, and they looked even more bored than the rest. They didn't interact with the others in any way, and they sat down whenever they had a chance. There was no enthusiasm for the protest in their eyes. He suspected they were just collecting a paycheck.

The third was the most concerning. He called him Lecter. There wasn't boredom in his eyes. Resting intensity is what came to mind. He was constantly observing. His attention would move from the passing traffic to the Fermilab Security booth in the distance to his own group. He had even locked eyes with Leo a couple of times. He was either a fanatic or some sort of security. Either case had scary implications about why he was here.

Leo picked up the cold coffee from the hood of his car and finished it off. He'd spent enough time observing, time to dig in and get dirty. He pulled out his lanyarded press credentials and walked across the street. Lecter watched him like a hawk as he walked up to El Capitan and introduced himself.

At first, El Capitan was guarded, but he turned on the charm. After Leo assured him that he was only there to do a human-interest piece and had a few softball questions he wanted to ask the various members of the protest, El Capitan began cheerily telling him how he got involved with Nadir and how important it was for research organizations to be transparent.

Leo eventually extricated himself from El Capitan and proceeded to wander amongst the Mob. He would single them out, ask his standard questions, and then pick another one from the herd.

El Capitan tried to distract him from interviewing Dee and Dum, but one of the Mob asked him a question, so Leo took the opportunity to question Dum. As suspected, Dum was a paid protestor and not a believer. El Capitan never noticed, but Lector most definitely did. His expression was inscrutable.

Leo wasn't sure he wanted to tackle Lector, but his problem solved itself. A plain gray sedan pulled up, and Lector broke off from the protest and walked over to it. Another man cut from the same cloth hopped out, and the two began a serious conversation. Leo immediately nicknamed the newcomer Vader. He no longer thought that either one was a fanatic. When Lector gestured in his direction while they conversed, Leo drifted back into the Mob and used his phone to casually snap a picture of the sedan's license plate as well as pictures of both Vader and Lector.

While Vader and Lector continued to converse, Leo turned his back to them and began taking pictures of the rest of the protestors with his actual press camera. He did plenty of "act normal" pictures but also let them ham for the camera and promised to email them to El Capitan so they could have copies. He was very careful not to get Vader and Lector in any of his shots, and when Vader made his way up to El Capitan, he put the cap on his lens and went back to just talking to the mob.

Leo looked over his shoulder and caught Lector getting into the gray sedan's passenger seat, and it swiftly pulled away. When he looked back, Vader seemed to be introducing himself to El Capitan. The introduction was brief, and Vader picked up a sign. He walked over and tried in vain to blend in. The Mob reacted like a wolf had just wandered amongst the flock. They clustered in little clumps trying not to act like they were avoiding him. To his credit, he was enthusiastic and friendly, and it didn't take long for his charm to ease the tension.

The Mob moved from nervousness to mild unease and eventually to acceptance in just fifteen minutes; Leo couldn't help but admire Vader. Whatever his actual purpose, the guy was pretty good at putting others at ease. He had the same seriousness and situational awareness as Lector. But Lector hadn't bothered to try and engage with the rest of the protestors. Vader took his protesting seriously, but he smiled and laughed and was actively chatting with The Mob.

It was time to see if El Capitan knew anything about Vader as casually as possible. "Excuse me, Miguel? Do you have time to chat?"

Jeff McIntyre

El Capitan smiled, seemingly impressed that Leo had remembered his name. "Sure man, what's up?"

Leo gently guided him over to a tree that was far enough away from the occasional chanting that it wouldn't interfere with their conversation but also far enough away that no one could hear them. He would be able to see anyone approach them.

"Let me say; I think you're doing a bang-up job here. Everyone is still enthusiastic, despite how long you've been out here. The signs are spot on, and everyone seems to be getting along. From what I've seen, no one is trying to start trouble."

"I appreciate you noticing. Sometimes it's like herding cats, but I do my best. With all the extra scrutiny on Nadir, we need to keep things nice and tight." El Capitan gestured toward the mob. "They're good kids, and they believe in this. I just need to make sure nobody does anything stupid. This is the part of Nadir that people need to see. Not any of that other crap."

"So, you're aware of the troubles between Fermilab and people claiming to be from Nadir?"

El Capitan's face scrunched up. "None of my kids would do something like that. Every one of them understands what's at stake. This is about getting positive attention, not starting a fight, and giving Nadir a bad name."

He pointed towards Dee and Dum, "So what about Steve and Jack? They don't seem like true believers to me."

152

El Capitan held up his hands in mock surrender. "Ya got me there. They get paid by the hour to help fill out our numbers when not enough volunteers show. We've got about five regulars we work with through a temp agency when needed. But honestly, it's a fairly common practice."

"And what about the new guy and the guy he replaced?"

El Capitan's eyes flicked nervously to the mob, and his voice lowered, "Hey uh, I'd rather not talk about them if you don't mind."

"Would it help if we kept it off the record?" He deliberately put his phone in his pocket and folded up his notepad.

"You can't print any of this, but I don't really know who those guys are." El Capitan seemed about to look back at the group again, but Leo stepped in front of his eye line.

"Tell me what you do know. I promise I won't use it in my story, but I need to know who I'm dealing with."

El Capitan turned to look out into the street. Not looking at The Mob, but not looking at Leo either. "Look, I don't want to get in trouble, but those guys bother me. The story from HQ is that a wealthy benefactor of Nadir sends these guys to assist with the protests and to act as mediators in case of any conflicts with Fermilab staff, the public, or police."

He nodded, "That seems fairly reasonable, but obviously, you have some concerns about them."

"Look, man, I did four in the Army, and I ran into guys like this. They're professionals. They're either military or a three-letter governmental agency, and I don't mean retired. They're on a knife's edge all the time." He gestured in the direction of The Mob through Leo's chest. "Lance, the guy that's here now, is all right, but they do shifts. All the other guys are here on a mission, and it has nothing to do with protesting Fermilab."

"Thanks for the info. Now act like you just told me a joke," and he burst out laughing.

El Capitan was stunned for just a second, but then he nodded and smiled, then started laughing too. The look of relief in his eyes was easy to see.

Leo grabbed El Capitan's hand and shook it firmly. "I'll make sure you get a link to download all the pictures I took for the team." He spun on his heel and started walking across the street towards his car, but he took a moment to wave a farewell to The Mob as he went.

Chapter 24

Sophia's mind raced. With all the things that had gone on in the last few days, her mind was everywhere. Everywhere except where it was supposed to be.

Rebecca had sent her a meeting request with no subject, and she was desperately scanning her email for an indication of what the emergency was. She wasn't due for her regular meeting with Rebecca for another three weeks at least, which meant something had blown up.

She had no idea what that could be. Even as she was frantically texting various project leads for one-line status updates, her mind was filled with visions of a dog the size of a car stalking her son as he played in the back yard. She knew it was a gross exaggeration. Most coyotes were smaller than your average large breed dog but try as she might, she could not convince her imagination to calm itself down. She wanted to scream every time she thought about it, which was every time she wasn't concentrating on work.

Her inner demons were whispering to her that she was a bad mother. Her son has an imaginary friend from being bullied. He might have torn up their lawn in an act of rebellion. A coyote attacked her son in their own yard in suburban Chicago. She couldn't protect him at school, and she couldn't protect him at home.

Her irrational internal mom wanted to quit her job and wrap her son in bubble wrap. Never mind the fact that they could never afford for her to do that, and doing so would almost certainly do more harm than good. She and Daniel agreed that they would not be overprotective parents. Tony needed to live and grow and succeed and fail. On top of all of this, she was obviously failing at her job in some fashion.

As she walked to the elevators, she stopped when she caught a glimpse of herself in a mirrored piece of wall art. She thought she looked like a wreck. Her makeup looked like it had been put on by a dropout from clown school. She had pulled her hair back into a ponytail this morning, but a couple of loose wisps had escaped. She paused long enough to re-do the ponytail. She didn't have her compact on her, so she did the best she could to clean up some of the untidiness in her makeup. She straightened out her blouse and then took a deep cleansing breath before continuing to the elevator.

As she rode the elevator up to the executive suites, she rechecked her email and texts for even the slightest hint of what might be waiting for her. Rebecca might like to chat with her about life from time to time, but that didn't mean she wasn't an exacting taskmaster. Sophia excelled at her job because she was always on top of the situation. Even if those projects were out of control, she liked to know what level of chaos they were in.

Anxiety and fear spiraled out of control in her mind. She had a knot in her stomach and was lightheaded as she stepped off the elevator and headed to Rebecca's office.

"Uh… hey, Chief," Sophia called out as she knocked on the door frame of Rebecca's open office door.

Rebecca was seated at her desk and was staring at her laptop with a slight frown. "Come in, Sophia, have a seat." She gestured at the seat across from her without looking up. "Give me just a minute to finish this up."

She instead walked over to a side table where Rebecca kept a pitcher of iced water and poured herself a glass. She stared out over the city as Rebecca typed away on whatever correspondence she was working on. Sensing that Rebecca was finished, Sophia walked over and stood in front of her desk, clasping the glass with both hands as if she didn't trust herself not to drop it. She locked her knees to keep from rocking nervously as she waited for her boss to address her.

Rebecca sighed and closed her laptop. A bemused expression crossed her face as Sophia continued to stand. "So, my dear. I'm sorry I didn't reach out to you sooner, but I wanted to know how your weekend was at the lake house?"

That simple question wrung everything out of Sophia. She gently and with great purpose set the glass down on the desk, collapsed into the chair, and started sobbing.

Rebecca jumped to her feet, alarmed. Not understanding what was happening but wanting to console Sophia, she walked around her desk and laid a hand on Sophia's shoulder.

"I am so sorry," she finally said through her tears. "I thought I was being called out on the carpet for something. I don't feel like I've been doing a very good job the last couple of weeks and thought something must have slipped through the cracks." Anger suddenly rose in her, "There's just been so much… BULLshit going on I haven't been able to focus."

Without replying, Rebecca grabbed a couple of tissues from a drawer, handed them to her, and calmly waited for her to regain her composure.

"Sophia, you are a strong and independent woman. You're intelligent and driven, but you are also compassionate. You love your husband and son. I know you're concerned about Tony's well-being, but what on earth could make you this stressed out? I hope nothing happened on the island. I talked to Elektra, and she seemed to think everything went swimmingly. She loved Tony, and that is not a woman who likes many people."

She didn't respond immediately. She sniffled, blew into the tissue, and then unloaded everything that had been happening. She glossed over "Bob" since Rebecca was already familiar with that, but she talked about the torn-up section of the yard. Tony had never acted up in that way, and this happened within days of them getting back from the island. He had seemed so happy that weekend, and even now, he was as cheerful as ever. When they asked him what happened to the yard, he denied knowing anything about how it had happened.

"On top of that, Tony was attacked by a god damned coyote! In our back yard!" She was still filled with heat, but doubt crept into her voice. "I mean, we live close to that nature preserve, but I've never heard of coyotes being spotted this far into the city."

"A coyote. You're sure it was a coyote?" Rebecca said, her voice flat.

She wiped the last tears from her eyes. "I mean, I didn't see it, but Daniel did. He was certain it was either a big coyote or a small wolf."

Rebecca stood up and began pacing behind her desk. She paused briefly and rubbed her temples. "Please tell me that Tony was unhurt."

"Yes, thank God. I'm sorry, Ms. Drake. I let this get in my head, and I've been worthless at work the last few days." She knew she sounded pathetic, but at least Rebecca didn't seem to be bothered by her work.

"My dear, do not apologize for being worried about your son. If something like this happens, just let me know what's going on. I'm rather fond of you and your family, but even if you were just any other employee, I want to know about incidents that are this impactful to your life." Rebecca grabbed Sophia by the arms and hauled her out of the chair. She looked her in the eyes and smiled. "Now. I want you to go home. Pick up your son from school and give him a big hug for me. Spend some quality time with him. Take tomorrow off. You can pull Tony out of school and spend it with him, or you can go to a spa and just relax. You need to leave this behind you. After all, what are the odds of a coyote attack in suburban Chicago? Be thankful that Tony wasn't hurt." Rebecca gave her a quick embrace and then released her. "Now, I hate to rush you out, but we're over the allotted time for this meeting, and I have some other issues to attend to. Go home. That's an order."

She could only nod, a little stunned. "Thank you for being so understanding. Oh, and thank you so much for the weekend at your house. It was lovely."

As Sophia turned and walked out and as the door finished closing, Rebecca's mask of pleasantry dropped. Her brow furrowed, lips twisted in a wordless snarl, and she swiped the glass of water across the room, spilling its contents across half her office, and the glass shattered against the wall.

Chapter 25

A tall, lanky Native American man crouched upon a hill overlooking a truck stop. His skin was weathered from years in the sun and rain. It covered wiry muscles earned from long days surviving. His hands were the kind of rough that only came from years of working with them. His long black hair had not a speck of gray in it. Bound in a simple ponytail to keep it under control and a wide-brimmed felt hat to keep the sun out of his eyes. He looked to be in the ageless land of late thirties to early fifties.

His boots were dusty and worn. Good boots that had served him well, but wear and tear had brought them near to the end of the road. His jeans were faded, not from some factory acid wash, but from long use and determined care. He wore a simple solid blue button-down shirt. Light enough to allow air to flow and wick away the sweat that came

Jeff McIntyre

from everyday labors. The top three buttons were undone, revealing a simple but thick silver chain with an amulet made of feathers, talons, and teeth.

He stared down at the comings and goings of the people and machines with a bored expression in his pale gray eyes. Waiting without really watching. Occasionally he would scan the horizon, but hours passed with no apparent change to this routine.

As he waited, a brief spring squall rolled through, soaking him to the skin, and despite the coolness of the air, he seemed to barely notice.

He was far enough away from the truck stop that most of the noises were muffled beyond recognition. Occasionally the squeal of air brakes releasing or the deep staccato of a tractor trailer engine braking would carry clearly to him. But mostly, he was left in silence.

Hall and Oates began singing "Maneater" from a leather holster on his belt.

He slowly pulled a cell phone from the holster, looked at it grimly, and then answered. "Hello, Rebecca."

"How dare you. What on earth possessed you to send one of your children after him? You, of all people, know what's at stake; how long I've been working toward this, and you would jeopardize it all to what? Punish me?"

"Relax, I knew the gnome would protect him. That's what he's there for, after all. A coyote is no threat to a gnome, and I knew the gnome would not harm Softpaws."

"Softpaws? You're naming them now?"

"Of course not. I would never presume to name them. That's what she calls herself."

There was a long ten seconds of silent fuming before she finally responded. "A Coyote, you don't think that's a little too on point? If you want to get my attention, there are easier ways to do it. A phone call, for instance."

"The coyote was the entire point. I wanted you to know it was me. You are too wrapped up in your schemes to see what is coming. I found him. If I can find him, so can the others, and there is no predicting how they will respond." In his mind's eye, he saw her pacing in short circles behind her desk as she tried to form a response.

Rebecca's sarcasm dripped through the phone. "I keep an eye on all of them. They're too wrapped up in their own petty schemes to worry about what I've been doing. Besides, his return benefits them as well as it does us."

"And that's the problem; they're dangerous enough. Frankly, I don't think the world needs magic. I'm certain it will cause more problems than we can possibly imagine. I think we're better off if he doesn't return."

"You don't mean that. You may not want magic to return, but how can you not want to see him again?" the disbelief apparent in her voice.

He pulled off his hat and dropped it on the ground. His tone softened. "It's been fifteen hundred years. I've found my own path. You know what he stood for, and I don't think he would approve of what you're doing."

"Your opinion on how an immortal who's been imprisoned by death for the last fifteen centuries is noted. I'm going to do what I must."

His voice hardened, "Rebecca, this is foolish. Let… him… go… It's been too long; how would he adapt to this world? What chaos will magic sow? What will these people DO to him?"

He pulled his head away as her voice screamed out of the phone, "I will NEVER give up on him, do you hear me? NEVER! If you're not going to help, you had better stay the hell out of my way." and the call disconnected.

He briefly considered calling her back but knew he'd blown his one shot to convince her. It had been a long shot, anyway. He rubbed his temples with one hand, then picked up his hat and placed it back in place. "Come Quickwind. Let's go find your mate." A white-muzzled coyote appeared out of the brush and sauntered to his side. It looked down on the human presence, whined, and shook from its head to its tail before looking up at him expectantly. They took one last look at the truck stop and the highway stretching into the distance before turning away and began walking south.

Chapter 26

Brian was trying to keep an open mind about how the Knights do things. The Table wanted an in-person overview of operations at the Large Hadron Collider, so he, Katrin, and Micah had volunteered. Katrin took care of the travel arrangements. The Geneva International Airport was a stone's throw away from CERN and the LHC, but Katrin had instead chartered a flight into the Annemasse Aerodrome. It was a smaller airport, but it was on the other side of the city from the LHC.

He was still getting used to driving in Europe. It was mildly claustrophobic compared to the big cars and wide expressways of the US cities he was used to driving in. The narrow streets and hectic traffic sometimes reminded him of a first-world version of Kabul.

The car that had been waiting for them looked not much larger than a shoebox, and he was beginning to suspect that this was a bit of mild hazing on Katrin's part. She had insisted that he drive to "get used to European traffic." When Katrin pointed out the two-door Honda Civic that was reserved for them, Micah shot her a dirty look, but he folded into the back seat without comment. This kind of juvenile behavior seemed a little beneath a secret quasi-military multinational organization, but it might be one way they keep from taking themselves too seriously.

"What was that?" He had been studying the GPS when he heard Katrin ask him a question.

"I asked what you do for fun when you're not investigating particle accelerators and nuclear science labs?" Katrin had a small smile on her face that made him feel like a cat toy.

"Oh, sorry. I'm still trying to deal with all this... this. Ya know?" He paused as he navigated through a busy intersection before continuing. "Ever since Colonel Larkin gave me The Deep End file, I've had a lot to think about."

Katrin's smile deepened. "I totally get it. I sicked up after reading it. I hadn't gotten any warning about what they gave me, and it turned my world upside down. Probably even more so than you."

"How on earth could finding out that Arthur, Merlin, and the Knights of the roundtable are real; be even worse for you than it was for anyone else?" he asked.

Katrin shrugged, "I'm a legacy."

He looked at her confused, "I'm not sure what that means."

"It means that I am a direct descendant of Gawain, and a member of my family has held a seat in the Knights of the Stone off and on since its inception. I took over from my uncle when he got cancer and decided to retire. He was passed the seat by my grandfather on his deathbed. I'm the 35th generation of my family to serve."

"Wow. You're right. That is definitely more messed up than what I went through." Brian admitted.

Katrin smirked, "Thank you, it's good to feel validated."

He did some quick math. "35th generation? That sounds a little light for fifteen hundred years."

Katrin's smile turned wicked. "Just because there are descendants of Gawain around doesn't mean they're worthy of holding a seat. We still must go through the vetting process, and there is still the pass/fail at the end of probation. Some of the things we have to do on behalf of the cause; well, I don't think my uncle Clive the baker would make a good fit. Glad to see you made it through."

"Yeah, me too. Considering who and how I was recruited, I should have suspected there was a trap door at the end. I guess I fanboyed over Colonel Larkin and didn't think too hard about the ramifications. It wasn't until I was about two paragraphs into The Deep End file that I realized that this was something I could get disappeared over." Brian paused briefly as the vision of the Lock bursting into flames flashed in his mind. "Didn't matter; while I didn't exactly know what I was signing up for, I still would have signed up for it, and the reasons haven't changed."

"So why did you sign up?" Katrin asked.

"Couple of reasons. I wasn't doing anything with myself. I was looking for a purpose, I guess." Brian poked the GPS to life before he continued. "But mainly, this magic shit scares me more than anything I've ever encountered or even been trained for, and I've seen some seriously heinous things. If I'm this afraid, imagine what your average joe on the street would be like. I am a soldier, and fighting the things others can't is what I do."

Katrin looked at him thoughtfully for a second. "I think you'll do just fine, Squire Cooke."

"Squire?" he responded as he eased the car into gear. "Isn't that a term for someone who is not yet a knight?"

Micah's deep voice finally made its presence known from the back seat. "Term of endearment for the newest member of the Knights."

Katrin poked him in the shoulder, "You'll probably get called that until Larkin kicks it. Lord knows he's never going to retire. The other knights have been calling me that for ten years, and I'm so glad it's finally over. Think of it as a bit of hazing by a bunch of old men."

He gave her the side eye. "And one woman?"

Katrin laughed. "Oh yeah, I didn't get called Squire Lancaster for a decade only to not get to use it on the next new recruit. I'm petty that way."

"I noticed your official dossier was a little light on details." He said. "You're one of the few sitting Knights that doesn't have a military background. How did you get your experience?"

Katrin didn't immediately respond. "She's an assassin." Replied Micah after the silence ran too long.

He was startled by the response and gave Katrin a questioning look.

"It's true." She said at last. "Don't look at me like that." She crossed her arms defensively and looked away from him and out the window as she spoke. "It's a family business of sorts. I allowed myself to be recruited into it as a rebellion against my father. My mother died when I was young, and my father left me to be raised by nannies and boarding schools. Enter my mother's brother. He's handsome, charming, lives a life of adventure. He starts coming around and introduces me to foreign languages and cultures, martial arts, shooting. I throw myself into these activities because he's exciting and enthusiastically encourages me like my father never will."

Katrin is quiet for a long time, then continues. "Turns out Uncle Reggie is a well-respected independent assassin. He takes contract hits for NATO alliance governments whenever they want plausible deniability. He was training me to be his partner. Next thing you know, I'm mostly solo because he's been recruited into the Knights when grandad passes away. Ten years after that, Reggie gets cancer and pulls me in to replace him."

The conversation lagged a bit as he made his way through a roundabout heavy with traffic. At least Katrin and Micah had the decency not to try and give him advice.

Katrin spoke up as soon he exited the roundabout. "Anyway, enough about me. You never did say what you do for fun."

"Uh, I do a lot of reading: throwaway science fiction and the occasional historical fiction. I especially like books with a bit of military flair thrown in, but frankly, I'll read about anything. Ever since I got recruited, I've upped my workouts. I wasn't exactly out of shape but I wasn't where I wanted to be."

Katrin reached over and squeezed his bicep. "Seems ok to me. I'm planning on hitting the gym at the hotel tonight before dinner if you'd care to join me. Workouts go faster with company." She half turned to the back seat. "You too, Micah. You're more than welcome to join me."

"No, but thank you. I have made dinner plans this evening with an old friend. You two enjoy yourselves."

As he jogged on the treadmill, Brian pondered the events of the day. He probably shouldn't have been surprised, but they had shown up to the security gate at the LHC, flashed the credentials they'd been given for this assignment, and been invited in and treated like VIPs.

Katrin later explained that the Knights made significant donations to CERN via one of their many corporate fronts and so were allowed to do periodic assessments on the progress of the experiment.

Brian didn't pretend to understand the science, but the presentation they'd been given had been geared for corporate executives, so he got the gist of how things were going. The LHC revamp was on track, but it would be at least a year before they would be ready for the next full systems power-up.

This gave them a benchmark, and based on the reliquary timetable, this gave them more than enough time to track down the Lock. When he got back to his room, he planned on reviewing the last reliquary timeline estimate and comparing it to what they'd been told at CERN. From what he could remember, it seemed like the LHC test was a highly likely candidate for the next Key Event.

He was running with his head down, concentrating on his breathing, when the treadmill slowed down and began a cooldown cycle. He lifted his eyes a bit and found himself staring squarely at Katrin's sweaty behind furiously pumping on the stair-climber right in front of him.

He quickly grabbed his towel and hopped off the treadmill turning his gaze away. As he wiped away some of the excess sweat, he admitted to himself that despite her being at least ten years older

Jeff McIntyre

than him, she had a nice ass. He hadn't initially been attracted to her. In the Knight's meetings, she had come off as brash and a bit arrogant. He sometimes felt like she was trying a bit too hard to fit into the good old boys' club.

Ever since they had arrived in Geneva, Katrin had become charming, flirty, and very touchy. It wasn't like she was coming on to him, but she suddenly became very likable and in turn, attractive. As soon as they had left the LHC to head to their hotel, she had returned to her normal brusque self, but his lizard brain kept imagining what she would look like naked.

He squashed the thoughts like a bug on a windshield. He was new to the Knights. Still getting a feel for how things work and, more importantly what the dynamics were between its highest-ranking members. He may be part of this organization for the rest of his life. Best not to rock the boat.

Katrin hopped nimbly off the stair-climber while it was still going full speed. She walked over and grabbed a bottle of water from the fridge. "Come on, Cooke. I've got something in my room I need to give you before tomorrow."

Brian draped the towel around his neck, nodded, and followed in her wake to the elevator. Katrin pushed the fourteenth floor and leaned back against the back wall of the elevator, still breathing heavily from the workout. The elevator rose swiftly, neither saying a word. The elevator walls were made of polished brass, but they had been worked with a texture that made the reflections slightly out of focus. As the elevator dinged for their floor, Brian looked up and thought he caught Katrin staring at him. When the doors opened, he stood aside and gestured for her to lead the way.

Katrin opened the door to her hotel room, and he followed. As the door swung shut behind him, she turned around and slammed him against the door. She grabbed both ends of the towel and pulled his head down to her for a ferocious kiss. After a moment, she released him and stepped back. "All right, I've made my intentions known. It's your move. And this is just some fun. I'm not interested in a relationship."

He paused for a second to catch his breath before responding. "Are you sure this is something we should do? Even without relationship complications, co-workers having sex together isn't usually a good idea."

"One benefit to being part of a secret organization is that there's no HR for anyone to complain to. We're adults, and so long as we treat ourselves professionally and don't let this get in the way of our duties, nobody cares who we screw." She walked over to the bed and kicked off her shoes. "Besides, if we can't keep things professional out of the bedroom, they'll send someone to kill us. They encourage this kind of thing. It makes pillow talk less dangerous."

Brian took two strides, scooped her up, and threw her onto the bed. She held up her hand as he

Jeff McIntyre

started to take off his shirt. "Don't let me forget. I have a dossier to give you regarding our assets in-region and a more detailed status report of the LHC from one of those assets on the inside."

Chapter 27

Leo was driving through the maze that was suburban Chicago. His phone was reading back to him the notes he had taken during his time at Nadir's offices. He was trying to think of ways to independently verify some of what he had learned there.

He was certain that a follow-up interview with Hank Lee would be rejected, so he would probably have to resort to some ambush tactics. He knew Hank's favorite watering hole, and it wasn't all that far from the Fitzroy home. Maybe later this evening, he would try to catch Hank after he'd had a drink or two. He'd turn on the charm and ply him with drinks. Apologize for the tone of the interview and ask him if he'd read the article. Now that the series had run, hopefully, Hank wouldn't hold a grudge. He had painted Fermilab and the HERBERT experiment in a very positive light. There was only a passing reference to Nadir and no mention of the incidents, so with luck, he would cut him some slack.

Jeff McIntyre

Sophia had called him up and asked him if he wanted to come over for dinner. Tony had been in a bit of a funk lately, and she was hoping that Uncle Leo would help cheer him up. Besides, Tony had been dying to tell Leo about everything he had done at Rebecca Drake's lake house.

As he pulled onto the Fitzroys' street, he looked up a block and a half to where their house was and saw Tony riding his bike on the sidewalk.

He was a good kid, and Leo was worried for him. When Sophia called him, she had filled him in on the bullying, the imaginary friend Bob, and, as if things couldn't have gotten worse, a potentially rabid coyote straying into their yard and going after Tony.

Up the street past Tony, a large pickup was heading toward them. It was driving a little erratically, and he saw the driver lean over to the passenger seat, and his head disappeared like he was trying to fish something out of the floorboards. Time slowed down. The pickup was coming from behind Tony, and veered toward the sidewalk where he was riding his bike. Leo hammered his horn. It got Tony's attention, and he waved as he recognized Leo's car. The pickup jumped the curb and bore down on Tony, and Leo could only watch his friend's son die. There was a loud metallic crunch, and the pickup lurched like it hit something, but Tony and his bike didn't hurtle through the air or get drug under the truck. Instead, Tony looked startled and lost control of his bike. It rolled a few more feet before he keeled over and landed on his side.

The Garden Gnome

He slammed on the brakes and flew out of his car, barely remembering to put it in park. He ran over to Tony, not knowing what he would find. The truck had stopped, resting half on and half off the curb. The driver looked like he'd been sucker punched. Tony lay on the ground, still straddling his bike. He was looking back at the pickup less than six feet away from him and said, "Wow, that was close."

Maybe it was the shock, but he burst out laughing. There was no damage to Tony's bike, and Tony seemed to be ok. He did a quick check for blood or broken bones, but other than a scraped elbow, he looked fine. "Don't move, kiddo. Just lay still." He gently extricated the bike from Tony and set it on the grass. He fired a quick text to Sophia, 'side of house now 911' and then actually dialed 911.

As he waited for an operator to answer, he motioned for Tony to lay still and then walked over to the driver's side of the pickup. The driver still sat there dazed. The remains of the airbag covered his steering wheel. His side window was cracked, and there was a smear of blood where his head bounced off the glass. There was a decent amount of blood running from a gash in his left temple, and he was mumbling, "the kids ok, he's going to be ok, I didn't hit the kid, he's gotta be ok, dear god, let him be ok."

He wasn't a medical professional, but he was pretty sure this guy was in shock. "Sit still," he yelled through the glass. "I've called 911." At that point, an emergency services operator answered the phone, and he began to convey what had happened. He saw

Jeff McIntyre

Sophia and Daniel round the corner of the house, looking up and down the street, trying to figure out what the emergency was. They spotted Tony on the sidewalk and broke into a run. He stayed on the line with the emergency services operator but walked over to where Daniel and Sophia could hear him as he explained the situation. Sophia was gently probing her son, looking for signs of injury. All the while, Tony, sensing how afraid his parents were, gently reassured them he was fine and patiently awaited paramedics to arrive to check him out.

Confident that Daniel and Sophia would care for Tony, he walked back to the driver's window. "An ambulance is on its way. Just stay still."

The driver groggily nodded his head. "Is the kid ok?"

He looked back at Tony and nodded, "Yeah, I think so. We'll get him checked out, but I'm not sure you hit him."

"Thank God. I was stupid; I'm just glad no one got hurt." He paused; a confused look came over his face. "If I didn't hit him, what did I hit?"

He shrugged, "I don't know." He walked around the truck to get a better look at the passenger side. The front fender and passenger door were crumpled in a distinctly round shape. The paint was horribly scratched, and smears of dirt were rubbed into the scratches.

He'd seen damage like this before. He had been driving with friends through the Black Hills of South Dakota in an area prone to rockslides. They had stopped to help a driver who had pulled off to the side of the road after a single boulder had come loose and collided with their vehicle as they were driving through. This damage looked just like that van had. "I really, really have no idea."

Normally, Leo didn't drink anything harder than beer during the week, but this evening's events had him nursing a bourbon. He was drinking it slowly because he still had to drive home tonight. Daniel was putting Tony to bed, and Sophia was making a half-hearted attempt to wash dishes.

Kids are amazingly resilient. Tony seemed unfazed by the accident. Why should he? He hadn't been hurt. Daniel had been uncharacteristically quiet, and Sophia had barely kept it together.

After the paramedics had cleared Tony and hauled the pickup driver off to the hospital for observation, Leo ran through everything he had seen to the responding police officer. The officer seemed as confused as Leo when it came to the source of the damage to the pickup. Still, it was pretty obvious that he hadn't actually made contact with Tony or his bike, and it was also obvious that neither Leo nor his vehicle had been involved in the accident.

He had a dashcam, downloaded the footage to his phone, and shared it with the officer; which only confirmed his account. The officer eventually gave up trying to explain what happened and blamed it on a light pole, even though the nearest pole had no signs of an impact.

Once everything calmed down, he kept Tony occupied to give his friends time to process what had happened without upsetting him. Tony was now in bed, and the drinks came out. "All right you two, in here. Sit down, have a drink, try to relax. That's an order."

Sophia flopped on the couch and pulled a nearby blanket around her like a shield. She shivered under the covers, but Leo doubted she was cold. He handed her two fingers of whiskey on ice which she gratefully accepted. He gave a bigger glass cut with cola to Daniel as his friend sat on the couch next to Sophia. She wiggled her feet under Daniel's butt and smiled at him.

"So, it sounds like you and my godson have been having a rough time lately. Is there anything I can do to help? I'm more than willing to Tonysit in the evening if you two want some alone time." He drained the last of his bourbon and sank into the chair opposite his friends.

Daniel and Sophia glanced at each other before Daniel responded. "Appreciate the offer Leo, but right now, I think we need to spend as much time with Tony as we can. This is just another shitty thing in a long line of shitty things we've had to deal with, but this whole thing with bullies and his imaginary friend. We need to be there for him, and we're in the process of trying to get some professional help. Soph and I no longer think that this is something we can wait out."

"I'm just glad he doesn't seem to be phased by the coyote or this. I don't think I can handle much more of this. At this rate, I'm half expecting his school bus to get into an accident." Sophia sipped at her drink; the corners of her eyes glistened, a single tear clinging to her cheek.

"Soph, I say this with utmost sincerity. If there's anything I can do to help, just ask. I'll be there. And please, keep me in the loop on whatever process the therapist recommends. I don't want to accidentally sabotage anything by overstepping." Leo grinned widely. "Uncle Leo admits he can be a bit much sometimes."

Chapter 28

Colonel Samuel Larkin, the current first seat of the Knights of the Stone, had known Nathan Smith for over forty years. Their relationship had gotten off to a rocky start. Nathan had been a CIA field agent that had provided him with intelligence on a high-value target in Laos. A General in the Laotian military with a sideline in drug production and trafficking. That intel had proven to be either unreliable or incomplete. Maybe both. It didn't matter, some good people got killed, and the bad guy got away.

He'd never liked working with the CIA. It was a necessary evil, and Nathan's failure had proven to him that it was an evil that wasn't worth the cost.

Nathan had taken the failure of that mission very personally. He read the after-action reports. He investigated the survivors. Went back to his sources. Verified the data he had to work with when he built the package for the strike team. Then he disappeared. Sam thought he had vanished into the black hole of the agency. Didn't think much about him except when he was mildly drunk and was kicking himself for the lost lives of that mission.

Six months later, Nathan walked into his office with two coffees and handed one to him like that was where he had been all along. He set a large folder on his desk and started to earn his trust back. Nathan hadn't been idle in the six months he'd been gone. He had been confident in the original mission, and when it went sideways, he had to find out why. He laid it all out in great detail. A translator vetted by Larkin's own people had been in the pay of the General they were after for over three years.

Not only had Nathan figured out it was the translator who had leaked the strike team's plans, but he also found out how the smuggler had been so savvy and disciplined to place a mole that deep and resist using any of the other information that he had undoubtedly been given.

It turns out that a Colonel in the People's Liberation Army had gone native rather than return home when China had withdrawn its advisors from the region. He had married one of the General's daughters and had been living and fighting for him ever since. This Colonel had been a very savvy intelligence operative in the PLA and coordinated a sophisticated counter-intelligence action to protect his father-in-law's operation.

Nathan laid all this out. Then he laid out an opportunity for payback against both of them. He had details on how they ran their operation. Precise details of how many troops they had at their disposal to protect their operations and what kind of equipment and weaponry they had at their disposal.

To sweeten the pot, he noted that the US military still employed the translator in question. No one else had been able to connect the dots to him. He planned to have him transferred back to Larkin's unit for the express purpose of planting misinformation.

Larkin was not about to be convinced over a coffee and a half-hour conversation. He took the file and told Nathan he'd think it over. He spent two days combing through the details and came to two conclusions. First, the operation was worth the risk. A little for payback but mostly to take two dangerous people and their entire operation out of play. Second, Nathan Smith was not someone you wanted to be on the wrong side of. He had been almost obsessive in the details, and his plan would decapitate a large, sophisticated drug production operation. Still, it was also dangerous, and there would undoubtedly be civilian casualties.

He eventually gave the go-ahead but with one caveat. No one knew this operation better than Nathan, so he wanted him with the strike teams in case they needed to adjust the plan on the fly. That turned out to be the best idea he'd ever had. Nathan's intel was spot on, but they didn't count on a visit from another Laotian general and his personal escort. That nearly doubled the number of hostiles they would need to deal with. With Nathan's help and

Larkin's approval, they made a smooth pivot and managed to succeed at their objectives with no casualties and only a few wounded.

When it was over, and they were discussing lessons learned over a couple of whiskies, he decided he needed to get to know this young man a little better.

"So why did you take this so personally? I've seen plenty of ops fail for various reasons, and I've seen plenty of Intelligence people walk away and dust their hands of the affair like it was no big deal."

Nathan didn't immediately respond. He offered Larkin a cigarette and then lit one for himself when the Colonel declined. He took a long drag and blew the smoke up to the ceiling. "Because I should have known it was too good to be true. Everything was fitting together too smoothly. A bunch of your men died because I didn't dig deep enough, and I can't forgive myself for that. I've had ops go sideways because of personnel issues, unforeseen circumstances, winds of fate. Hell, I even had one blow up on us because a hooker walked in at the wrong time. But this one, this one was on me. I did the due diligence, but I could have and should have done more."

"I suppose I can understand that sentiment, but greater men than you have walked away from a losing proposition and just cut their losses." He stared down at his whiskey glass as if wishing it were bigger. "But you. You couldn't let this go, and I want to know why."

185

Jeff McIntyre

Nathan took another drag off the cigarette. "I've never gotten men killed because of something I did or didn't do. I don't really feel like I've redeemed myself, but I can feel a little better that those bastards are off the table and that those deaths, the deaths that I'm responsible for. They weren't for nothing. I also knew I would have to convince a hardass like you to give me a second shot. THAT was probably the hardest part."

He rarely thought of Nathan until years later. He had been a member of the Knights of the Stone for nearly a decade when one of their members was killed during a key event, and they were looking for a replacement. Nathan Smith's name popped into his head as though there could be no other choice.

Nathan met all the criteria and was quickly approved and invited. He and Nathan had developed a good working relationship that transformed into a deep friendship. His attention to detail had been invaluable, and he had become something of a savant when it came to the artifacts in the reliquary.

For the last thirty years, Nathan had been cataloging all accounts related to the artifacts and the timing of key events into a cohesive playbook. Prior to this, the Knights had become incredibly dependent on two artifacts in particular. Castor's Hummingbird increased in temperature as Key events approached and began to glow when it occurred. The Broken Blade of Excalibur could be used as a crude compass to lead them to The Lock. The closer it got to the Lock and the closer the Key event was, the easier it was to home in. In the presence of the Lock after a Key event, it would supposedly burst into a ghostly blue heatless flame.

Relying on these two had gotten the job done. But as Nathan frequently pointed out, it was clumsy and had led to several missteps and minor catastrophes. Under his guidance, they now had a full accounting of all artifacts and all known interactions with Key events. He had also increased the number of sensors in the reliquary by a factor of ten and had two teams of analysts ready to process all the new data they would receive as the date of the Key event approached.

All these thoughts rolled through his head as he and Nathan wandered from station to station in the reliquary making observations of the various relics. The sensor data was captured automatically, but standard operating procedure required that each of the relics be observed and directly interacted with by a minimum of two Knights each week once any of them started reacting. Normally this duty was handled by Nathan and Katrin, but with Katrin out on assignment, he had offered to help. It had been a while since he had been in the reliquary. It was good to see these physical reminders of what was at stake.

"Did you visually inspect Excalibur yet?" Nathan asked him from across the room.

"Not yet." He replied. "I'm getting old, and I was reminiscing. I didn't know you were in a rush."

"I'm not in a rush, but you're old and sometimes need prodding." Nathan quipped with a smile.

He chose not to respond to the younger man's jab as he walked over and unlocked the lid of the Excalibur display. It was a rectangular plexiglass box with a hinged lid that used pressure gaskets to form an airtight seal resting atop a marble pedestal specifically designed to hold it securely. Inside was a narrow length of metal that was horribly corroded, almost to the point of being unrecognizable. If it had been as beautiful as its legends claimed, it certainly didn't look the part now.

It was completely submerged in the unfiltered water of a freshwater lake. Despite the contrariness of putting a metal sword in water, it was the only substance that seemed to retard the rust that was slowly consuming it. Because he knew what he was looking at, he could make out the broken tip and the barely eight inches of remaining blade. The guard was merely a ring of rust that indicated where the blade ended, and the hilt began. The tang was mostly exposed as the handle had almost completely corroded away. The pommel was a rough lump at the end; if it had been decorative, the details had long been covered in corrosion.

He did not attempt to remove the blade from the water as that was reserved for when the Key event was closer, but he tried to make careful observations of the general condition of the sword. He looked at his tablet, compared archival pictures to what he saw before him, and made careful notes. There didn't appear to be any change, but he did notice a few flakes of rust in the bottom of the case. He wasn't sure if that was normal, but that seemed worrisome when it came to this particular artifact. He took his notes, snapped a few pictures, and then reclosed and locked the case.

"So, what were you reminiscing about?" Nathan asked as they both approached the case for Castor's Hummingbird.

"I was thinking about how we met." He looked down into the case. He'd seen this relic many times from the video feeds and Nathan's reports. Under a large heat-resistant glass dome, a fist-sized chunk of amber with almost no impurities rested on a ceramic platter. At its center was a hummingbird, trapped in what appeared to be mid-wingbeat. It was as beautiful as it was impossible. It was also emitting heat. Three separate lasers monitored its temperature at fifteen-minute increments. The current readings of all three showed that it was stable at 114 degrees Fahrenheit.

Castor's Hummingbird was the most important relic they had when it came to predicting the timing of a Key event. Its temperature would steadily increase as the time approached until it burst into flame at the same time the Key event occurred. The amber itself never burned away, and the fire would stay lit until the Lock was killed. At this point, the fire would immediately extinguish, and the amber would return to room temperature. Based on past observations, with its current temperature as a baseline, the Key event was twelve to eighteen months away. After over four decades in the Knights, the game was on again. They all needed to be on their toes.

"You must be getting senile if you're thinking about that. Reflecting on events from forty years ago. We have a few more pressing things to worry about, don't you think?" Nathan did a few quick checks of the instruments on the Hummingbird's case. "I haven't gotten to Excalibur yet; anything interesting I should be on the lookout for?"

"A few flakes of rust in the bottom of the tank. I don't know if that's normal or not, but I took note of it." He leaned in close to the glass and inspected the amber of the hummingbird. The rising heat radiated through the case from the relic, but he couldn't find any visual differences.

Nathan stopped perusing the instruments and began rifling through files on his tablet. "That's odd. I'll have to check the histories, but I don't recall Excalibur ever shedding rust before. It might be nothing, but I'll look into it."

"The only thing I have left is the Family Stone." He walked to the far corner where a simple slab of sandstone about the size of a dinner plate lay on a velvet inlay on the top of another marble pedestal. The only noteworthy thing about the stone was the two figures visible on its surface. A combination of engraving and painting, the pigment was a simple red, but the images had first been scratched into the stone. Perhaps the ancient artist was hoping it would lend the image more permanency. Carbon dating of the pigment had put a rough estimate of between 10000 to 12000 BCE. A man stood on the left, a woman on the right, arms extended, and hands clasped.

As was typical, there was not much to report about the stone itself. He knew that the stone would begin to glow as the Key event approached. It was not as useful as the Hummingbird because the lumens it released seemed to ebb and flow with no predictable pattern, and it didn't start glowing until about a week before the Key event occurred. This didn't give them much time to react, so it was mostly kept as an object of curiosity.

Nathan joined him at the plinth. "I've installed three multi-spectrum cameras to monitor this thing. I keep hoping that one day we might be able to pull more information about timing from them, but honestly, we have so little data other than pictures of it glowing that it might take a hundred years before we have enough data sets to be useful."

He peered closely at the stone and thought he saw a shimmer. His chest clenched in panic. "Nathan, do we have imagery of this thing in the dark?"

Nathan nodded, "We do. I can't say we've done a fantastic job of studying this particular relic, but we have normal light, daylight, and artificial light; and we have infrared and UV images in pitch-dark environments. The last Reliquary Seat suspected that maybe it was solar powered, so they did a full light based workup on it, but it didn't reveal anything we didn't already know."

"Do me a favor, hit the lights." He motioned to the bank of switches on the opposite side of the room without taking his attention off the stone.

Nathan peered at the stone but couldn't make out what Sam was seeing. He made his way across the room, slapped the switch bank, and the room plunged into darkness. Several small red LEDs were scattered around the room associated with various cameras and instruments, but otherwise, the room was pitch black.

He looked back to where Sam was standing and could vaguely make out his outline. He was still hunched over, peering at the stone, but he shouldn't be able to see him at all. He pulled out his phone and used the active screen as a weak light to guide him through the maze of pedestals, then shut off the screen when he reached his friend's side. They both stared down at the dim light emanating from the stone. The stone emitted light, but the graven images did not, leaving them in stark relief against that pale yellow glow.

Nathan had seen hundreds of images of this stone and read volumes of reports on the observations made of it in the events leading up to a Key event, as well as after the Lock had been opened. None of them had hinted at the circle of children, hands clasped, that surrounded the man and woman.

Chapter 29

Daniel and Sophia walked into Tony's room. Tony looked up from the video game he was playing inquisitively. Daniel leaned up against the door frame while Sophia walked over and sat on the end of the bed. "Sweetie, we want to talk to you about Bob and some of the things that have happened lately."

Tony tensed a little "don't be mad; he's just here to keep me safe."

Daniel frowned. "I know you think that, bud, but we're worried. It's our job to keep you safe, not his. We want you to understand something. Bob isn't real; your imaginary friend can't keep you safe."

Tony's eyes grew wide, and then he started giggling. If anything, this made Sophia and Daniel even more worried. Tony saw that they weren't laughing with him and quickly settled down. With childlike seriousness, he looked at each of them. "Mom... Dad... Bob isn't imaginary, he's a gnome, and he's in the back yard."

Daniel shook his head slowly, "Tony, we've talked about this; garden gnomes are mythical creatures. People make ceramic statues of them and put them in their garden because they think they're cute, but they're not real."

Tony sighed the exaggerated sigh of a ten-year-old. "He's real, and I can prove it," He hopped out of bed and stormed past them, heading down the hall. Sophia stood up and gave her husband a worried look.

Daniel shrugged, "We better follow him." They slowly turned to follow in the wake of their son as he turned the corner to head downstairs.

Tony's head popped around the corner near the baseboard with an exasperated look on his face. "C'mon, hurry up!" The head popped back around the corner, and the soft rumble of Tony's feet running down the stairs carried back to them. Despite their son's urging, Daniel and Sophia slowly followed their son down to the kitchen. With worry apparent on their face as they saw their son standing in front of the backyard door, hands outstretched, beckoning them to stop. "First, you have to promise not to be mad when Bob tracks dirt into the kitchen."

Daniel frowned at his son, "Bud, if you bring in one of Mrs. DeLuca's garden gnome statues, you'll make her mad and upset your mom."

Tony stomped his foot in irritation. "Can I prove to you that Bob is real or not?"

Sophia looked at Tony worriedly and sighed. "If there's a mess, we'll clean it up together. What are you going to show us?"

Tony held up his hands again. "Wait here; I'll be right back." Tony opened the door to the back yard and took two steps into the darkness. He waved at the motion sensor above the door, and the yard was flooded with light.

Sophia sat down at the kitchen counter. "I think we had better find a counselor for him."

Daniel took a couple of steps toward the back door so he could keep an eye on Tony. "I don't disagree; I just wish we could have handled this ourselves."

Tony had walked over to the row of bushes that made a soft fence between the lawn and the side street. He appeared to be having a serious conversation with it. "Imaginary friends are often caused by emotional stress. It feels like we've failed him on some level." Daniel had half turned to talk to Sophia, but movement at the corner of his eye caused him to turn his attention back to Tony. He saw his pajama-clad son marching imperiously across the yard, headed toward the open back door.

Walking timidly behind him was something impossible. He was very short, barely a foot tall. His face looked kindly and wise with ruddy cheeks and a long white pointed beard that hung past his rounded belly. He wore a thick, white woolen shirt, a red pointed hat with matching trousers, and suspenders with large black buttons. He had black boots that seemed cartoonishly large for his small frame. You almost couldn't tell what color they were because they were clad in copious amounts of rich dirt and small pebbles. It looked as if some Black Forest witch had breathed life into a typical ceramic garden gnome.

Daniel would have asked him to remove his shoes, but the absurdity of what he was seeing had momentarily stunned him. Seeing Daniel's reaction, Sophia stood up to get a better look at what he was seeing. She let out a strangled shriek as Tony and the gnome entered the kitchen.

Tony glared at his mother in annoyance. "Mom, don't be rude. Bob, this is my mom Sophia and my dad Daniel. Mom, dad, meet Bob."

The gnome took a step forward, leaving a trail of dirt behind him. He swept off his hat and bowed deeply. In a surprisingly deep but cheery voice, he said, "It is my great pleasure to meet you. I am Burbalobonomicus." Tony giggled, and Bob looked at him side-eyed. "Tony finds it easier to call me Bob."

Daniel woke up enough to react. "Tony, I... think... you'd better let us talk to Bob alone for a while."

Tony looked apprehensive, "Be nice to him; he's my friend."

The gnome shooed Tony towards the stairs, "It will be all right, Tony; your parents and I have some things to discuss."

Tony slowly edged towards the stairs, worried that a fight might break out if he wasn't there to mediate. Daniel escorted his son to the stairs and waved him hurriedly up, never taking an eye off the strange creature. When he heard Tony's door shut, he grimly moved to confront the oddity in his kitchen.

The gnome raised its hands in a calming manner. "You must have questions, but let me spin my tale for you first. I assure you I am not what you think, more than you can imagine, and above all, I am no threat to you or your family."

Daniel's gut reaction was to throw this thing out and call the police. But with all the strange things that Tony had attributed to 'Bob' of late, his curiosity was getting the best of him. He could sense fear in Sophia, so he stepped over and grabbed her hand. Sophia clasped his hand fiercely. He pulled her to him and gave her a reassuring hug, and she squeezed him tightly.

Bob hmphed quietly to draw their attention back to him, "May we please all sit down. I promise to answer as many questions as I am able, but this may take some time." Daniel and Sophia stepped back from each other and hesitantly nodded in agreement. The gnome gingerly sat down in the middle of the kitchen, settling into the small clumps of soil he had tracked in. "I apologize for the mess, but unfortunately, it is a part of my nature."

Daniel and Sophia, seemingly spellbound, lowered themselves and sat cross-legged on the floor so as not to tower over their diminutive guest. "Excellent!" Bob proclaimed. "This is going far better than I could have hoped. I must say that despite your fears, you are both acting with a considerable amount of decorum considering the circumstances."

Sophia opened her mouth to ask a question, but the gnome swiftly held up his hand. "Please, my dear. I promise you can ask questions but let me have my say." Sophia closed her mouth slowly and then quietly nodded. Bob tilted his head to the side, closed his eyes briefly as if gathering his thoughts, and then began to speak. His voice was warm and kind, but there was a rumbly roughness to it.

"First off, I am not a diminutive human being with a penchant for dressing as lawn ornamentation. I am also not a hallucination, a practical joke, a special effect, or an 'imaginary friend.' I am a gnome, a magical creature who is a guardian of the earth and soil. A keeper of secrets and lore. Your legends of my kind go back over five hundred years to the verdant forests of Central Europe, but in truth, we are far older than that. I have been tasked with keeping Tony safe until he is ready and able to protect himself." Bob had been leaning slightly forward as he spoke, but he then leaned back, put one hand on his hip, and then gestured with the other up and down at himself, "I also don't look anything like… this."

Daniel seemed confused and opened his mouth, then seemingly not wanting to interrupt, quickly closed it again.

Bob chortled, "It's all right. You may now ask questions."

Daniel and Sophia both opened their mouths to speak, "what do" "who" Sophia stopped and gestured to her husband to proceed. "What do you mean, you don't look like this?"

Bob smiled, "That's as good a question as any to start with. The answer is complicated. Magic is absent from the world. Because there is no magic, I, a magical creature, cannot be perceived by you in my true form. Tony told you that I am a gnome, which is quite correct. But over the centuries, humanity's concept of a gnome has evolved into this. Your mind perceives me like this because this is what you think of as a gnome. When magic fully returns, only then will you see me as I truly am."

Daniel poked Sophia. "I know we both have a million questions; you ask one." Sophia leaned forward with a serious look on her face. "What did you mean when you said you were tasked with protecting Tony? Who tasked you, and why does he need protection?"

Bob squirmed a little but then sighed. "I knew I would have to answer this, and I will to the best of my ability, but I must caveat this. Remember that part about being a keeper of secrets? There are some details I am not allowed to divulge. I will tell you as much as I can, but some of this will have to be in generalizations."

Sophia grimaced. "Fair enough, but I need to know who or what is threatening my son. That is not negotiable, or we will find a way to rid ourselves of you."

Bob raised his hands defensively, "If I can eventually convince you to trust me, I hope you will come to understand that I only want the best for him." Bob paused briefly before continuing, "First, you must understand that amongst magical creatures, there is a hierarchy. The details of that don't really matter; just know that it exists. In the grand scheme of things, I'm fairly high up, but at the top heap are creatures called the ancients. They are powerful enough to be awake when magic is gone. I am powerful, but I am not powerful enough to be awake in the quiet times. One of these creatures woke me and imbued me with some of their power so that I could watch over and protect Tony from, well, anything."

Sophia considered what he said. "So what Tony said was true? You drove off the coyote? You saved him from that idiotic driver?"

Bob smiled and nodded. "I also kept him safe from a Yellow Jacket sting or two and caught him when he fell out of the oak tree."

Daniel shook his head wistfully. "I told him to stay out of that damn tree. I thought he had gotten it out of his head."

Bob shook his head. "Not until he fell out and nearly landed on his head."

A quizzical look came across Daniel's face, "Hey, um, not to sound indelicate, but how could you have possibly caught Tony? He's at least twice your size."

Bob smiled coyly, "A gnome must keep some secrets. In truth, I am a magical creature. I am both stronger and faster than this form would lead you to believe."

"So, you won't tell us who this 'Ancient' is?" Sophia asked.

The gnome shook his head slowly, "Unfortunately, I'm not allowed to divulge that secret. They will tell you when they feel the time is right."

"You've sort of told us the who, but you haven't really told us the why? I mean, it's great what you've done for Tony, but why does this Ancient care about Tony? What could he possibly be in danger from?" Sophia's agitation increased as she spoke.

Bob spoke gently, trying not to spook them. "I wish I could tell you, but I'm not allowed to divulge that. I think you deserve to know, but all I can do is ask the Ancient if I can reveal that to you."

Despite Bob's gentle demeanor, Sophia looked troubled. At that moment, Cleo appeared from around the corner of the fridge. Without hesitation, she sidled up to Bob and walked a tight circle around the gnome, rubbing her head against his back and wrapping her tail around him. Bob chortled, reached out, and stroked the cat's tail as she completed her circuit and headed back out of the kitchen. Sophia was startled by Cleo's reaction to Bob. The cat was a ghost whenever they had other people in the house.

"Bob, I appreciate your candor. You've given us a lot to think about. Since you seem comfortable there, I would appreciate it if you'd return to the back yard if you don't mind. Daniel and I have a lot to discuss."

Bob nodded and stood up, "But of course. If you have any questions, you know where to find me.

Again, I apologize for the mess. Could you... open the door for me?"

Daniel stood up and crossed the kitchen, stepping over the dirt trail and pulled open the door for the gnome. Bob swept off his hat and bowed deeply to Sophia, still sitting cross-legged on the floor. "It has been a pleasure, madam. Fear not; I take no offense at your reaction. I would expect nothing less considering the circumstances." Bob spun on his heel, placed the hat back on his head with a flourish, and marched out the door and into the night.

Daniel locked the door behind him, turned and leaned his back against it, and stared up at the ceiling. Sophia stood up and poked her husband. "Go get Tony. We'll go to Leo's and sort this out. I don't want to stay here until we decide what we're going to do about this. I'll grab a few things and meet you in the garage."

Daniel woke from his reverie with a start and nodded in agreement. They went up the stairs side by side; Daniel stopped at Tony's room and quietly opened the door. Sophia could hear him gently rousing their son from sleep as she headed down the hallway to their bedroom.

Sophia grabbed a bag from the closet and began stuffing it with a change of clothes for them both and then headed into the bathroom and grabbed a few essentials off the counter. She snatched a hair tie and began sweeping her hair back into a ponytail. As she did so, her eyes locked with herself in the mirror. There stood a short, dark-haired woman with her mother's warm face and her father's deep green eyes, barely holding it together, right on the verge of tears. Her head sunk, and she slammed her hands on the counter and braced herself to keep the sobbing at bay. Her chest heaved, and she shuddered before getting herself under control. Clenching her entire body with determination, she turned her back on the mirror and headed back into the bedroom.

She walked into the closet and grabbed a step stool. She placed it at the back and climbed two of the steps so she could reach the highest shelf. With little décor, she swept several shoe boxes from the shelf onto the floor and reached for what she knew was there but couldn't quite see. Her hand grasped the cold steel of her father's double-barrel shotgun.

It had been decades since he had taught her how to shoot the monstrosity and had not given it much thought until he had left it to her in his will. He knew she didn't care for guns, but he also believed that his daughter should know how to take care of herself. She hadn't been able to bring herself to get rid of it because it was a part of him.

With his voice in the back of her head, she cracked the breach, verified that it wasn't loaded, and then snapped it shut. She reached back up, grabbed the ancient box of double ought shells that had come with the gun, and carefully climbed down the stepladder. She grabbed the bag off the bed and went downstairs and into the garage.

Daniel's eyes widened when he saw what she was carrying, and he hesitated briefly when she motioned to him to pop the trunk. Sophia stomped her foot, and he quickly fumbled at the controls as she marched to the back of the car. She threw in the bag and gun, gently tucked the shells into the bag, and zipped it up. She slammed the trunk closed and then got into the passenger seat. "Not a word." Daniel frowned at her, looked back at Tony, who was groggily asking where they were going, and slowly backed the car out of the garage.

Ancient eyes watched the steel machine back out, the sharp glare of its headlights briefly blinding them as it backed onto the street, lurched forward and rapidly disappeared into the suburban maze. Then the eyes sank into the earth and vanished as if they had never existed.

Chapter 30

Leo stared at his cell phone suspiciously. The conversation he had just had might have been the strangest conversation he had ever had with Daniel. Which was saying something considering they went to college together, shared more than a few illegal substances during that time, and Daniel had a knack for pranks.

The things that had been happening to Daniel and his family 'could' be the most elaborate prank he had ever pulled. But the way he had sounded on the phone was eerie. It was a mixture of awe and fear. Add that to the rumblings about a gnome and Tony, with Sophia angrily telling him to wrap it up and concentrate on the road, and Daniel seemed all too serious.

He began using his reporter brain to process what Daniel had told him previously, the snippets of tonight's conversation, along with the event he had personally witnessed. He mulled it over as he got out

pillows and blankets and began inflating an air
mattress he kept around for when his brother stopped
by unexpectedly. He grabbed three beers from the
fridge and cracked one open for himself. About the
time he finished his beer, he heard them pull into the
drive. His reporter instinct had come to a very
startling conclusion. That Daniel was either crazy or
deadly serious.

He turned on the porch light and opened the
front door. As the Fitzroys got out of the car, he noted
that Tony was fast asleep in Daniel's arms, Daniel
looked lost in thought to the point of distraction, and
Sophia had the scariest look on her face that he had
ever seen. She also appeared to be carrying a
firearm pathetically disguised underneath a
sweatshirt. This was definitely not a prank.

He beckoned them inside and closed and
locked the door behind them. "I've got the couch in
my office made up for him." Daniel nodded and
strode down the hallway with Tony softly snoring in
his arms. Sophia set down what she was carrying,
and Leo saw the distinctive double barrels of a side-
by-side shotgun peek out from under the sweatshirt.

"I'd ask how you're doing, but that makes
things obvious." he pointed at the gun. "I think I'll start
with what's going on and why you feel you need to
carry that with you."

Sophia didn't say anything at first. She picked
up the beer, took a few sips, and then stared intently
at the label as if she wished it were something a lot
more potent. She shook herself out of her reverie and

began to speak. Leo listened intently, making mental notes of questions he had but didn't want to interrupt. By the time she ended with a ", and that's when we headed here," he had picked up Daniel's beer and downed the whole thing. He didn't remember picking it up or taking a drink. Daniel was back and standing to his left with the same stunned look he'd had on his face when he arrived.

"I… um… shit. If it were any two other people, I would say you're both insane, but even he," flipping a thumb at Daniel, "wouldn't be dumb enough to try this as a prank."

Daniel gulped, "I don't think I'm creative enough to come up with something like this. It was like something straight out of a movie, the first act of a horror movie. This kind of stuff just isn't real. Right?"

He stared at the bottle, lost in thought. He wandered into the kitchen, grabbed three more beers, and then handed them out before replying. "So, let's eliminate the obvious explanations. He wasn't some sort of super hologram or light show?"

Sophia shook her head. "Definitely no; he tracked dirt into the kitchen, which Cleo walked through. We could see him, hear him; he smelled of freshly turned garden soil, and although none of us touched him, I'm pretty sure I heard his steps on the floor."

He nodded, "Ok, what about an elaborate robot or animatronic toy?"

It was Daniel's turn to shake his head, "I've seen some pretty sophisticated robotic technology as part of inter-university presentations. Even the most advanced still make a ridiculous amount of electro-mechanical noise. Other than some fairly clompy footsteps, he was completely silent."

"Last but not least. Is it possible that he was some sort of little person?" he asked.

Daniel and Sophia looked at each other, and both slowly shook their heads in the negative before Sophia answered. "We talked about that on the way over, so I googled the shortest people in history. There have been a few people who were less than two feet in height, but they all had very obvious signs of physical deformity. That stature takes a toll on the body. 'Bob' had none of that, and I swear he was barely a foot tall. He literally looked like a flesh and blood garden gnome, ruddy cheeks, round belly, and all."

He contemplated their situation while they all sat quietly. A small flash of insight scared itself into his thoughts. He frowned and turned to Daniel, "All right, history boy. What are myths?"

Daniel was stunned for a moment. He quickly recovered and frowned deeply. "What does that have to do with what happened tonight?"

He casually chucked his bottle cap at him and replied, "Humor me. I want to talk to Professor Fitzroy."

Daniel growled at his friend but formulated a response. "Myths are morality tales. They use the supernatural to provide a context for natural events we don't understand or in some cases to provide a basis for some sort of worship."

"So, they're a lie we tell ourselves to explain the unexplainable and to give us a reason for doing the ridiculous in the name of the Flying Spaghetti Monster?" he asked.

Daniel nodded. "Basically, yes. Almost every myth is tied to some form of worship or reverence of the supernatural creatures involved in the story, and almost every story is either a direct morality play or an explanation of nature, such as be good, or Santa Claus won't give you gifts or Zeus creates lightning storms when he's angry so we must make sacrifices to him."

"So, if a myth is a lie, there is one universal truth about lies. The best ones have a kernel of truth in them. You've had two unexplainable events happen in close proximity to Tony, and now an unexplainable creature has come forward and explained them. We've eliminated the most likely cases, although I won't completely eliminate sociopathic little person from the pool. That leaves us with the unlikely possibility that you have a magical gnome living in your back yard." He turned to Sophia. "If that is a true statement, I think you have to take what he has told you as truth until you can prove otherwise. I totally get why you brought the gun now."

Sophia shook her head, "It's not that simple. If he isn't what he says he is, he's dangerous." She closed her eyes, and her hands curled into claws as she spoke. "Even if he's telling the truth about himself and… and... magic, that doesn't mean we can trust him. The only thing I do believe is that my son is in danger. Either from a magical lawn ornament, a sociopath dressed as one, or from some unknown threat that we know nothing about."

He looked into Sophia's eyes and saw that they were brimming with tears, but her jaw was set, and there was a fierceness behind the tears. "Look, we're not going to solve all life's mysteries tonight. It's late; you two are exhausted. Get some sleep, call in sick tomorrow, and we can talk about what you want to do next after you've gotten some rest."

Chapter 31

The din in the conference room at the headquarters of the Knights of the Stone was unbearable. All the Knights except for Larkin were in the room, and at least three separate shouting arguments were going on at the same time. Brian kept quiet. He still understood very little about what was going on. As the new kid, they still didn't have him looped in on all of The Knight's business, but he knew something momentous had happened with the reliquary. Nathan had sent out the details of what he and Larkin had discovered. When Brian compared it to Nathan's reliquary playbook, there was no corollary. Whatever was going on was new, and that had all of the Knights in a literal panic.

He was surprised that they weren't more collected about this. From his perspective, the Knights versus the return of Magic was a war that had been waging for over fifteen hundred years.

Panicking just because things weren't going to plan wasn't going to accomplish anything. He and Nathan seemed to be the only ones that weren't losing their shit.

Nathan was trying to calm Katrin down. She was currently yelling at Tabari Hamid. Tabari had been in the middle east searching for other magical artifacts that might be useful in detecting Key Events or the Lock when the last meeting had occurred. He had flown in last night after getting Nathan's update on the reliquary. When he arrived for the meeting, he had casually mentioned that he had been followed while in Cairo but had no idea what agency or government was responsible.

Tabari was surprisingly calm in the face of Katrin, loudly lecturing him about fieldcraft and the solemn responsibility of the Knights to maintain the secrecy of the order. He explained that when he realized he was being followed, he took four separate flights using three different identities before driving from Munich to Brussels for this meeting. He was surprisingly patient, considering he had twenty hours of flights, nine hours in a car, and had come to headquarters as soon as he arrived in town. But his patience was beginning to wear thin. His accent was getting thicker, and he was punctuating some of the conversation with Arabic swear words as he became more and more agitated.

On the far side of the room Stephen Mercier, the second seat, was in a heated discussion with Viktor and Matz. Brian had no idea what their argument entailed, but it sounded particularly harsh to his ears as they were all speaking in German, and their volume seemed to be increasing in steady increments.

At the end of the table to his right, clustered the remaining Knights. Mikah, Maya, Duncan O'Connor, and Hsin Zhang were speaking in low tones, although it seemed Maya was doing most of the talking.

Brian had never actually met Duncan or Zhang in person before. Their expertise lay in field operations, and they were both running active task forces. Duncan was responsible for the full-time monitoring of the LHC particle accelerator at CERN. It was his team that he, Katrin, and Micah had liaised with while they were in Geneva, but at the time, Duncan had been in France doing some legwork on the ITER Fusion reactor.

Hsin Zhang's presence here was frankly amazing, especially on such short notice. He had spent the last decade surveilling and actively sabotaging North Korea's nuclear weapon and ballistic missile programs. It was undoubtedly one of the most dangerous of all the Knight's posts, but he was there as a representative and with direct orders from the Chinese government's Ministry of State Security. Brian was certain it had taken a lot of political favors and a decent number of bribes to get Zhang here as quickly as he did.

He was thinking about joining the group at the end of the table to listen in on what Maya had to say when Colonel Larkin entered the conference room. Most of the talking died away, but Katrin continued to rail away. If anything, her voice sounded louder and bordered on the edge of panic with all the other conversations gone.

Colonel Larkin slammed a fist on the table, which caused Katrin's mouth to snap shut. In a calm voice, he said, "Please be seated. We have much to discuss."

Like cowed children, they all shuffled to their respective seats and settled in. Larkin didn't speak for what seemed like hours but was, in fact, only a couple of minutes. "Every generation of the Knights of the Stone has faced adversity. Every Key Event is different, and every Lock is found in different circumstances." He glared around at each face around the table before continuing. "Listening to the panic emanating from this conference room makes me wonder how many of you should have been failed during the vetting process. Now, let's start working the problem. Nathan, let's skip the usual bullshit, please. Record it, but this is an emergency meeting; we don't need a roll call or minutes. Let's just start with the latest you have from the reliquary."

For his part, Nathan only looked slightly miffed that they were going to skip formalities. "I'm going to assume you've all read the brief, but at a high level, the temperature of the Hummingbird continues to progress as expected. Based on the known pattern, the Key Event should be somewhere between twelve and eighteen months away. One thing to note is that in the normal forty to fifty year timeline between key events, the Hummingbird is indicating that this would be on the low end of that time scale but still within the known values of previously recorded Key Events."

Nathan used a remote to fire up the large monitor at the end of the room. "This is the reliquary camera view of the Family Stone. Some of you may not know, but there hasn't been much research done on the stone beyond standard observational records. It has always been unpredictable in the luminosity it generates and in its timing. It tends to ebb and flow randomly as the Key Event approaches. However, it has never before been observed to glow more than a month before the event. Even more troubling is that the husband and wife reliefs are well recorded, but there is no record of the band of children that has now been revealed."

Viktor spoke up. "Love the detail, Nathan, but what does this mean?"

Nathan looked like he was about to continue with more technical details, but the look Larkin gave him caused him to pause. He gave a deep shrug and continued, "The long and the short of it is, our most reliable relic is still saying we have plenty of time, and our most unreliable relic is doing something weird."

Stephen's face instantly turned red. "Merde! Why in the hell did you slam the panic button, Sam? This sounds like a fire drill if ever I heard it." The French expletive followed by unaccented English threw Brian off for a second, and he had to stifle a laugh.

Larkin took a deep breath. "Why? Because we're on the edge of a Key Event, and I don't like surprises. It's one thing to say that one of the relics is acting a little strangely. It's another to say that one of them is doing something that has never before been identified in over a thousand years of observation. I, for one, don't want to leave this room until we've agreed to a change in our operational cadence. I don't want to be caught with our pants down. From personal experience, we don't want another Pyramid test situation, and we definitely don't want another battle of Aleppo. You can call me paranoid, but all it costs is time and money. We don't know how much of the former we have, but we have lots of the latter."

"I agree with Samuel," Katrin interjected. "If we continue to operate under our standard operating procedure and things go sideways, there's no telling what damage could be done. In fact, I think we should enact Vanguard protocols immediately."

Several people shifted uncomfortably around the table. Brian had never heard that term before, nor was he familiar with Aleppo other than it was a city in Syria, but he didn't think now was a good time to start asking questions.

Nathan switched the screen to a presentation. "Samuel and I have worked up the framework of an agenda. It's not set in stone, but it's something to help get things rolling along. First, I'd like to review our current financial status, as that should alleviate any concerns about our ability to escalate readiness. Any objections?"

All present nodded their agreement, seemingly eager to begin doing something.

Brian followed Larkin back to his office. They had been at it for over four hours and had now split up so that people could get something to eat and get away from one another. Every one of the Knights had very dominant personalities and strong opinions. It made coming to concrete decisions time-consuming, but in his opinion, they were starting to make good progress on a game plan for adjusting their operations.

Colonel Larkin poured two glasses of bourbon on ice and slid one of them across the desk to him. "I appreciate you being levelheaded in there. Viktor, Stephen, and Katrin seem to be a little 'overwhelmed' by this."

He closed his eyes and took a sip of bourbon. The Colonel knew how to pick the good stuff. "Not a problem, sir. Frankly, this is just the intelligence gathering and planning phase. I'm not sure why some of them are getting so worked up about this."

Larkin nodded his agreement. "You're new, so you don't yet understand. For most of them, this has been a dream job. Carte Blanche expense accounts, freedom to live their life however they want, a lifestyle that most people never dream about. But now the reality of what we're responsible for is staring them in the face. They'll be fine once things start moving, but for now, they're just trying to find their footing."

He set down his glass. "Colonel, I have a couple of questions I didn't want to ask in front of the rest of them as I feel like these are probably things I should already know."

Larkin laughed, "I wouldn't worry about looking like a fool for asking questions. Not asking questions is what will make you look foolish."

"I'll have to keep that in mind. What happened in Aleppo?"

"That's actually an excellent question. The details are not in the files I gave you. Aleppo was the closest we came to the destruction of the Knights. In 1138, near the end of the Christian occupation of Jerusalem, a series of massive earthquakes struck the city of Aleppo in Syria. The Knights and its forces had been involved with the various factions of the crusades. At the time, almost all the Knights of the Stone were European Christians, and Aleppo was a Muslim stronghold. There was no way we would be able to infiltrate a Muslim city with weapons, so we were trying to encourage the various knightly orders to invade Aleppo so we could assassinate the Lock."

"This sounds like a recipe for disaster. Why didn't they just sneak in, identify the Lock and then hire assassins?" Brian asked.

"Because most of the Knights were drinking the Crusade Kool-Aid, that's why. They thought they could kill two birds with one stone. Take one of the more powerful Muslim strongholds and kill the Lock.

219

Win-win. Unfortunately, by the time they garnered enough support for their plan, the earthquakes began. Aleppo was devastated by a series of earthquakes that occurred over an entire year. The Christian leaders saw it as a sign that God was punishing the Muslims, so why interfere."

The colonel stood up and paced a bit as he continued the story. "It was six months before they could assemble a force large enough to assault the city. Our best guess was that the Lock had been awake and preparing the entire time. The Christian armies were slaughtered by the Muslim forces and the monsters and demons that the Lock had summoned. We lost our best artifact for tracking the lock, and eleven of the twelve were killed. The only saving grace was that they managed to kill the Lock before being overrun, and the youngest member had been left behind to guard the reliquary. That one young man was able to rebuild the order quickly enough so that they were ready fifty years later when the lock returned."

"Don't we have Excalibur? I thought that was the best relic for tracking the Lock."

Larkin shook his head. "It's the best we have right now. It buzzes in your hand when you've got it pointed in the right direction, and it gets the job done. There was an Egyptian scarab necklace that, when worn, told you the exact distance and direction to the Lock. We've spent centuries trying to re-find that necklace, but it's probably in some wealthy person's private collection gathering dust."

"So, what are Vanguard protocols, and why haven't I been told about them?" he asked.

Larkin gave him a wicked grin. "That, my boy, is because you are the Vanguard protocols."

His blank stare made Larkin laugh out loud.

"I shouldn't laugh because this isn't going to be particularly fun for you. We never deploy all of our resources to any one potential threat anymore. We'll have backup on the ground on each continent. Two full-fledged knights with their respective teams ready to go in each region, but we obviously don't know where the Lock is going to be. Those teams will continue their operations with slight modifications based on our current discussions, but someone has to babysit Excalibur, so we know the second it's active."

"So, how did I get picked for this illustrious position?" He suspected this might be the Knights of the Stone equivalent of latrine digging duty. "I am kind of new at this."

Larkin finished off his drink before answering. "We choose whoever is the most combat effective at the moment. I suppose you could go break your leg, and it would probably fall on Micah, but we've deemed you to be the tip of the spear."

He shrugged. "Doesn't seem so bad. It's not every day you get to hold one of the most legendary weapons in history."

Larkin smiled and shook his head slowly. "Remember when I said we need to know the second it becomes active?"

Jeff McIntyre

"I'm going to have to sleep with it, aren't I?" Brian groaned.

Larkin nodded with a grim smile. "It's much worse than that."

Chapter 32

Daniel and Sophia woke to the sound of giggling and the smell of breakfast. By the time they threw themselves together and wandered out to the kitchen, Leo already had a mound of pancakes a foot high. Tony was cheering on Uncle Leo's pancake flipping show while he munched on a fresh shamrock-shaped cake.

"Morning, you two; coffee is ready, and so is breakfast." Leo pointed to the kitchen chairs. "Have a seat, eat something, and then we can chat about Bob. I've been doing some thinking, and I have some ideas, but they can wait until after caffeine."

After many pancakes had been devoured and at least two pots of coffee inhaled, Leo put Tony to work washing dishes so the adults could talk.

"With all the weirdness that is Bob, I think we need to try and sort things out as logically as possible." He pointed at Daniel, "First is research.

Jeff McIntyre

Find out everything you can about gnomes. The origin of the myth, their description, habits. The story of gnomes started somewhere; let's go back to the beginning and see if we can put any of this in context. If there is a kernel of truth to the legend, it's probably in the original stories about them."

"Seems like a reasonable way to start. It will give me something to do besides twiddle my thumbs." Daniel responded.

"Part two, with your permission, I'd like to interview Bob." He said. "One of you will need to ask him if he's ok talking to me and if he knows what a reporter is."

Daniel waved his hand across his throat, "Whoah whoah whoah. We do not need a story out of this; we need this out of our life. What is interviewing him going to accomplish anyway?"

"Relax, I would never print something like this." He pointed at Sophia. "She would kill me, and no one would believe me anyway. The interview will help me shake out the truth. If this is a con artist, I'll figure it out. It's kind of my job. If he is what he says he is, his stories will be deep and complex. Possibly with historical context that can be verified."

Sophia spoke up, "Ok, Leo. That sounds like a decent plan, and I trust you not to throw our family under the bus."

He turned to her, "The last part is not as straightforward, and I'm not sure you're going to like it."

Sophia stiffened. "If it helps us figure this out and bring some sanity back to our lives, I'll do whatever it is."

He had expected no less. "You have to convince Bob to prove he's a magical creature."

"How in the HELL," Sophia quickly looked towards the kitchen and lowered her voice. "How in the hell am I supposed to do that?"

"I don't know, but if he wants to earn your trust, he has to do… something. From what you told me last night, he was respectful and overly deferential to you in particular." He put a hand on her shoulder. "Besides, you're Tony's mother, and if he wants to prove that he's telling the truth and not a threat, he needs to convince you more than anyone. He can't just say 'I'm a magical creature' and expect you to just accept that."

Tony wandered in from the kitchen, "Whatcha talkin about?"

Sophia patted the couch cushion next to her, and Tony walked over and plopped down. "Tony, we're talking about what to do about your friend Bob."

Tony scrunched up his face, "What's the big deal? He's my friend; he protects me."

Daniel walked over, sat on the coffee table in front of Tony, and put his hands on Tony's knees. "I know this is tough sport, but this isn't as simple as having a friend who's there for you and stands up for you. Bob shouldn't exist. We can't simply take at face value what he's saying."

"I finally made a new friend, and you're going to chase him away!" Tony's shoulders slumped, and his head sank.

"Sweetie, it will be ok. We just want to spend some time getting to know Bob. This is all new to us, and we just want to make sure that you're safe." Sophia reached out to Tony to pull him in for a hug, but he wrenched away and jumped up.

"No! You're just going to ruin everything. Can't you just leave him alone?" Tony bolted out of the living room and ran to the back door.

He moved to go after him, but Sophia interjected, "Don't. Let him go. I'll talk to him in a few minutes after he's had a chance to cool down a bit."

Daniel stood up with a sigh, "Do you want me to stick around and help calm him down?"

"No, go do your research. I think he and I could use some one-on-one time." Sophia stood up and curled into her husband's waiting arms. After a long embrace, he kissed the top of her head and then let go.

"Give me a call if anything comes up," and Daniel walked out the front door.

"Soph, I'm going to hop in the shower. I have to run out and cover a story, but rest assured, I'm going to spend some quality time thinking about what questions to ask a mythological creature. Let me know if you or Tony need anything."

Sophia stared off toward the back door where her son had fled before turning to respond. "Thanks,

Leo; I appreciate your help. I know how ridiculous all this must seem."

He shook his head, "Honestly if all this had gone down and you hadn't come to me for help, I would have been very disappointed in you. You guys are family. We'll do what we need to do to get through this… whatever this… is."

Sophia sat back down and checked her phone as Leo headed for his shower. There were no work emergencies yet, so she started making notes about what she might say to Bob. The sheer ridiculousness of trying to formulate questions to ask a magical gnome should one suddenly appear in your life made it impossible to keep her thoughts straight. One ten-minute conversation had turned the world upside down, and she feared there was no path to flipping it back over.

After several minutes of staring at a blank screen on her phone, she sighed, got up off the couch, and followed in her son's footsteps. Leo had opened a window in the door to let in some fresh air, and two voices carried on the breeze, one young and one deep and gravelly.

Sophia clenched at her chest to get the panic under control before it started and then slowed her approach and tried to eavesdrop without Tony or Bob noticing her.

Jeff McIntyre

"They don't trust you; they're going to try and get rid of you." Tony's voice was ragged from crying. Sophia reached for the door to go and comfort her son, but Bob's voice made her pause.

His voice was gentle, consoling. "That is not going to happen. I made a promise to you, Tony. I would stand by you until you no longer want me. But you must listen to your parents. No one cares for you and wants to protect you as much as they do."

"But Bob, you're the only friend I have." Tony sobbed.

Bob gently chided him, "Bah, don't you think you're exaggerating a bit? This 'Uncle Leo' seems like a stand-up fellow. You have Cleopatra; long may she reign. She is always there when you need her. And what about Joe and Takahashi? From what you told me, they seemed to be very friendly to you."

Tony sniffed. "Adults don't count. Cleos cool, I guess."

Bob's low chuckle made Sophia smile in spite of herself. "Despite appearances, I think you have a chance to turn the tables on those bullies at school. Turn them into allies rather than enemies. They seem to crave attention, and if you give it to them in the right way, I think you may be surprised."

"Bob, promise you'll never leave me."

"I promise, as long as you want me around, I will be here for you."

Sophia took a few steps back to give them time to react and then shouted towards the open window, "Tony, can you come in and talk to me?"

There was a brief pause before he responded, "Yeah, I'm comin." Shortly the door opened with no sign of a gnome in tow. Tony's knees were covered in dirt, but Sophia pretended not to notice as she took his hand and walked him back to the living room.

Chapter 33

Deb wandered around the perimeter of the crime scene. The police had cordoned off the area and were doing a good job of keeping the crowd under control. There wasn't much for her to do here. She'd checked in with the supervising detective, and the forensics specialists were already doing their job by the time she got there. She didn't think they'd find much useful, but she didn't want to muck about until they'd had a chance to do their thing.

It was a standard large metal trash dumpster, common behind every strip mall in America. Green with two large plastic lids that could be flipped up and back when trash was deposited or when the dumpster was picked up to be emptied. It had been painted green, but most of the paint had been scorched away. The lids had melted and then burned away as the fire had raged. Oddly, she could still read "Lou's Trash Service" emblazoned on the side. The fire had damaged that section, but it was still legible. The smoke had stained the cinderblock of the building, and it looked like the heat from the fire had been intense enough to damage cabling that was attached to the building's roof.

The air smelled… bad. Burning trash has a uniquely awful smell that varies depending on the contents. The air held the unmistakable scent of burnt plastic, but there were undercurrents of cardboard, various chemical smells, and oddly curry. The Saffron Grill, one of the tenants of the building, was undoubtedly the source of that particular aroma.

There was nothing extraordinary about this building. It just happened to be a stone's throw away from the Fermilab campus.

The forensics technicians largely ignored the dumpster as it was still smoldering. She was certain they would give it the once over in due course. For the moment, they were focused on the graffiti that had recently been sprayed on the wall ten feet to the right of the dumpster.

"HERBERT must be stopped" in bright yellow and white spray paint was emblazoned in foot-high letters. The dual colors and a couple of flourishes seemed to indicate that it was from someone familiar with street graffiti. The paint was fresh enough that it was still wet in places where the artist had over-sprayed. Forensics was canvasing the ground, searching for anything left behind by the perpetrators.

Her phone buzzed in her pocket. She pulled it out and saw the text message, "I'm behind you. Come chat when you have a minute." She turned and saw Leo Schafer standing behind the police line staring intently at his phone, most likely hoping she'd respond. She glanced around quickly and saw that the police had things well in hand. Rather than respond, she slipped her phone back into her pocket and walked over to him.

As she approached, he put his phone away. He nodded down the police line to where it ended at the building wall. No bystanders or police were standing there, so she adjusted her path and met him where their conversation could be more private.

"Thanks for the heads up, Agent Kazdin. Not the most exciting scoop I've ever gotten, but I still appreciate you keeping me in mind for anything related to this."

She nodded in agreement. "No, not the most exciting, but definitely worrying. This will accomplish exactly what Nadir wants. It's going to unnerve the staff at Fermilab, and all it cost them was two cans of spray paint and a gallon of gas." She turned and waved at the police presence. "This is all a waste of time. The odds of them turning up any meaningful evidence that will help in this investigation is practically nil."

Leo grinned. "Can I quote you on that?"

"No, you may not," Deb said sternly. She turned and surveyed the scene. "Leo, there's not much point in you hanging around. If you want to take some pictures from back here, you're more than welcome. I'll send you the parts of the police report that are available for public consumption as soon as I get them."

"That would be great, but that's not why I came. Oh, don't get me wrong, I'll take the report and use it in my article, but I have something for you." He handed her a heavy manila envelope. "That took some wrangling to put together. I now owe Bears tickets to a friend of mine who's a forensic accountant. Worth it because I'm still not sure how he managed to put this together. Go ahead and look through it when you have the time, but I can give you the highlights."

She opened the envelope and peered inside at what must be half a ream of paper documentation. "You couldn't have sent me a digital copy?"

"Uh, no. He's kind of paranoid about digging around the finances of Security firms known for black ops and government contracts. Anyway, the gist is that Titan Security's presence is funded by Infinity Financial."

"That's surprising. Really surprising. Why does an investment firm care about a particle accelerator experiment? They're publicly traded, so how in the hell did their Board of Directors approve of that?" Her excitement rose. "If we can confront them about this, even if it's behind closed doors, we might get them to admit to what's going on."

"Well, let me clarify." Leo held his hands up to slow her down. "It isn't IFI exactly. It's their CEO,

Jeff McIntyre

Rebecca Drake. She has dug deep and has been a major donor to Fermilab for the last few years. That was how my buddy figured out what was going on. The details on how he tracked it down are in there."

Her excitement drained away. "It's still useful. I'll try and verify this, but if it pans out, I owe you one. I wish I knew what it meant, but it gives me a direction to head."

"Hey, before I head out," Leo interjected. "Can I show you a couple of pictures?"

She looked at Leo curiously. "Pictures? Of what?"

"Not of what. Of whom. I was interviewing Nadir protestors, and there were a couple who didn't strike me as the 'Fight the good fight liberal millennials' that made up the bulk of the group. Frankly, they looked more like they were in your line of work. If I stepped on someone's toes, I'd like to know whose." Leo pulled out his phone and brought up one of the better pictures he had taken of Lector and Vader. "I managed to take a couple of snaps of them without them noticing."

She took Leo's phone and zoomed in and out on the picture. She then flipped through some of the other images he had taken of the protestors and handed it back to him. "You've got good instincts, although those two aren't exactly blending in. Definitely law enforcement or military. Send me those pictures, and I'll see if I can figure out who they are. If some other agency is working Nadir, I and, more importantly, my boss will want to know."

Leo nodded as he fiddled with his phone. "Hey, if everything pans out with that IFI lead, you get to buy the next pizza and beer."

"I think I can do better than beer and pizza." She said over her shoulder as she walked away.

Chapter 34

Leo took out his phone and hit record on his note app. "Mr. Esposito, thank you for agreeing to see me on such short notice. I wanted to get your official response to the incident of arson that occurred near the Fermilab campus. I also wanted to know if you were ready to release information regarding the internal investigation of your team?"

Alvaro Esposito's tired smile spoke volumes. "In some ways, I wish we had found someone to lay the blame on, but everyone checked out. If any of our members aren't who they say they are, they're very good at misdirection. Our background checks turned up nothing untoward, although we've forwarded that information to the FBI so they can verify if there's anything we missed. And, if any of our members are secret radicals, they're very good liars. We've done personal interviews with every employee and active member. The responses are a mixture of horror and fear. No one seemed nervous or dodgy, and we didn't get any 'they deserved it' rhetoric."

He was surprised at how relieved he felt. "I'm glad to hear that, although I agree it might have been easier if you had found a scapegoat. Hopefully, the FBI will figure out who IS responsible. Have you looked into any ad-hoc protestors? People, who aren't officially signed up with Nadir but have a habit of habitually showing up at your protests?"

Alvaro's smile faded, but he nodded. "I'm assuming you're referring to our paid seat warmers?"

"Yes, but not just them." He agreed. "I was also thinking about true ad-hoc protestors and the security consultants that have been showing up outside Fermilab."

"You are very good at your job Mr. Schafer." His smile had returned with grudging admiration. "I'm glad I trusted you." Alvaro leaned back in his chair and unconsciously smoothed his mustache before continuing. "To answer your questions regarding non-member roles. All our temps are regulars, and we perform background checks and interviews before hiring them. None of them have been flagged as interesting, and their information has been forwarded to the authorities for thoroughness. Our Team Leaders have been tracking ad-hoc protestors for the last several weeks. There is little we can do about them, but we did take notice of regular repeats and forwarded that information to the authorities as well. As far as the security contractors are concerned, one of our benefactors hired them and put them at our disposal. Our security has vetted them, and I have no concerns about them."

"Are you aware that Titan Security Services is also providing additional security support to Fermilab?" he asked.

Alvaro's eyes raised slightly, but then he nodded his head. "I was not aware, but I shouldn't be surprised. Titan is a very large company. In a combat theater, this would be considered a conflict of interest. But in this case, Fermilab and Nadir both want to avoid any incidents. If their services can help de-escalate the situation, I'm all for it." He pushed a piece of paper across his desk to Leo. "We're not resting on this either. That is a memo that went out to the team yesterday."

Internal memorandum, not for external distribution:

Dear Team:

These have been difficult days. As many of you know, Nadir has been the subject of an active investigation by the Federal Bureau of Investigation, as well as several "objective" stories across several forms of media, both traditional and social.

I ask that you all be strong, as we are far from done with this ordeal. We must continue to fight the good fight but at the same time be disciplined in our interactions with the public, press, the authorities, and in particular, those organizations that we have chosen to protest. Any recognized member of Nadir that is found to be breaking our code of conduct will be censured with the possibility of dismissal, and we will fully cooperate with the authorities and their investigations. I would ask that all of you take the time to review our code of conduct and treat this situation with the utmost seriousness.

I am also pleased to report that we have concluded our internal investigation, and at this time, we have no reason to believe that any of our current team members have been involved in any provocative activities.

Lastly, if you have any information regarding persons or organizations involved in the disturbing incidents that have occurred around Fermilab facilities and staff, please feel free to send me, aesposito@wearenadir.org or security security@wearenadir.org an email. You don't need to provide any details; just make us aware that you have information, and we will reach out to you.

> Regards,
> Alvaro Esposito
> President and Chief Activist

A wise man can see more from the bottom of a well than a fool can see from the top of a mountain - Anonymous

He skimmed it, "Not for external distribution?"

Alvaro nodded, "Yes, I'd appreciate it if you would not publish it, but if you have any questions, I'm more than happy to answer them."

He liked Alvaro, but he was also still wary of him. He hoped that he and Nadir were both on the up and up about their goals, but he couldn't yet give them the benefit of the doubt. "I appreciate your candor Mr. Esposito, and I'm pleased that you are continuing to push your team and that you are cooperating with the authorities. But I only have one more thing I wanted to talk to you about. Are you aware of the arson incident that occurred near the Fermilab campus?"

Alvaro's lips twisted, and his brow furrowed. "I saw a blurb in the news, but it was pretty sparse on details. I wasn't aware that I needed to respond."

"You should be prepared to release a statement." He pulled up a picture on his phone and showed it to Alvaro. "By this evening, all the news agencies will be reporting on the graffiti that was found near the fire. This message, 'HERBERT must be stopped,' was spray painted nearby."

Alvaro took a deep breath. His head lowered, and his eyes closed as he exhaled. He shook his head briefly before returning his eyes to Leo. "Thank you for the warning. I can't tell you off the cuff our precise response, but I will try to express our consternation at these continued threats aimed at Fermilab and reiterate that Nadir espouses peaceful protests and lobbying our government and industry as the only means of accomplishing our goals. Threats, damage, and violence are unacceptable." He opened a drawer and pulled out a bottle of bourbon and a couple of glasses. "Drink?"

He shrugged, "Sure."

After filling the glasses with ice cubes from a mini fridge behind his desk, Alvaro poured a couple of fingers' worth of bourbon into each glass and then handed one to Leo. "This is terrible news. Whoever is behind this isn't letting up, and this marks an escalation over previous incidents. Sooner or later, someone is going to get hurt. This isn't what I want, Leo, but there's too much at stake for us to just back off. Fermilab is acting irresponsibly."

"I don't understand the science enough to have an opinion." He took a sip of the bourbon. Alvaro had good taste; it was very smooth. "But I agree, their reaction to your protests is not normal."

"Don't print this, but if things get worse, I will back down." An angry grimace crossed Alvaro's face. "I don't think I could live with myself if anyone got hurt over this. The thought of how the HERBERT team will be feeling once they hear of this makes me sick to my stomach. The scientists and technicians are good people being driven by poor leadership."

He held up his glass toward Alvaro. "Here's hoping that throughout all this, cooler heads will prevail."

Alvaro held up his glass in response, and they both downed the last of their drink.

Chapter 35

$$E = MC^2$$

Hank Lee had been monitoring the latest low power tests of the HERBERT ring when the overhead system paged him to come to the administrator's office. He didn't even know the paging system still worked. He couldn't remember the last time they'd used it. That's what cell phones are for.

When he got to the office, Agent Debra Kazdin had been waiting for him. She gave him a quick overview of the arson and graffiti that had been found behind a strip mall just a few blocks from the campus. She assured him that she would get to the bottom of this before things escalated and reassuringly answered his questions before departing.

As he walked the long sterile hallways back to the HERBERT lab, he kept trying to come up with what to say to his team that could somehow alleviate their panic. He wasn't coming up with much. He just hoped that they would hear it from him first.

His hope was in vain. Gossip, especially panic-inducing gossip, had the ability to defy the special theory of relativity regarding the speed of light in a vacuum.

As he entered the lab, a small cluster of people had gathered around Yuri, who was talking loudly and gesticulating wildly in the way that meant he was aggravated.

Hank paused in the doorway, took a couple of deep cleansing breaths before anyone noticed him, and then walked up to the assembly and inserted himself. He held up his hand in Yuri's face. "Please stop. We may as well address this for everyone right now. I know what happened at the Saffron Grill; let's please not indulge in any idle speculation. Let's get the rest of the team over here, and I'll tell you what I know and what the plan is."

Yuri cupped his hands and bellowed to the techs at the control station. "Yo! Grab everybody and get them over here. Boss wants to talk to us."

Hank rolled his eyes but smiled when Yuri turned his attention back to him. "Thanks, Yuri." Then he waited patiently as word spread around the various monitoring stations. People in other rooms slowly filtered in and joined the group. Hank gestured for everyone to spread out into a large circle so everyone could see him. He was short, after all and didn't want to shout through people.

When the last technician joined the ring, he addressed his team. "I'm sorry to report that there has been another troubling incident. Fortunately, no one was hurt. A dumpster behind the Saffron grill was deliberately set on fire, and graffiti saying, 'HERBERT must be stopped' was left on the wall near the fire."

Hank raised his hands as people started to speak. "Please, let me continue. The FBI is directly involved in the investigation. Agent Kazdin informed me that there is an entire task force working with our security teams on ways to improve campus security. Local police will be increasing their presence on the campus and surrounding neighborhoods. We will receive additional security contractors, and anyone who requests it can get an escort to and from their home." Hank lowered his hands before he continued. "Now, I know this makes you nervous, and I don't blame you. I will reiterate, if any of you have experienced any incidents recently, please bring them to my attention. Any information we can provide to security and the authorities may help them get to the bottom of whoever is responsible for these threats."

Someone shouted, "We all know it's Nadir. Why don't they just round those people up!?"

"We know nothing of the sort. Unless someone can prove otherwise, that group of protestors has been at our front door for weeks, and there hasn't been a single incident that I'm aware of." Hank's voice was pleading. "Please, they are entitled to their opinions as well as their fears and prejudices.

Jeff McIntyre

We can only prove them wrong, and for the love of non-Newtonian fluids, please don't approach them. I don't want any tempers getting lost. On either side."

Yuri chimed in, his deep Russian baritone rolling over half a dozen other voices. "Do you think we should delay the experiment, boss?"

Hank shook his head. "No, Yuri. Let's be realistic; we have a garbage fire and some spray paint. This wasn't an assault or sabotage. Out of an abundance of caution and to help people get away from this place for a bit, I'm calling it for the day. No night shift either. Go home, spend some quality time with your family. Come back in the morning refreshed. I want to do a full ring test tomorrow." There were a few groans from the crowd.

"Folks, I understand. As if we needed any more stress in our lives. This project means a lot to all of us. The sooner we get a full power test under our belt, the sooner all of this pressure goes away. Successful test, no end of the world, Nadir has nothing to protest. Trust in the process and trust in me. We'll get through this. Now go home."

Katrin walked into Micah's office, the fury on her face evident. "We've barely set up shop here, and you authorize this stupid little stunt? What on earth did you hope to accomplish with trash burning and graffiti?"

Micah stroked the hairs of his goatee as he responded, his words clipped from his South African accent or maybe from frustration. "I was hoping to get them to 'slow their roll,' as you say. All our efforts to date have only caused them to accelerate their efforts in the same way that the Key event seems to be accelerating."

"We don't even know that it is accelerating; you're just guessing." Katrin paced around his tiny office. "We're supposed to be a team; the least you could have done was give me a heads up."

"Perhaps that was a little unprofessional of me. I'm not used to working with peers." He picked up a vape pen, took a long drag, and then exhaled around his words. "Not a guess, a working theory. I'm going to run with it until I see fit. We get daily updates on the reliquary, and if the activities at Fermilab change and there is some sort of corollary effect on the relics, then I will have proven my point."

Katrin crossed her arms across her chest. "I'm not used to working and playing well with others either, but we just got here. Just some consideration, please."

"I apologize, my dear. An opportunity presented itself, and I pulled the trigger, so to speak." Micah paused, then pointed at her accusingly. "You seem to work well with the Cooke fellow. Or is it that you seem to play well with him?"

Katrin grinned. "It's always fun to play with new toys. You didn't seem to mind when you were the object of my attention."

"I must admit it was an interesting way to get inducted into the Knights." Micah waved at the air with his pen. "The old guard don't approve of your dalliances."

"If you ask them, they'll disapprove, but you note no one has tried to stop it. They can grumble all they want about it, but they'd rather we sleep with each other than have any outside relationships. Sex, or worse, love; in our business is a huge security risk." Katrin stopped pacing and plopped down in a chair. "You know that Maya has been banging Mercier and Petrov. I think she has a thing for older men."

"Where you have a thing for younger men. I believe the Americans would call you a cougar." Micah said accusingly.

Katrin grinned impishly but quickly returned to seriousness. "So, if this arson ploy doesn't have the desired effect. What's the next step?"

"I'm putting together a series of contingency plans. A measured set of escalations that will put more and more pressure on not just Fermilab's security and staff but on law enforcement as well." Micah flipped his laptop around for her to look at. "I've started at the end. I could use your assistance putting these together and refining the details."

Katrin scanned what was on his screen. Her eyes got wide, and she let out a low whistle. "Full breach of the facility with a mixture of actual Nadir members and special operatives led by one of us.

Ballsy, I like it. What's your plan to deal with security?"

Micah took another puff on his pen and exhaled it toward the ceiling. "That is one of the things you can help me with."

Chapter 36

Rebecca Drake sent her assistant Jason the instant message, "Status Report. Now." She knew it would take him a few minutes to gather what he would need, so she poured herself a glass of wine, kicked off her shoes, and waited. It was a simple red import, not particularly expensive, but it was from a middle eastern vineyard she was fond of.

Her eyes wandered around at the various art pieces and artifacts she had decorated her office with. It humored her to surround herself with items from her past. Most people discounted them as the typical show of extravagance that often filled top-level CEOs' offices, but every one of these had meaning to her. The simple earthenware bowl on her side table had cost a sturdy blanket and two goats.

Her reverie was interrupted as Jason entered her office. He marched up to her desk and stood in front of it at attention with a sheaf of papers on a clipboard and a couple of folders waiting for her to acknowledge him.

She sat down her glass of wine before addressing him. "Let's start with Nadir."

"Yes, ma'am." He flipped a couple of the pages on his clipboard over and began reading. "The team assigned to Nadir continues to make regular reports. Their story about providing security to ensure the protester's safety is secure. We have the names of all active protestors, and they have identified two people as moles. They are still doing a workup on them but should have it put together by tomorrow."

"I want our own people to do a workup. Contractors are fine, but I'd rather independently verify their findings." She picked up her glass and took a sip. "Also, let's get a pair of investigators to tail the moles. No offense to the Titan boys, but looking inconspicuous isn't exactly their strong suit."

Jason made a couple of notes on his clipboard. "It will be done. Also, in their latest report, they identify a reporter who is showing above average interest in the protest and protestors." He stepped forward and placed a folder within her reach. "That is a quick dossier I had put together on the reporter. He's a tech reporter, and this type of story is outside his usual purview."

"Thank you. That is unfortunate but not surprising considering the events that have transpired. What about HERBERT?"

Jason flipped to a different page of his notes. "Hank Lee's latest report indicates that they are still behind your requested schedule, but the increased funding and amenities we've provided are helping them to narrow the gap. At this point, they are five days behind schedule; but that's down from thirteen days as of the last report." He consulted another page. "Titan is also reporting that everything is in place on their side and that they have been engaged by the FBI as expected. They are confident they can deal with any potential threats. There was an undercurrent of resentment towards interference from the FBI, but they assure us they are fully cooperating."

"Any suggestions on how we can squeeze more out of the Fermilab team?"

"I would suggest a bit of patience, ma'am. Their timeline is improving, and any additional stress may cause us to get diminishing returns. You want them to limp across the finish line, not implode within sight of it."

Rebecca's eyes narrowed, but she nodded her agreement. "Fine. For now. As far as Titan, reiterate to Phil Baxter that he is to fully cooperate with the FBI. I'm sure they're already suspicious about Titan's involvement; we don't need them getting suspicious enough to dig into our business. If he doesn't, I will personally put his nuts in a vice."

Jason winced but nodded and made another note. "Of course, ma'am."

"The Knights. Any progress?"

Jason hesitated. "I… don't want to get your hopes up, but we may have finally gotten a break."

Rebecca leaned forward; her eyes narrowed. "Spit it out. Either you have something, or you don't."

"It's incredibly convoluted, and it still needs lots of verification, but one of your agents has been tailing an Iraqi archaeologist by the name of Tabari Hamid. Mr. Hamid is well respected in the field and has spent most of his time excavating in Syria, Egypt, and Iraq. It came to our attention that Mr. Hamid has a standing request to several known antiquities dealers that he is interested in a very specific type of artifact. These artifacts correspond with items you have also expressed interest in."

"Pull our agent off him immediately. I don't want to arouse his suspicions. Effective immediately, you are to operate under the assumption that Tabari Hamid is an active Knight of the Stone." Rebecca collapsed back into her chair, her mind racing. "The Knight's resources are vast, so we need to tread carefully. I want you to employ a firm out of Turkey, I forget what their name is, but I'll send it to you once I dig it up. We've never used them before, but I've heard good things, and they can't be tied back to any of our operations. The goal is to very delicately identify everyone that Tabari Hamid operates with. I want three levels of connections established within a week and full background workups on anyone with a military or paramilitary background."

Jason made a few more notes and then spoke. "Might I suggest activating the Cyprus accounts and fund this new operation from them? I believe that's what you intended them for."

"Agreed. Be prepared to destroy those accounts and burn the Turkish firm the second we get any indication that the Knights are on to them." Rebecca finished off her wine. "Jason, don't forget to burn all that paperwork you're so fond of using after you've gotten things in motion."

"Of course not. I would never be so careless." He paused again and looked distinctly uncomfortable before continuing. "I hate to be a bother, Rebecca."

Rebecca came to attention at his use of her name.

Jason looked down at his feet. "I am becoming… tired again."

She stood up and came around the desk and lifted his head. "My poor thing. I am so sorry. My head has been so wrapped up in all these things that I've neglected you. I rely so heavily on you that I would be lost without you." She wrapped her arms around his waist and laid her head against his chest. "Contact Joe. Tell him we'll be flying to the island next weekend. By that time, most of this should be behind us, and I can get you back in fighting order."

"Yes, Rebecca. Thank you."

Chapter 37

Micah Krieg's mind drifted to the plains of central Africa. He spent several years as a mercenary in the Democratic Republic of Congo and South Sudan. It was an unfortunate reality for that entire continent that if you were experienced at war, there was always a place for you. He had been fortunate that despite a few skirmishes, he rarely saw combat. He had been careful to whom he pledged his skills, and he refused to work for factions that were eager for conflict.

Despite the inherent danger of the work, he considered his time there one of the best periods in his life. There was a primal beauty to sub-Saharan Africa. To wake up in the morning to the roar of a lion or the trumpet of an elephant. There was nothing else like it.

He'd been born and raised in South Africa but couldn't escape from there fast enough. His family had a long and unfortunate background in Apartheid and, before them, the Boers. He didn't share his family's racist tradition, but it was impossible to convince people to see past his name. He couldn't fault them for their justifiable anger, so he joined the military when he was eighteen.

The South African National Defense Force had enforced integration. Bullying, harassment, and racism were harshly dealt with regardless of who initiated it. There had still been some incidents. His name made him a natural target for anger with a long memory. He had served seven years with distinction and did his best to earn the respect of his fellow soldiers. But a particularly ugly incident forced him to end his career with SANDF.

Thus began his career as a mercenary and his love for the wilds of central Africa. It was times like this when the sheer stubbornness and ignorance of the individual members of the Knights, that his mind drifted back to those simpler days. The back of his mind noted but largely ignored the bickering going on in the video call. It was the same arguments they'd rehashed on every call since the Family Stone had started glowing. Everyone was looking for an action plan, but no one knew what action to take. Well, he had a plan, and he sat silently, waiting for Nathan to yield him the floor so he could present it. He caught himself stroking his facial scar, where it cleaved his beard. It was an unfortunate affectation he'd developed and could never shake.

The little heads on his screen bored him. It wasn't that he didn't believe in the Knights' goals, but the politics made him want to disappear into the wilds again. Twelve strong-willed personalities from such diverse backgrounds working toward a common goal was admirable, but in truth, they rarely agreed on anything. The stress of the approaching Key Event was taking its toll, and everyone thought they had the best idea. Except all of their ideas involved some variation of sitting on their hands until it was too late.

"Micah has an action plan he wants to present for dealing with Fermilab." Nathan finally intoned.

"Thank you, Nathan. Katrin and I have developed a series of events designed to increase tension between Nadir and Fermilab." Micah screen-shared his presentation. "I'll send this out to all of you after the meeting so you can peruse the details, but under my authority, we have already begun steps one through four. These first steps are merely a moderate escalation of what we've already been doing, and they involve no direct conflict with either side."

Colonel Larkin spoke up. "Before anyone objects, Micah is theater commander for North America. In addition, his early steps were vetted and seconded by Katrin and myself. So please, no bitching about process."

Micah couldn't help but smile. "Thank you, Colonel. I'm presenting this because steps five and six represent a significant escalation over our previous activities." He flipped through the presentation until he reached slide five. "Five involves an 'assault' of the Fermilab facilities. We have

identified and recruited a small number of Nadir
volunteers, who we will supplement with a group of
mercenaries in invading the Fermilab complex. The
intent is to sow chaos via minor larceny and
vandalism. No one will get hurt, and no damage will
be done to the facilities. A few of the Nadir people will
be apprehended by the authorities."

Matz Schoeller's harsh German accent broke
through. Matz wasn't on video, he hated video calls,
but he had joined the audio portion. "What makes you
think you can successfully breach the facility with the
enhanced security they have in place?"

"The public nature of the Fermilab facility
makes it impossible to stop what we're planning." He
flipped to a later slide where a map of the facilities
was displayed. "We're not going after the lab
complexes where most of the extra security is
deployed. We plan to have multiple escape vehicles
in place for our personnel, and we will deliberately
strand a few Nadir members to be scooped up as
scapegoats."

Nathan Smith chimed in. "Before we get too
into the weeds on some of the finer details, please
show us step six. This is quite an escalation of our
previous activities, and I can only assume step six is
an even bigger move."

"Quite." He flipped the slide with the highlights
for the final step. "Not to mince words, but this is a full
breach assault. For step five, we're only using about
half of the Nadir members we've recruited. For this
plan, we're calling in the rest and half a dozen fringe

fanatics who Nadir wouldn't accept. We'll have a full strike team disguised as protestors. These are all experienced operators, and they will be led by me. While the actual protestors sow chaos and draw attention to themselves, my team and I will penetrate the main HERBET lab and plant a significant amount of explosives. I estimate the damage will set them back one to two years."

"What are your plans on dealing with security?" Nathan asked.

"We will be armed with lethal and non-lethal weapons. Non-lethal will be the primary method, but I'm taking it upon myself to injure one of the primary scientists. This is a backup in case the explosives don't do as much damage as we hoped. A bit of trauma should set them back on their heels."

"This is frankly ridiculous. Are we really to the point of such mayhem already?" Maya Abrams spoke up. Her voice was strained, and she squirmed uncomfortably before the camera. "I thought our charter, our history, has been to use violence as a last resort. Micah, you are planning on leading the strike team personally. In this day and age, can we afford to risk one of our own? This seems to be excessively risky."

"Maya, I appreciate your concern. But frankly, with the state of the reliquary, we don't know what's going on." Colonel Larkin poked at the camera as if to emphasize his point. "North Korea is nowhere near ready for another nuclear test. CERN isn't scheduled for another power-up for at least another year.

Jeff McIntyre

Fermilab is the most likely Key Event on the horizon, and I think it behooves us to bring that experiment to a halt until we get a better read on those artifacts." He leaned back. "And as far as violence as a last resort? I think you need to re-read our histories, Maya. We do what we must when we must. Whatever it takes to stop the Lock from being awakened."

Katrin broke in. "We also have developed an asset within the Fermilab security forces. They've already been helpful in identifying holes in their security plan that we can exploit. Micah's plan is ingenious. We are exploiting one hole in step five. Their reaction to step five, we believe, will create another hole at the start of step six that the strike team will exploit to succeed with the primary objective."

"Thank you, Katrin. You will also see that I'm recommending that we automatically activate Vanguard as soon as step five is enacted. If we decide to move to step six, it might be on short notice, and we should have Mr. Cooke in place as a failsafe. Feel free to review the presentation and reach out to me if you have any further questions. I suggest we reconvene tomorrow and bring the plan to a vote once you've all had a chance to review the details." Micah pondered the faces on the screen. He resisted the urge to smile. He could tell that he'd won them over. An action plan, even an aggressive and risky action plan, gave them something to latch on to.

Chapter 38

Daniel stepped into the back yard of Leo's house. He cupped his hands and shouted. "Bob? Can we talk, please?"

A bush to his right rustled and the top of a small red cap popped up through the foliage. The behatted bush shook itself like a cat waking from a nap in the sun, and the hat glided to the front of the bush, and the diminutive gnome poked his head out and looked around cautiously. Seeing only Daniel, Bob stepped out.

"Greetings Daniel. I see my attempt at being unobtrusive has been less than successful." Bob swept off his hat, bowed deeply, then replaced his cap and stood up in a single smooth motion. "How may I be of service?"

He crouched down to not tower over Bob. "Sophia and I would like to talk to you further. Also, with your permission, our friend Leo would like to speak with you as well."

Bob let out a deep sigh. "Daniel, I was really hoping to keep the knowledge of my presence to just your family."

"Leo is family; in every way that matters. He cares about Tony's welfare as much as if we were related." Daniel rolled back and sat down with a grunt. "Look. You've said that this is about Tony. I wished we had asked you more questions the other night, but you were a bit of a shock. We've had some time to think, and we hope you have answers. Hell, if what you're saying is true, I may *never* run out of questions, but all three of us want to talk to you."

Bob nodded as he considered Daniel's question. After several long seconds, he nodded more affirmatively. "Very well, Daniel, but I would like to request a change in venue, so to speak. Leo's back yard is not as private as yours, and I'm not particularly comfortable indoors for any length of time. Why don't all of you go back to your house, fix yourself a lunch, and we can enjoy the lovely Spring weather while you ask your questions." Bob smiled. "If you do not wish Tony to listen in on the conversation, he can at least be occupied in his room."

Daniel nodded. "That's not a bad idea." He stood up. "Look, Bob. You've been nothing but helpful so far, but frankly, this whole situation is bizarre beyond understanding. Even if we end up believing everything you tell us, we're still not sure we should trust you."

"I completely understand. It may seem counterproductive to you, and I apologize for the deception, but this is exactly why I tried to remain hidden from you." Bob picked up a dead stick from the grass. "Trust is as fragile as this." He bent the small branch until it snapped. "I don't want to do anything to endanger the goodwill you have already given me. A lesser man might have tried to call in authorities or harm me. No, Daniel, your caution is understandable and justified. I hope to earn your trust, but I know that it must be earned. Go home. I will meet you there in a while."

Leo and Daniel had marched Tony up to his room. They stood shoulder to shoulder and had given strict instructions for him to stay in his room while the adults had an adult conversation with his un-imaginary friend. Tony, in turn, had admonished them with arms crossed and a foot stomp to be polite to Bob. He was his friend and deserved to be treated kindly for everything he had done. They had assured him they would be nice to Bob if he promised to stay put until they called for him.

Jeff McIntyre

Sophia had been downstairs hiding her father's shotgun. This whole situation still made her nervous, and she wanted to make sure it was easy to get to but would still be no risk to Tony. She settled on putting the shotgun unloaded on the floor behind a bunch of buckets and cleaning products in the pantry. She hid the box of shells behind a bunch of canned vegetables. Tony might rummage for a snack, but he certainly wasn't going to pick green beans or peas.

Sophia had laid out a large blanket in the grass, and she, Daniel, and Leo lounged there, eating sandwiches and drinking iced tea while they waited for Bob to appear.

Leo took a deep gulp of his tea and then spoke. "I'm not going to record this because I don't want to spook him, but if half of what he told you is true, this could be one of the most momentous conversations in history. I'm not proud to admit that there is a terrified hamster running circles in my stomach." He straightened his back and shifted from side to side, hoping to somehow physically ease the tension he felt in his mid-section.

Daniel punched him in the arm. "You'll be fine. What tack are you going to take with him?"

"I'll apologize in advance." Leo rubbed the spot on his arm in mock pain. "I'm going to be, let's not say adversarial, but it will be rapid-fire questions to throw him off balance. It's a little rude, but it lets me be the bad guy. Let's start with your question Daniel. I'll take it from there. His answers should help

264

inform some of my questions. When I'm out of gas, we'll let you finish up, Soph."

Sophia nodded but didn't respond. She scanned the yard looking for signs of the gnome. At the back of the yard, where their landscaping backed up against the forest preserve, she saw a bush begin rustling like a small animal moving through it. She pointed in that direction for the other's benefit. "I think he's here."

The bushes parted, and the diminutive gnome stepped out. He saw them, smiled, and cheerily waved before marching across the yard toward them.

"What color is his outfit?" Daniel whispered.

"Red hat, green shirt, and red pants," Sophia replied.

Leo's gaze jerked at her in surprise, and then he whispered. "Blue hat, red shirt, green pants."

Daniel shook his head and sighed. "So, we weren't crazy. I see a red hat, green shirt, and blue pants." He then waved back at the gnome.

When Bob got closer, small twigs and leaves crunched under his footsteps. "I didn't know if you were hungry, but I made an extra sandwich if you'd like it."

Bob's face lit up with a smile. "Thank you so much, but alas, I am not hungry. But that was very considerate of you." He marched over to Leo and bowed. "And you must be Uncle Leo that I've heard so much about."

"Pleasure to meet you too, Bob. I'm afraid I'm the one that instigated this. Daniel and Sophia are worried about you, and I'm here to try and help them determine what you're all about." Leo gestured to a spot in the yard where Bob would be the center of attention for all three of them. "Why don't you have a seat?"

Bob nodded with a smile. He plopped down in the indicated spot and then wiggled his behind in the grass to make himself more comfortable. "Let us proceed then."

Daniel was sitting with his knees up. He leaned forward and crossed his arms across the top of them. "I've done some research on what I'll call the documented origin of gnomes. What can you tell us about Paracelsus?"

"Ha! I should have known you would do your homework." Bob giggled and slapped his knee. "Poor mad, brilliant, wonderful Paracelsus."

Leo couldn't help but be amazed by what he was seeing and hearing. Such a small creature, laughing and talking with such a deep gravelly voice. He would have thought the combination would be deeply unsettling. Instead, he found it comforting. The little gnome was frankly adorable. He wasn't sure if that was some magical effect, the normal human instinct to want to coddle cute things, or maybe Bob was simply that charming.

"About five hundred years ago, Paracelsus was wandering through the Black Forest of Germany when he stumbled upon a very rare phenomenon. I believe it was created by some human wielder of magic long long ago, for it seems unlikely that anything like this could exist naturally." The gnome leaned forward; his voice lowered as if he were letting them in on a precious secret. "Imagine a large circle of Birch trees in an almost impassable forest wall. An almost impossible to find path zig-zags through their trunks and leads you to a wide forest clearing. A small babbling brook winds its way through the clearing, where it plunges over a cliff in a magnificent spray and lands in a pool so deep and clear you would think it was glass. A breeze whips across the pool without seeming to disturb it. The pool is bordered by a sheer cliff wall adorned with crystals on one side and a field of rocks and boulders on the other. In the midst of the boulder field is a fissure that rends the earth, and from it, fires roil upward, created by a pool of magma just below the surface. In this place, earth, fire, wind, and water meet, and it is where I met Paracelsus."

"So, you said that magic is gone from the world. How long has it been gone?" Daniel asked.

"In your reckoning, almost fifteen hundred years," Bob said sadly.

Daniel looked skeptical. "You said this place was created with magic. But how could such a place exist without magic?"

"I'm going to give you your first lesson in how magic works." Bob took a deep breath before continuing. "Imagine that magic is like running water moving over the world. It has a source, and from that source, it flows. As it moves across the earth, it encounters rapids, pools, and falls. Everything that a river does. In some places, it is weak, and in others, it is powerful and swift. In addition to its blending of elements, this clearing is a natural well. A deep hole where magic collects. For a thousand years, the four of us waited in that clearing. Feeding from the well, hoping for magic to return."

"The four of you? I'm assuming a salamander, an undine, a sylph, and you; a gnome?" Daniel asked.

"Exactly so, Daniel. We had fled there when it became apparent that magic would take longer than we expected to return." Bob stroked his chin thoughtfully. "There is a natural ebb and flow to magic. It comes for a time, say forty years or so. Then, without warning, it will begin to wane. It's as if the tap from which magic flows is turned off, and it slowly fades away. Then, after a similar amount of time, the tap is opened, and magic begins to flow over the world."

"Can I cut in for a second?" Sophia asked. "Who is Paracelsus and what are salamanders, undine, and sylphs?"

"Sorry, hun. I should have given you the backstory. The very first written reference of gnomes was from a sixteenth-century German physician and philosopher named Paracelsus. He documented encountering elemental creatures that he believed were important to the natural order. He was brilliant and odd. Gnomes were associated with the earth; Sylphs were creatures of air, Undines were water, and Salamanders fire."

"Paracelsus was a beautiful soul and a brilliant man. He was also extraordinarily eccentric. In another time, he might have been a powerful user of magic." Bob ran his fingers through the grass, and his attention drifted as he spoke. "He visited us many times, and we taught him much about magic and magical creatures. But every time he used what we taught him, he depleted the well and shortened our time. We eventually asked him not to return. Not that it made much difference. Shortly after he left, the well ran dry, and each of us in turn, began our slumber."

"When and how did you re-awaken?" Sophia asked.

"This is treading some dangerous ground that I can't speak in too much detail about, but it was about five years ago. An Ancient came to me and offered to feed me in exchange for protecting Tony. I agreed, and shortly after, they brought me here to keep an eye on him."

"Bob, we've only lived here about six months. You've been in Chicago for almost five years? Daniel asked.

Bob chuckled. "I'm very glad you moved here, Daniel. Trying to keep an eye on him while you were living in your downtown apartment was not very much fun."

"How can the ancients be active when there's no magic, and what do you mean feed you?" Leo asked.

"Remember how I described magic like water?" Bob asked. The three of them all nodded.

Jeff McIntyre

"Each magical creature has a small well inside them that holds magic. We feed from that well. That's why magical creatures don't just disappear or die as soon as magic stops. The size of that well varies wildly. Generally speaking, the bigger the well, the more powerful the creature. The veil between wherever magic comes from and here is a wall. When the tap between here and there is open, there's enough magic for everyone, and we constantly replenish our well. There are a very few that we call Ancients. The Ancients not only have their own well, they are a pinhole crack in the wall. They are constantly fed a dribble of magic which allows them to survive. They can't often expend that energy to do anything fancy, but it sustains them. The Ancient put magic in my well so that I could stay awake, and it has sustained me for these last five years."

The three of them sat there contemplating what Bob had told them up to this point. Bob sat patiently waiting, a small smile on his face. At last, Daniel nodded and pointed to Leo, "You're up."

Leo nodded. "All right, Bob, I'm going to ask you a series of questions. This isn't particularly polite conversation, but hopefully, it will allow us to get through some facts and details in short order. Are you ok with this?"

Bob nodded. "But of course, Leo. If this is what you wish."

"I appreciate your understanding." Leo took out his phone and consulted his notes. "Let's get started. What is your name?"

The Garden Gnome

"Burbalobonomicus"

"What is your species?"

"Gnome of the Gnomi"

"In simplest terms, what is a Gnome?"

"A magical earth spirit."

"Where are you from?"

"Chicago," Bob smiled. "But I dwelt in central Europe for a very long time."

"Where is magic?"

"I don't know."

"How long has it been gone?"

"Approximately fifteen hundred years."

"Will it return?"

"Yes."

"When?"

"Soon. Although I don't know specifically."

"Who is your benefactor?"

Bob smiled. "I can't tell you that, Leo. Nice try"

"Had to give it a shot. Why were you sent here?"

"To protect Tony."

"To protect Tony from what?"

"Anything that is a threat to him."

"I want to protect him as much as anyone, but why do you want to protect him?"

Bob briefly paused. "Because he is the source of magic."

"What!" Sophia almost yelled. "Bob. Tony is just a boy; how in the hell can HE be the source of magic?"

"I am sorry, madam. This information is why I was a little late arriving here. I didn't know specifically

271

why the Ancient wanted me to protect Tony. So, I asked them. They revealed this to me, and I demanded I be allowed to tell you this." Bob took his hat off and looked down into it with a tinge of embarrassment. "I had my suspicions but no real proof. I just knew that the Ancient wanted Tony protected. Over the years, I've become very fond of you and your family. I wish I could have told you sooner. Given you more time to prepare. Tony is about to become the most important person in the world, and there are those that would seek to do him harm."

Leo spoke up. "About to? Do you mean he's not currently the source of magic? Obviously not; there is no magic. So can we stop him from becoming the source?"

Bob shook his head. "Unfortunately, no. The ebb and flow of magic into this world is tied to the life and death of one human. That human's soul has been born and reborn countless times. This time that soul is in Tony, and it is only a matter of time before they re-awaken, and magic returns."

Sophia was in shock; she could barely bring herself to ask. "Does… does that mean we lose Tony when that happens?"

"I don't believe so. Not exactly." Bob's deep gravelly voice became soft and calming, as if not wanting to spook a startled animal. "He will still have all of Tony's memories and experiences, but he will also have lots of other memories and experiences."

They all sat there in stunned silence. Even Bob seemed unsure of what to do next. Daniel wrapped his arm around Sophia as she silently shuddered with suppressed tears. Sophia finally patted Daniel's chest and pushed him away. She wiped the tears away and scrubbed her hand on her jeans. "Bob, if what you say is true, our lives are about to change in ways we couldn't possibly imagine. I appreciate all that you've told us. I wish I could say I don't believe you, that this is all a lie or that I'm in a dream. But unfortunately, I think I do believe you."

They sat silently for perhaps a minute before Sophia finally broke the silence again. "Bob, can you… prove to us that magic exists?"

Bob's expression had been sorrowful, but at Sophia's question, his eyes brightened, and he smiled just a bit. "Yes. Yes, I believe I can." He placed his hat back on his head and then stood up. "Please, follow me."

The three of them slowly climbed to their feet and followed the gnome across the yard to the edge of Tony's sandpit playground.

"Allow me to apologize for the mess I made of your yard when I chased off that coyote. The least I can do is repair the damage." Bob went to his hands and knees, his tiny hands grasping the soil at the edge of the large tear in the yard.

It was still mostly barren soil, but a few weeds were starting to grow in scattered patches. As they watched, Bob began to sing. It wasn't loud, and it

273

didn't sound like his voice. It was as if someone had created a piece of music from the sound of gravel pouring into a series of different sized glass bowls. It was tonally complex and seemed to swell as it progressed. Sophia reached out and grabbed the hands of both Daniel and Leo. They were so enthralled by the singing that the soil starting to move, caught them by surprise. Spreading in waves from his hands, the larger clods of dirt began to break down into fine soil and the tear slowly filled in. The weeds were pulled under, and then grass began to appear, swiftly growing to six inches in height. At the edge of the lawn sat a large Hibiscus that had been split in half. Dead leaves and branches where the shrub had been damaged began to shake free from the bush and fall to the ground. New growth swiftly filled in the hole, and the bush swelled; the leaves wriggled as they grew. Finally, the bush exploded with large, vibrant red blooms.

Bob stopped singing and sat back on his heels, admiring his handiwork. He looked back over his shoulder and smiled. "Sorry about the singing. It isn't necessary, but something I just like to do when I'm growing."

"It was beautiful, Bob," Sophia said quietly.

Chapter 39

Deb was a little anxious. She kept adjusting towels in the bathroom, readjusting the flower arrangement on her entry table, wiping down every horizontal surface in her kitchen and living room, and fussing about which files she felt she could discuss with Leo and which ones she should keep undercover.

This was a big step for her. She had never had anyone in her apartment since she had moved to Chicago other than the building superintendent and the movers. She did some mental exercises to keep herself occupied and, at one point, deliberately skewed files out of one of the folders so that everything didn't look so perfect. It bothered her, but she ignored it.

Her apartment was a bastion that helped her manage her OCD. She was able to keep things here under control. That way, when things got out of control everywhere else, she had a place to retreat to where everything was as she expected. Although it

was no longer debilitating, it was always there. Her
mind still felt the patterns, but she could ignore them.
It was rejuvenating to come home to a neat and
orderly place where she would not be criticized or
pitied.

She would have preferred meeting Leo
somewhere else, but with all the legwork she had
been doing, she had hardly spent any time in the
office, and while a lot of her casework was online,
she had an affection for hard copy. Her co-workers
gave her endless amounts of grief for it, but it
sometimes helped her thought processes. She could
share her hard copies with Leo, and they could
review the whiteboard she used to track her head
space on things that needed follow-up.

After circling her apartment for the third time,
she finally stopped long enough to pour a glass of
wine. She refused to let an interloper's presence in
her sanctum unnerve her. This was good; it was
going to be fine, everything was fine.

She sipped from her glass and ran down
some of the things on her whiteboard like she had a
thousand times before as she waited for Leo to
arrive. True to her word, beer and pizza had been
replaced with wine and veal parmesan from a family-
owned restaurant down the street. The delicious
smells from her oven began to waft through the room
when her doorbell rang.

When she opened the door, Leo was standing
there with a folder in one hand and a bottle of wine in
the other. "Sorry, I'm late. It took longer than I thought

to pick out a wine. I wasn't sure what we were having, so I decided to bring a nice rosé and… what is that wonderful smell emanating from your apartment?"

She took the bottle from him and let him inside. "Thank you, but I can't take the credit. I'm not much of a cook, but Mama Morello's has amazing pre-made meals. They don't advertise it, but if you ask nicely, they'll whip something up that you can just throw in the oven. I have to limit how often I go there because Mia, the actual Mama of Mama Morello's, is determined to fatten me up. I have a hard time saying no to their cheese ravioli, and she always sneaks half a loaf of garlic bread into every one of my orders."

"It sounds like she's adopted you. The next time you're in the mood for eating there without homework, give me a call, and you can introduce me." Leo set his folder on the kitchen counter. "That sounds like the kind of local place I love to give my money to."

"We can break into your rosé if you prefer, but I've already got a burgundy open." She held up the bottle and presented the label for his inspection.

Leo waved his hands and didn't even pretend to inspect the label. "I'm not a wine expert. I know a guy who fancies himself a liquor store sommelier. He convinced me that rosé goes with anything. Let's stick with your burgundy; we can save my bottle for another time."

She poured a glass for him. "Shall we eat first? Then we can dig into work."

Leo smiled in relief, "Thank God. I was hoping you wouldn't make me concentrate while smelling this. My stomach would judo throw me across the room."

Deb laughed, "Well, I'm sure our concentration will be fine after a couple of glasses of wine combined with an Italian-induced carb coma."

Leo was rinsing the plates from their feast. He turned his head and nodded at the folder on the counter. "Go ahead and look through the stuff in that. My accounting buddy has dug up a couple more interesting tidbits."

Deb picked up the folder and flipped through the sheets. She walked over to the couch as she read and sat slowly down.

He dried his hands and wandered around her apartment. He was reminded of the pictures he had found of her. The same practiced smile like a mask to hide who she really was. Her apartment was a reflection of that mask. Just enough tasteful furniture to barely fill the space. Artful decorations were located at strategic places. There was no cohesiveness to them, nor did there appear to be anything that might have a personal connection. No pictures of family or friends, no souvenirs from a spontaneous trip or life experience, and nothing that might be a cherished heirloom or chintzy keepsake. The mask of her apartment was created so it would look like a well-adjusted adult lived here and not in a spartan undecorated apartment like a recluse. The one exception was her graduation certificate from the FBI. It wasn't placed prominently but in a place where she would see it frequently.

"We're killing trees with all these hard copies." She yelled back at the kitchen, thinking he was still there rather than examining her decor.

He slipped into the living room to join her. "I'll plant a couple of trees when this is all over. Besides, this is safer for my buddy and us." He plopped down in the chair across from her and made air quotes, "The NSA sees all."

Deb's eyebrows raised at that, and she grinned. "You're not wrong. I'm assuming none of this is admissible in court."

"Ha!"

"That's what I thought. I'm going to have to try and verify this stuff in other ways." She flipped back and forth between a couple of sheets. "So, Rebecca Drake has been making sizable donations to Fermilab for what? Five years?"

"That's what it looks like. I mean, I get rich people spreading their money around doing good if it makes them feel better. But why particle physics and why HERBERT? From everything I've heard, the LHC at CERN is the flavor of the decade when it comes to particle accelerator research."

Deb shook her head. "That's not even the weirdest part. To my knowledge, Fermilab is wholly owned and gets one hundred percent of its funding from the Department of Energy. It seems highly unusual, for what is essentially a governmental agency, to accept donations from a private individual."

He stared at the ceiling and ran his fingers up and down through his half-shaven scruff. He knew it was an annoying habit, but it helped him think. When he looked back at Deb, she was looking at him with a narrow-eyed contemplative look. "What... what are you staring at?"

Deb pointed at his face. "You should not go around with three days of scruff. Either shave regularly or grow a beard. Stop half-assing it; it makes you look old."

He squirmed a bit at the pointed critique of his appearance. He dropped his hands from his face as an odd thought raced through his mind. "Uh, Deb. You do know I'm gay, right?"

"I wouldn't be a very good detective if I hadn't figured that out by now. I'm pretty sure you and I have the same type, albeit on opposite sides of the fence." She tossed his folder on the coffee table between them and leaned back. "You're about ten years older than me. I like athletic, well-groomed, clean-shaven men. They need to be mature but funny, and I prefer they be a little older than me. You like athletic, well-groomed, clean-shaven men that are mature for their age but funny and a little younger than you. I've caught you checking out men that I was checking out."

"Well shit, I never caught you checking anyone out," Leo admitted

Deb's eyes glistened with amusement. "I check everyone out, but my reasons are government business, and I only occasionally look at their butt. Anyway, let's get back to the actual reason we got together. Shall we?"

Leo nodded. "So, I looked through some of your files while we were eating."

"I noticed," Deb said dryly.

He ignored her sarcasm. "Titan Security is providing services to both Nadir and Fermilab. That's entirely too coincidental. If Rebecca Drake is providing all this funding for HERBERT, it's likely that she is the one footing the bill for Titan at Fermilab. Is there any way we can confirm that?"

Deb nodded. "I think so. I just need to corner Hank Lee. He's been very cooperative, and I have no reason to think he won't be forthcoming if I ask him. Provided Phil Baxter isn't around to babysit."

"Phil Baxter? Is he with Titan?" He asked.

Deb sighed deeply, "Yes, and he's an extra steaming pile of crap unto himself."

"Well, forget him for the moment. I don't want to lose my train of thought. If Ms. Drake is funding Titan at Fermilab, is it possible she's also funding them for Nadir?"

"That is an excellent question, but I know for a fact that a large chunk of Nadir's funding comes in the form of" It was Deb's turn to do air quotes. "Anonymous donations. You and Alvaro seem to be getting along pretty well. Why don't you just ask him? I'd have to get a subpoena to get that kind of information out of them."

He sat quietly, thinking about what they had discussed during the evening. "Do you mind if I ask you a personal question?"

Deb picked up her glass of wine and took a sip. "I might need this, but sure. Go ahead."

"You have a lovely apartment, and I don't want to sound rude. But it kind of feels like a museum. Is there a reason for that?"

Deb took a larger swig of wine before answering. "When I was a teenager, I used to wash my hands more than fifty times a day. I would arrange silverware in precise formation and then have a panic attack if anyone bumped them before they were ready to be used. I counted... everything. Ceiling tiles, floor tiles, bricks, M&Ms. It came to a head when my mom came home to find that I had skipped school to count the fibers in my bedroom carpeting."

"I'm no expert, but that sounds like really, really bad OCD." He looked around her apartment. "I would say you're pretty well adjusted." He grinned. "I mean, you're still a bit anal, but your personal interactions seem pretty normal."

"It took years of medication and therapy to get me there." Deb took a deep drink of wine. "By the time I graduated from college, I had weaned myself off the meds. They never would have accepted me in the FBI if I hadn't. But I was compensating in other ways. As it was, I barely scraped through the psych evals. If it weren't for a couple of mentors pushing me and believing in me, I would have been washed out."

"I would say they were good judges of character who could read more than the cover of your book. From where I'm sitting, you are an excellent detective, and I bet you piss all your co-workers off."

Deb laughed. "It sounds like you've been talking to some of them." She looked at him suspiciously. "Have you?"

He threw up his hands in surrender. "You got me, but you gotta promise not to be pissed off at him."

Deb crossed her arms across her chest. "I'm not vindictive, Leo, but you will tell me who you've been talking to and what they told you about me."

Leo smiled and shook his head. "All right, all right. Jake Phillips is a college buddy and close friend of mine. I wanted to know who was working the Nadir case, and he gave me your name. He also called you a pain in the ass, but so is he, so I didn't hold that against you."

Deb uncrossed her arms and smiled wryly. "Well, I'll be sure to be a bit more of a pain in the ass to Agent Phillips in the future. I'm not upset; I've been called much worse."

"Don't be too hard on him; I plied him with alcohol before I asked," Leo admitted.

"Oh, I'll keep this one in my pocket for now and use it when it's most inconvenient for him." She smiled. "Well, it's getting late, Leo. Do you want any of the leftovers?"

He stood up and patted his stomach. "Oof, no. My stomach says yes, but my abs say not if you ever want to see me again, so I appreciate your attempt to fatten me up, but I'll pass this time. Thanks, though." He walked towards the door, and Deb followed him. He turned in the hallway before she closed the door. "Thanks for dinner, and thanks for letting me get to know you. I can imagine that it is not that easy for you. I'll give Alvaro a call tomorrow and try to squeeze the information about his donors out of him. I'll let you know if I find anything." He turned to walk away.

"Leo, keeping my apartment orderly and free of clutter and distraction helps me to rejuvenate and keep my OCD under control. But it is the last vestige I keep of my old therapy regimens. Having you over was a kind of first step in getting rid of that. I appreciate your understanding and not showing pity." Deb leaned against the door frame. "Most people treat me like an alien or a freak when they find out."

Leo nodded his head sadly. "My Granny Tina was an absolutely amazing woman. She was very special to me for a lot of reasons. But she suffered from anxiety and depression her entire life. When dementia began to set in, they seemed to become magnified. Watching her endure that in the last few years of her life was the hardest thing I've ever had to do. But on one of her lucid days, her last best day, she spoke to me with a self-awareness I had never seen before or since."

Leo's eyes drifted away, and a small smile came to his face. "Leo, my boy. I know you don't want to see what is happening to me, and I don't want you to remember me like this. But I need you to be here. You don't need to speak, just hold my hand and be present. Some days my mind doesn't know who you are, but my heart always does. I'm descending into a hell of my mind's own creation, and I really don't want to go alone. But don't you dare pity me. Just be here and know that I love you no matter what happens." Leo looked up to see Deb's eyes welling with tears. "I'm sorry; I didn't mean to upset you. It's just ever since then; I try not to pity anyone for their challenges. I only try to understand them and be there for them if they need it."

Deb scrubbed the tears out of her eyes with the palms of her hands and then wiped her hands on her jeans. "You have a nice butt, Leo. It's too bad you bat for the other team." She held out her hand. "I guess we'll just have to be friends."

Leo laughed and took her hand. "You've got a nice ass, too, Deb."

Chapter 40

F: Esposito, Alvaro
T: Williams, Jacob; Marino, Valentina

Mon 4/18/2022 6:24 am

Jake, I need an update on where we are in the investigation of the names that have been provided by our team leads. I want any details we can dig up on their involvement assembled and in the hands of Agent Kazdin by end of day Wednesday.

Tina, book a meeting for Jake and I to go over the details sometime tomorrow afternoon. Thank you.

Alvaro Esposito | President | Nadir
aesposito@wearenadir.com

The Garden Gnome

F: Williams, Jacob
T: Esposito, Alvaro; Marino, Valentina

Mon 4/18/2022 7:47 am

Still in progress boss. Here's what I have so far:

Application information on subjects that attempted to join Nadir but were rejected.
Complete dossiers on all former members that were ejected with cause.

I'm still compiling all of our bench warmer contractors' details. And I'm still waiting on details for the Titan people. I should have them sometime tomorrow afternoon.

The real sticklers are the people who have had no official affiliation with us. The legwork is going very slowly. I've only got confirmed details on half a dozen. That's another twenty or so that we only have names and descriptions. I've asked the supes to get pics of these people if they show up at the protest sites, but for the time being, I'm having to do a lot of guesswork.

Jake Williams | Director of Security | Nadir
jwilliams@wearnadir.com

Jeff McIntyre

F: Esposito, Alvaro
T: Williams, Jacob; Marino, Valentina; Aguilar, Miguel

Mon 4/18/2022 8:14 am

Adding Miguel;

Jake, I appreciate that this is a difficult task, but we need this nailed down. I'll call Titan and make sure you have their information by this afternoon. I need you to focus on getting the contractor information completed.

Miguel, I've attached Jake's list of unaffiliated people that have been joining Chicago metro protests. I need you to reach out to all protest team leads. Go over the list and ask them to rack their brains for any additional information. They should also reach out to all active members that are on site today. I don't care if we rattle some trees. The unaffiliated are the ones I'm most worried about, and we need as much information about them as we can get. I need this completed and to me by the end of business today.

Alvaro Esposito | President | Nadir
aesposito@wearenadir.com

Alvaro Esposito's cell phone rang with the hard brass opening of Gloria Estefan's Conga. He

288

smiled. His daughter had gotten ahold of his cell phone and changed the ringtone again. He might keep this one for a while. Leo Schafer's name popped up on the caller ID. His smile dimmed. It's not that he didn't like Leo but talking to the press right now was not exactly high on his list of things to do. Still, better to get this over with.

He reignited his smile before answering. "Hello Leo, it's nice to hear from you. Is there something I can help you with?"

"Hey, Alvaro. Sorry to bother you, but I have something I wanted to talk to you about." Leo's voice was low, contrite. He either had bad news, or he was going to ask something he didn't think Alvaro would want to answer."

"Sure, Leo. I have a few minutes. What's on your mind?" he asked.

"Let me start by saying this is off the record. This isn't for an article; I'm just trying to help with the investigation."

Now he was intrigued. In their few conversations, he had felt that Leo was a pretty straight shooter. This level of intrigue was not what he had come to expect from the reporter. "O... K... I'll answer what I can, Leo. But no promises."

"Fair enough. Can you confirm that Rebecca Drake is funding Titan Security's presence at your protests?" Leo's question sounded more like a statement.

He paused. He liked Leo. On a certain level, he trusted him... somewhat. Even off the record, this was probably not something he could share. "I don't think I can answer that, Leo. Most of our contributors want to remain anonymous. If I thought it would help the investigation, I would consider it, but I don't think it will."

"I understand your position, but I'm just looking for confirmation. The FBI will find out sooner or later. But if they have to subpoena it out of you, it might slow the investigation down." Leo paused, letting him consider what he was asking of him, then continued. "If you tell me, then I give a non-official confirmation to the FBI, and you're an anonymous source. If there is a subpoena, it will be after the fact to seek confirmation, but in the meantime, Agent Kazdin can continue her investigation under the assumption that she understands the situation going on in Titan."

He paused for effect, but he had already made up his mind. "You make a compelling argument, my friend. Yes, Titan is paid for by Rebecca Drake. They report to us, but I'm assuming they also report to her. I do not consent for this information to be used in any publication, and you did not get this information from me."

An instant message from Tina, the receptionist, popped up on his computer. *You have a call waiting for you sir.*

He resisted the urge to sigh. It's already been a busy day, and he hadn't even had coffee. "I have to let you go, Leo. I hope that helps grease the wheels."

290

"Thanks, Alvaro, I'm sure it will." the call disconnected.

He replied to Tina. *Who is on the line?* He really wanted to go get a cup of coffee and a bagel before he had to deal with any more drama.

His blood ran cold as Tina typed out *Rebecca Drake sir*

F: Williams, Jacob
T: Esposito, Alvaro

Mon 4/18/2022 8:32 am

What the hell Alvaro. Miguel isn't cleared to do research on our members. He's just a field supervisor. You're asking him to essentially interrogate all of our active supervisors and protestors. I think you're asking a bit much of him. And why is this such a huge priority all of a sudden?

Jake Williams | Director of Security | Nadir
jwilliams@wearnadir.com

Jeff McIntyre

F: Esposito, Alvaro
T: Williams, Jacob

Mon 4/18/2022 9:02 am

I'm sorry for the stress this is causing you and your team Jake, but I'm going to say this once. Get it done. I'm no longer content to wait until Wednesday. No one is going home today until I have a package ready for the FBI that I'm satisfied with.

We are in a war for our survival. There is an active federal investigation that we need to be assisting with in every way we possibly can. I've been on the phone with some of our top contributors, and to say they're not happy is like saying the Sahara is kind of dry. We need to be able to say that we did everything in our power to help get to the bottom of this. If one of our active members IS involved, I'll hang them out to dry myself. There's no room in Nadir for radical activism.

Alvaro Esposito | President | Nadir
aesposito@wearenadir.com

Chapter 41

Samuel Larkin re-watched the video of the Las Vegas fiasco in 1980. He did this from time to time to remind himself of what was at stake. It had been forty years since there had been a Key event, and he still remembered the cold terror he had felt as he witnessed the Lock kill his fellow Knight.

Lucius Wright had been young, intelligent, idealistic. All of that despite being a Vietnam veteran who had been involved in the evacuation of Saigon. He had been barely thirty when the Lock had set him on fire with magic. He hadn't died quickly either. Sam had extinguished the fire as soon as the Lock was dead, but Lucius had suffered third-degree burns over eighty percent of his body. He spent three agonizing days in an ICU burn unit before his heart finally gave out.

Now, another Key event was upon them. He was older, maybe a little bit wiser. But he was slower, fatter, and he no longer had the sharpness of his youth. The years had dulled him. Too much time spent as an administrator. He was no longer an operator, and that made him feel ill-prepared. Despite all the sacrifices he had made over the last forty years, he wasn't sure that the Knights were ready. They all knew what was at stake, but the attitudes on display on their now daily calls did not fill him with confidence.

The only saving grace was that they did have a few sharp knives in the sheath. Micah, Katrin, Brian, and Duncan were all still finely honed. That made the rest of them seem all that much more embarrassing in their indecisiveness and foolish grandstanding. He had hoped this crisis would strengthen them, but instead, it seemed to expose their weaknesses. The Knights of the Stone were not ready, and he had no one to blame but himself.

Nathan Smith walked in as he was throwing himself a well-deserved pity party. "Anything new?"

He shook his head but didn't say anything.

"Chatterbox. I don't know about you, but I think a bourbon is in order." Nathan began pouring two glasses from Sam's side table. He slid one across the desk to his old friend and then sat down. "Drink that now. You look like someone kicked your dog."

He flipped his laptop around so that Nathan could see the screen. Frozen in time was Lucius Wright, immolated and flailing helplessly as he fired into the Lock.

Nathan grunted and said, "I see you're celebrating your past successes."

He shot Nathan a dirty look. "We're not ready for this. We've spent too much time with finance, research, lobbying, and administrative bullshit."

"You may not be ready, old man, but the rest of us will do our part." Nathan tipped his glass to his forehead in a half-assed salute. "You're not giving us enough credit. Don't get me wrong; I'm pretty sure Tabari and Viktor are shitting themselves. But they're not combatants, and neither are you." Realizing that his glass was already empty, Nathan walked over and grabbed the bottle, and refreshed their glasses. "We, the elder statesman of the Knights, have done our part in preparing our organization and our people for the trials before us. Let the kids handle the field work."

"These daily update calls are bringing me to my wit's end. Two months ago, we were a well-oiled machine. Everyone took their jobs seriously, and we functioned as a coherent team." He took an angry swig of his bourbon. "Now all anyone does is demand updates from the reliquary and bitch about how no one is doing what they're supposed to be doing."

Nathan smiled at his friend across his glass and shook his head. "You're just upset that you won't be directly involved. It's about to get real, and you're too old to get into the thick of things. You're itching for some action."

He smiled wryly. "I'm an old fool, but not that much of a fool. I'm not upset about not being involved. I'm upset that I'm in no condition to be in the action. I'd be a liability, and I know it. I should have remained sharp."

"I'm glad you didn't," Nathan said. "Because then you would be in the shit. There should be some perks to getting old. Just sit back and wait like the rest of us old farts."

Sam's phone was sitting on his desk next to his laptop, and it began to vibrate. He looked down and saw that it was Brian Cooke. He answered the call and put it on speaker. "Hey Brian, you're on speaker. I've got Nathan in my office as well."

"Good. That should speed things up. It's time. Call an emergency meeting so you can discuss next steps. Excalibur began vibrating about ten minutes ago." Brian paused briefly to let them absorb that. "It's strongest on a bearing of west by southwest and a downward pitch of about fifteen degrees. I used the web tool Nathan gave me, and it's definitely North America, so it seems Fermilab is likely. "

Nathan hovered over Sam's phone. "Brian, how strong would you say the vibration is? Barely detectable, pager strength, or uncomfortable to hold?"

Brian barked a laugh. "Who knows how strong a pager buzz is anymore?" He continued before they could respond. "I get the gist; it's still barely detectable. That's why I didn't call immediately; I needed to convince myself that it was, in fact, vibrating."

"Ok, just so you're aware, the buzzing will increase the closer you get in both time to the Key event and proximity to the Lock. Then it will suddenly stop, and you'll be able to sense the direction in your hand. If you actually take the sword into his presence after he's been awakened, it will likely burst into flame." Nathan explained.

"What do you mean, likely?" Brian asked.

"There are some conflicting accounts on that particular subject, but…" Nathan began to explain.

He interjected before Nathan got rolling. "Look, Brian. Get that thing sealed up in its tank and get ready. I'll call your drivers to come to pick you up and get you to the airport. They've been on standby, so it won't take long for them to get there."

"Already done, sir. The tank is sealed, and I've got my things. I texted the drivers already, and they should be on their way up." Brian replied. "But you can call the pilots and give them a destination, so they have time to file a flight plan."

Nathan chimed in. "I'll handle that. I'll also email you the full Excalibur write-up so you can know what to expect from it. I'll leave you one word of warning, it's in the docs, but I want to reiterate. Do NOT attempt to harm the Lock with Excalibur. It gets… mad if you try to do that. Just use it to find him."

"Um, thanks for the safety tip," Brian said. "I'm not sure I want to know what happens when you piss off a legendary magic sword."

"Brian, you have our utmost confidence. You can never be completely prepared for something like this. Just remember your training." He hit an icon of a big red button in the upper right corner of his laptop screen. "I've just fired off the emergency meeting invite to everyone. You can join if you're able, otherwise, get your ass to the airport, and we'll let you know what the outcome is."

"Thanks, I'll drop and join the call," Brian replied, and the call disconnected.

Even with the emergency request, it took about fifteen minutes before everyone joined the video call. He tapped his desk impatiently while they waited. Nathan, in the meantime, had switched to water so that he would be slightly less buzzed by the time things got started.

When the last face finally appeared, he resisted the urge to sigh but began to relax. "All right, folks. Brian is reporting that Excalibur has activated and is indicating a location in North America. That makes Fermilab the most likely candidate. He is already en route to the airport where our plane is standing by to take him to Chicago."

He paused to let that information sink in before continuing. "I'm still planning on keeping a team on standby here in Europe just in case this isn't what we think it is. For those of you that are involved in the contingency plans for Fermilab, I expect a status report in my inbox within the hour. Now, does anyone have anything they want to address before Brian gets on the plane?"

The video call exploded as half of them began asking questions and talking over one another. He calmly muted everyone and waited until the angry faces stopped yelling at their screen. "Are we through? Enough bullshit, people. I'll reach out to each of you individually, and we will get your concerns addressed. Is there anything urgent that the team in North America needs?"

Micah raised his hand and nodded, so he unmuted them all. "Go ahead, Micah."

"Thank you, Nathan. I would like permission to go directly to step six of my previously approved plan. Full breach." Micah was unconsciously stroking the path through his beard made by his scar. "If Excalibur is active, our time grows short."

Nathan spoke up. "According to the histories, the Key Event should be somewhere between one and two months out. I think we have some time."

Micah shook his head vigorously. "I disagree, Nathan. The inconsistency of the reliquary could mean we have less time than usual. I think we have to press forward and take Fermilab off the table. I want discretion on this. Katrin and I will reach out to our mole within Fermilab and ask for an estimate on the timing of the full power test of HERBERT. But if that test is supposed to occur any time in the next two to three weeks, I want permission to move forward. This isn't my primary plan. We have the extraction team ready to go, and a safe house in Saskatchewan has been prepared. But I want to vote now on giving me discretion to launch phase six."

He admitted that he found it difficult to argue with Micah's assessment. He wanted not to have to kill the Lock, but he remembered full well what the consequences would be if they got it wrong. Better to make a mess and clean it up after the smoke has cleared. "I second Micah's request. All those in favor?"

The younger members all immediately raised their hands to camera height, each palm down. Nathan placed a hand on his desk, palm down as well. One by one, the other members did the same; Stephen, Maya, Matz, Tabari, Zhang, and finally, Viktor.

"Very well. Micah, you have your discretion. I'll be reaching out to each of you in turn." He ended the video call and immediately dialed Brian's cell phone back. "Cooke, is there anything you need from Nathan and I before we start herding the cats?"

It was difficult to tell on the cell connection, but Brian's voice sounded slightly embarrassed. "No sir. Thanks. But uh… can I stop sleeping with my hand in the tank of water?"

Chapter 42

Deb's mind raced like a rabbit with hounds at its heels. Leo had followed up to let her know that Rebecca Drake, CEO of IFI and one of the most influential people in finance, was funding Nadir and was most likely providing the additional Titan Security personnel at their protests.

When she told Reynolds her plan to question Ms. Drake, he had been skeptical that she would accept. Neither Ms. Drake nor IFI was under investigation. And even though there was an apparent conflict of interest in her donations to Nadir and Fermilab, there was nothing illegal about it. It might seem suspicious considering everything that was happening, but they didn't have any admissible proof that she was involved. The odds of getting a judge to issue a warrant to force that information out of either organization seemed unlikely. They would have to have reason to suspect some sort of malfeasance, and really all she had was a gut feeling that there was something off about the whole situation.

Luckily her boss felt the same way. They were both surprised when IFI returned their call and gave her an appointment first thing this morning to interview Ms. Drake. She wanted to make sure she kept her line of questioning succinct and to the point. Reynolds had been very pointed in his desire to not anger someone as powerful as Rebecca Drake.

Although it was unlikely that Ms. Drake would admit to anything inappropriate, Deb hoped that her gut would help her decide if it was worth the time and resources to dig up what was really going on.

Deb found herself contemplating the incredibly handsome assistant seated at a desk outside Ms. Drake's office. When she arrived and introduced herself, he flashed a movie star smile that almost made her blush. His clothes were neat, and he was clean-shaven. He could have been pulled off the cover of GQ. But there was a gentle slowness to everything he did. It could have been deliberateness, but it almost looked like she was watching him on video that had been slowed to two-thirds normal.

He slowly looked up, and she was so engrossed in her thoughts that she didn't have a chance to look away. Their eyes locked, and his crystal blue eyes twinkled as he flashed his brilliant white smile at her. "Ms. Drake will see you now, Agent Kazdin."

Deb jerked to her feet and smiled awkwardly at him. "Thank you, Mr...."

"It's Jason, ma'am, just Jason."

"Thank you, Jason." Deb kept her eyes locked forward as she walked over, opened the door to Ms. Drake's office, and entered.

"Good morning, Agent Kazdin. I hope I didn't keep you waiting too long. I tend to lose track of time. Jason has to keep me on track."

Deb walked across the office and extended her hand as Rebecca circled her desk to meet her. "Thank you so much for agreeing to speak with me, especially on such short notice."

They shook hands, and Rebecca offered her a seat and then returned and sat behind her desk. "Of course. I made it a priority when I heard the FBI wished to speak with me. I assume this has to do with my private funding of Fermilab and Nadir?"

Deb sat motionless; the fleeing rabbit in her head tripped and fell. "I'm sorry. How did you know what I wanted to speak to you about?"

"My dear, I knew it was only a matter of time before I was approached about my donations. With all the negative attention on the entire affair, I'm surprised it took you this long."

"We've been focused on the people on the ground, and it only recently came to light that you had a financial interest in both organizations." Deb pulled out her phone. "Do you mind if I record this conversation?"

Rebecca shook her head in the negative. "Of course not. I have nothing to hide."

Jeff McIntyre

Deb took a deep, cleansing breath to clear her head before she spoke. "First, let me start by saying the FBI is not accusing you of any wrongdoing. While unusual, the monetary support you have provided to Fermilab is not illegal. Nor is there anything wrong with your donations to Nadir. The reason I'm interviewing you is to ascertain why you are involved in financing organizations at odds with one another. It would seem to be something of a conflict of interest."

Rebecca shook her head again. "Not at all. You see, I am a fan of science. I am also a proponent of transparent and responsible science. If you've done your research, you know that my funding of Nadir goes back to its founding. But my relationship with Fermilab started almost five years ago."

She considered what Rebecca said. "Do you have any direct input into the operations of either organization?"

Rebecca smiled and shook her head again. "I do receive status reports from Fermilab on how things are progressing with HERBERT, but I do not have direct conversations with their team. As far as Nadir is concerned, I get thank-you notes and their newsletter. Although I have met and had very pleasant conversations with Mr. Esposito, the only recent contact with them has been to offer a security firm to defuse any situations that may arise during their protests."

"Ah, Titan Security. Let's discuss that. As I understand it, they are providing security for both

Nadir and Fermilab. Are you the one funding that additional security?"

Rebecca smiled. "I am. I have had dealings with Titan in the past, and when the situation became tense, I took it upon myself to offer their services. It seemed prudent for there to be professionals with no skin in the game available to be the cooler heads should any confrontations occur."

How long had Ms. Drake rehearsed these responses? "This all seems entirely reasonable." She replied. "Too reasonable. I've done my research, and you've been funding Nadir since day one. I find it hard to believe that you helped found that organization and have no input into who and how they protest."

"As I said. I've had conversations with Alvaro about his goals and his plans. I wanted to know what he was going to do with my money. I find him to be a fascinating man and worth the investment, but I've never told him how to run his organization." Rebecca's voice hardened. "Science unburdened by responsibility is a danger to the entire planet. If Alvaro believes that Fermilab is acting irresponsibly in how they are conducting the HERBERT experiment, then he has the responsibility to call them to task."

It was Deb's turn to shake her head. "That's where the conflict of interest starts to rear its ugly head. Why don't you just suspend funding for HERBERT and call Fermilab to account if you think Nadir is correct?"

Jeff McIntyre

Rebecca sighed. "I'm not a scientist, are you? I can't pretend to understand what has Alvaro worried about HERBERT. I know that the Fermilab team is passionate about their experiment, and none of them would continue with the experiment if they were at all worried about the risk or the ethics of the project. What I want is a peaceful resolution and for Nadir and Fermilab to come to the table and work this out." Rebecca stood up and walked over to a hand-turned earthenware bowl on a side table. It had no decoration but looked like it had been well used. "This bowl is underestimated by everyone who comes into my office. It is one of the first known examples of wheel-turned pottery. Despite its relatively intact appearance, it is almost eight thousand years old. The little-known story behind it is that it represents a technological improvement that revolutionized and then destroyed an economy."

Rebecca sat back down at her desk before she continued. "The pottery wheel was kept a secret by its creator. This technology was so revolutionary that it destroyed the trade of all other potters. No one wanted anything other than his wheel-spun creations. This led to a shortage in available pottery because he couldn't keep up with the demand of an entire trading region. His competitors eventually killed him and set his home on fire, destroying the wheel without understanding what it was. It would be centuries before the technique was rediscovered. Scientific advancement scares those who don't understand it, and they often react poorly rather than try to understand the thing they fear."

"Thank you, Ms. Drake. I appreciate you taking the time to answer my questions. You've been very helpful." Deb picked up her phone and stopped recording. "Ms. Drake, I've gotten what I want for my inquiry, and I don't want to be adversarial. As I said, you're not under investigation, but can I ask you a question for myself and not for the FBI?"

Rebecca considered her carefully and then nodded slowly.

"Can't you just pressure Fermilab to come to the table and talk to Nadir? I've talked to Mr. Esposito, and all he wants them to do is slow down and do some due diligence. Things would certainly de-escalate if they would just talk to one another."

"I do put pressure on Fermilab. Every day. But short of cutting off their funding, I have very little I can do to influence them directly."

For the first time in the entire interview, Deb was sure that Rebecca Drake had just lied to her.

Chapter 43

Rebecca walked down the pathway from the grass airstrip that led toward the house. Jason followed quietly behind her with a small duffle bag in his hand. It was bright yellow with a cheap screen-printed logo that said Tito's Gym and Est. 1978 that encircled a large cartoonish barbell. She knew Jason had a habit of shopping at flea markets, garage sales, and thrift shops. She had no idea what possessed him to purchase that.

Takashi knew she didn't like to be ferried unless she had luggage, and Jason always packed light, so he hadn't come out to meet her.

Joe would have the plane ready to head back to the city as soon as she was done here. She had too much to do, and being without Jason now meant she had to handle most of it herself. She sighed, not too loudly, but Jason was very attuned to her.

"Is there anything wrong, Ms. Drake?" He asked. His voice was slightly clipped; like he'd had too much to drink but was trying very hard not to let it affect his speech.

"No, Jason, but thank you for asking." She stopped, grabbed his hand, and continued walking.

Jason followed with an almost childlike smile on his face. His head sunk, and he stared at his feet as he walked but said nothing more.

When they, at last, approached the house, Takashi and Elektra came out to meet them. Takashi had her large fleece robe flung over his arm. It was a bit chilly tonight, a kind but unneeded gesture.

"I appreciate the sentiment, Takashi, but you know I don't need that." She gently admonished him.

Takashi bowed deeply. "I know you don't need it for the cold, Ms. Drake, but I know this drains you, and I thought you might want to wear it while you nap."

Elektra rolled her eyes but said nothing.

"That's very considerate of you, but I'm heading back to the city as soon as we're through." She patted him on the arm. "I would appreciate a ride back to the airstrip, though."

Takashi bowed his head sharply. "Of course, mistress."

Elektra cleared her throat before speaking. "How are your preparations going?"

She started to smile and then stopped. It had been forced, and Elektra had known her long enough

Jeff McIntyre

to know that. "As well as can be expected. Fermilab, Nadir, and Titan all seem to be under control."

Elektra's brow wrinkled. "You don't seem happy about that."

She shrugged. "I'm not. That part of things is going too smoothly. Titan even thinks they've identified who within Nadir is a plant by the Knights. They have not been this successful for this long without being cunning adversaries. I will have to go hands-on for the remainder of this. I've already put IFI in the hands of one of my Vice Presidents, and I have a doppelganger and an itinerary that puts me in Florida for the next two weeks."

Takashi asked. "How is the little Entei? How is Tony?"

She smiled, "He's fine, thankfully. There were some odd goings-on recently. Coyote has found him and sent one of his pets to remind me that Tony isn't safe."

Elektra's eyes grew to slits. "I don't believe it. He would never harm Tony."

"I'm sorry to say that he admitted it to me after the fact." Rebecca clenched her hands into fists. "That boy can be seriously frustrating at times." She suddenly smiled. "He gets that from his father, I suppose."

Elektra and Takashi laughed while Jason stood there quietly with his head still bent as if he weren't listening but was instead focused on his toes.

310

"To make matters worse, as if some random cosmic pile of crap dropped out of the sky, a truck jumped the curb and almost hit Tony." She raised her hands to calm them. "He's fine. In both cases, the gnome did his job."

"Perhaps luck is with you for a change," Elektra said. "And as far as Coyote. I'm sure he had no intention of harming Tony. As you well know, he is the master of hard lessons."

Takashi spotted something over her shoulder, gently squeezed Rebecca's arm, and then pointed. She turned and saw a lanky Native American man wearing a broad hat, blue shirt, blue jeans, and cowboy boots who had stepped out of the tree line and walked slowly toward the group.

Coyote stopped six feet from her. He kneeled, removed his hat, and bowed his head as he spoke to the ground at her feet. "I am sorry for any offense I may have caused. I only did what is in my nature. I still wish you would abandon this path. But if you are intent, then I will aid you in any way that you wish."

She walked up to him slowly. The anger rose in her as she imagined a feral coyote ripping a ten-year-old into mangled pieces. But she clamped it down and took a long deep breath. She could never stay angry with him. His ways were strange, but his intentions were pure. Always the teacher. She rested her hand on his head. Then reached down and pulled him up and stepped into him for an embrace. "I will be bringing him here. I could use your help defending this place from the Knights' inevitable assault."

311

Coyote pushed her out to arm's length. "I will defend him with my heart, my mind, and my will."

She couldn't help but smile as she stared up at his face. She stepped out of his hands and turned back towards Elektra, Takashi, and Jason. Takashi had a broad smile on his face, and Elektra was standing on her toes with her hands up to her face, which was covered with an enormous grin. She couldn't help but laugh as Elektra tiptoed up, arms extended toward Coyote.

Elektra giggled. "Dolos, you old fox. Gimme a hug."

Coyote grabbed the old woman in an enormous hug and swept her off her feet. "Dolos. I haven't been called that for an age. And it's 'old Coyote,' thank you very much. I've been called that for far longer than I was called Dolos." He gently set her back down.

"Bah!" Elektra smacked him lightly on the chest. "You'll always be Dolos to me."

"I should probably tell you," Coyote said as he picked up his hat and put it back on his head. "Out there, when I have to deal with civilization, I go by Carl Running Eagle."

She almost laughed out loud at that. "I can't see you as a Carl, but thanks for the warning."

Coyote's face turned serious. "If your plan is to bring him here and prepare for a siege, what do you plan to do about his parents?"

Her smile faded. "I will take him from them as soon as the HERBERT test has fulfilled its purpose.

They're good people and have done a good job raising him, but he won't need them anymore, and they certainly can't protect him. Once he's recovered, I'll ask if he wants to reunite with them; but there's too much at stake to leave him in their hands. Frankly, their lives are already in danger. I would take him now, but I don't want to traumatize Tony."

"It's a dangerous gambit. You have no idea what his state of mind will be. He's been away for a long time." Coyote said. "What if he doesn't remember us?"

"Don't you worry." She rested her hand on his shoulder and squeezed. "When magic returns, he'll remember."

Coyote's face looked pained as he asked. "Are any of the rest of the Kin aware of what you're up to?"

"No. A few of them have abandoned all ambition. Those that haven't, I keep a close eye on." She stepped away from him and kneeled amidst a small clump of blooming daisies. Their faces looked at her disapprovingly. "None of them have done anything out of the ordinary in the last several months… Speaking of being aware of what I'm up to. How on earth did you find Tony?"

"You're the one who started acting out of the ordinary." Coyote walked over to Jason and began looking him up and down. "I got suspicious when you relocated your company headquarters to Chicago. Eventually, I was able to sense the Gnome. Once I saw what you had him doing, I figured out the rest."

He turned back to her. "Jason's running on fumes. I'm assuming that's why you brought him out here."

She stood up and brushed bits of grass off the knees of her pants. "Indeed. Plus, when fully charged, he will be useful in the fight against the Knights. I suppose we should get him taken care of. Takashi, is everything ready?"

Takashi nodded. "Hai. The growth has been pruned back to a safe distance, and the fire pit has been swept and cleared of debris."

She turned to Jason. "Jason dear. Go to the fire pit and prepare yourself. I'll be right behind you."

Jason did not respond. He turned and began shambling toward the tower end of the house. He started methodically removing his clothing as he walked, stuffing each piece into the yellow duffle bag as he removed it. By the time he reached the tower's edge, he was completely naked. He then rounded the curved edge of the tower and disappeared.

She quickly disrobed and handed her clothes to Elektra. "Please be a dear and swap these out for something more comfortable. It's going to be a long night. I still have to fly back to the city. Coyote, things are going to be moving very quickly. Can you stay here until this is over?"

Coyote shook his head. "No, I have a few things to take care of. But I will leave one of my children here to keep an eye on things. I think Elektra will like Swiftwind. I can be here quickly enough." He turned to walk towards the woods.

She stopped him with a hand on his arm. "Thank you. I can't tell you what it means to me; to not be alone in this."

Coyote nodded solemnly and then walked into the tree line, quickly disappearing. Elektra had already disappeared inside the house, but Takashi stood there watching as Rebecca's naked form followed the path that Jason had taken. He stood there waiting patiently until the tree line beyond the tower became visible and the tower's edge was illuminated with a flickering light. Soon a light smoke began to drift around the edge of the tower. He smiled and nodded, then headed toward the house.

Chapter 44

Deb fidgeted nervously. The anticipation of violence always put her senses on edge. But waiting for all the teams to report that they were in place and ready was literally pulling her soul from her body.

She had sent a text to Leo to give him a heads up about what was going down and asked him to wait a good hour before showing up. She probably shouldn't have notified him beforehand, but texting back and forth with him had kept her hands and her brain busy for a few minutes.

It was difficult to judge emotion or intent in raw text, but his concern for her was apparent when he closed the conversation with a simple 'be safe.'

That platitude had helped more than she was willing to admit.

An anonymous tip had been called into her office. Nadir is staging an attack on Fermilab from a vacant tire shop three blocks from the campus. Be there at 7 pm, and you can intercept the conspirators before they strike.

Her boss Agent Reynolds had hastily assembled a crew of undercover surveillance who monitored the comings and goings of the building in question. They confirmed that several known members of Nadir plus a few adjacent malcontents were converging there.

In the meantime, they had gathered two Chicago PD SWAT teams and three FBI tactical teams. Half a mile away were another two dozen officers and agents, paramedics, and fire crews standing by at a local fire station to move in for backup, crowd control, and emergency response, depending on how things went down.

It seemed like hours since her team had gotten into position in the back room of a restaurant that shared an alley with the back of the target. It had been less than twenty minutes, but time flies when the adrenaline is pumping.

She was adjusting her tactical vest for the nineteenth time when she heard Reynolds's voice squawk over the radio. "All teams are in position; teams one through three move in. Four and five hold for my signal."

One through three were approaching from across city streets, so they would move first. Once they had crossed the gap, he would signal for her, in team four and team five, to move to their adjacent alleyway entries.

"Four and five proceed to position."

317

Jeff McIntyre

Deb held her pistol at tactical ready as the agent in front of her threw open the door. She moved through and into the alleyway covering the passageway North. The first thing that hit her was the overpowering smell of blood and bowels. In the dim light of the alleyway, she could barely make out an unmoving mass twenty feet up the alleyway that might be a corpse, but it was difficult to know for sure. She hissed to the two team members assigned to bring up the rear. "Phillips and Daniels hold here and cover the alleyway." She fell back and took up position right behind breach as everyone formed up and waited.

The only sound was their breathing for the ten seconds before "Now." came over the radio and her team burst into the repair shop. At least thirty people were gathered inside. Most of them were completely shocked by the sudden appearance of law enforcement. From Deb's perspective, she saw at least five of them tense as though they were about to spring into action. Thankfully they chose not to resist. Those five slowly and deliberately raised their hands, then dropped to their knees and placed their hands behind their heads. This was not their first rodeo. The rest of the group was stunned into inaction but did as they were told when instructed by officers.

Before things were even fully organized, she rushed up to Reynold. "Sir, we need to clear the alleyway. I think we have a situation there."

"What kind of situation? Reynolds asked.

"Judging from the smell, I'm guessing a body. Phillips and Daniels are covering the alley, but I want to clear it and make sure no one contaminates whatever happened back there."

Reynolds nodded. "Do it. We've got this under control. I'll call in a forensics team but feel free to do a walkthrough. You know the drill. Take two more agents to assist with the clear and establish a perimeter."

Deb rushed back to the alley door while throwing a "Yes sir." over her shoulder. She pointed at two agents with assault rifles that were in a covering position near the door. "You two, with me."

As they reentered the alley, the stench hit her again. Phillips and Daniels were still crouched back-to-back, their eyes fixed in opposite directions with their tactical lights on and firearms at the ready. They both glanced briefly in her direction as she and her two backups entered the alley.

She gestured to the two behind her to proceed South. "Clear that way to the street and then fall back to here." The passageway to the south ended a mere fifty feet from their position before it dumped into the street. Both switched on their tactical lights due to the dim lighting, then separated to opposite sides of the alleyway and proceeded in a tactical hunch, slightly staggered from one another. One would move forward and sweep his light into each cranny opposite him, then pause, and the other agent would repeat the maneuver from his side. It took them only a few minutes to reach the street.

Jeff McIntyre

They both peeked out into the street, scanning for threats, then turned back and gave her an all-clear before making their way back to her position.

"Two by two, rifles first. I'll hold middle." She whispered. Without discussion, the two rifle-equipped agents moved forward, and Daniels turned around to face North. Now with two agents on each alley wall, one forward of the other. The agent in the rear placed a hand on the back of the man in the lead and covered over his shoulder with a pistol. Deb took a position dead center of the alley but behind the two groups.

As a group, they moved slowly, not speaking. She gave the mass a wide berth. She flicked her light at it and confirmed her worst fear. It was the head and upper torso of a man, its lower part a ragged mess. A trail of blood led to a nearby storm drain. Her attention jerked ahead when she heard Phillips make a low retching sound." Their lights had illuminated the other half of the body a good twenty feet from where the torso lay. "Focus. Keep clear of it." was all she could say. The stench was overpowering. The team shifted to avoid the legs and the bloody mess that streamed away from it. They slowly progressed the entire length of the alleyway to the South. No other bodies, people, or obvious signs of what had caused the devastation behind them.

They didn't exactly relax, but they all stood up from their tactical movement and glanced around. Deb spoke into her radio. "Alley clear. Taking up perimeter positions." She turned to address her ad

320

hoc team. "You two keep anyone out of this end. Daniels, Phillips; you two head back and keep the South end secure. I'm going to start a walkthrough. Daniels, can I get your flashlight?"

Daniels carried a larger natural light flashlight on him for just such occasions. He smiled sheepishly as he handed it to her. "Just don't turn that thing on until we get to the other end. I don't want to lose my night vision. Or get a good look at what we've got back there."

Deb gave them a thirty-second count before she turned on the light and began sweeping the area. The first thing she found was the remains of two security cameras that covered the alleyway. They had been ripped out of their roof mounts and were lying in pieces on the ground. As she scanned the ground and walls, she saw all the typical hallmarks of an alley. Scattered bits of trash that either missed dumpsters or got blown in. There were several dumpsters scattered the length of the alley. A few abandoned pallets leaned against the walls. She checked the steel security doors that lined the alleyway, and they were all secure.

There was a layer of built-up dirt that had accumulated in the crevices. The drainage of the adjoining buildings did not do a very good job of keeping the alleyway clean, but a light sprinkling earlier today had left everything in a muddy mess. The footprints of her team as they made their way up and down the passage were obvious. She took pictures of the various sets of footprints and made a mental note of which ones she knew were from her and her agents.

At last, she circled the lower remains. She felt a hard lump form in her stomach as she surveyed the scene. A splatter of blood revealed where they had smacked against the wall, and then streaks down the wall led to where they had come to rest. The lower torso and legs looked like they'd been thrown against the wall. The legs were tangled limply across each other. Ragged tears of flesh and remnants of shattered rib cage gave way to shredded bits of intestine.

She circled the center of the alleyway and made a careful approach to the other half of the remains. The head was unblemished. The upper torso, however, shared the same ragged and torn look that the lower torso had. There was no indication of other footprints other than the victims. Maybe the forensics team will find something. She quickly scanned the head and face and saw no marks or contusions. The man appeared to be in his late thirties or early forties. Full head of slicked-back brown hair with only a few hints of gray. He had a well-groomed full mustache and beard. There was a long distinctive scar that started below his left eye. It missed his mustache but carved a path through his beard on its way to just under his jawline.

She stared into his icy blue, lifeless eyes. She had seen several bodies post-mortem. A couple in person at crime scenes. A dozen or so in morgues. Perhaps a hundred in imagery. During training, the

FBI had made her look at a lot of bodies. It occurred to her that she had never seen a victim look as surprised as this one.

Chapter 45

Brian was driving south from DuPage airport in a rental car. It had taken a little longer to get to Chicago than he wanted, but because they had wanted to avoid international customs, the pilots had first landed at a small airfield in northern Michigan. They had played some shenanigans with the locals that kept them occupied while he and one of the pilots switched to a local plane they had rented and then just jumped across the lake.

DuPage was the closest airport to Fermilab, and as soon as he landed, he knew they were in the right place. The vibrating of the sword had switched to a sort of mental compass in his head so long as he was touching it. Excalibur was no longer in its lake water tank. It was resting in an open case on the seat next to him.

The existence of magic was a hard pill to swallow. Reading the histories of the Knights of the Stone, watching the video of the Lock awakening in 1980, even seeing the relics generating heat and glowing in the reliquary, there was still a level of disbelief. Any of those could be explained away. The histories a work of fiction, the video created with modern editing techniques, the relics simple, special effect props. But the sword at his side, the sword that those histories said was the legendary blade of Arthur, King of the Britons.

Two weeks ago, it had been a rusted rod that was only eight inches long with no edge to speak of. The guard was nothing but a decayed metal ring. The hilt and pommel had been completely gone, with only a stub of rusted metal remaining of its tang. He had spent those two weeks in constant contact with that sword, hoping and praying it wouldn't vibrate. He had even slept with his hand in an elbow-length glove, completely submerged in the sword's tank so he could maintain that contact. Imperceptibly slowly, the rust had flaked away, the blade grew, and the hilt appeared from nowhere.

Now, the hilt was whole. Silver wire alternating with soft leather straps ran the length of the hilt, which had the distinctive four finger ridges of Roman swords. Two half disks, tarnished bronze but completely intact, made up the guard and pommel.

Jeff McIntyre

The blade was now full length with sharpened edges and a fierce point. There were still bits of rust and corrosion, but there was less of that each time he looked at it. It reminded him of a Gladius, but to his untrained eye, it seemed longer than what he expected for that type of sword. Other than the bits of gold in the hilt and on the pommel, there was no other adornment. It was a simple, dangerous-looking weapon.

He reached out and touched the hilt, and the presence of the Lock was like a lump in his head. The road he was taking was straight South, and the Lock was in that direction but slightly to the East of his current heading. His GPS made it apparent he was heading for the Fermilab campus.

That surprised him somewhat. One of the things the Knights had discovered about the Lock was that he was inexorably drawn to the Key Event. If he was that close, the Key Event could be frighteningly soon.

His phone rang, and he answered it on speaker without looking at it. "This is Brian."

Colonel Larkin's voice came from it. "What's your status, Cooke?"

"I'm about," He scanned the GPS on his phone. "Fifteen minutes out from Fermilab. The sword is leading me straight to the campus."

"I'm going to try and send you backup, but I don't have an ETA." Larkin's voice lowered. "Brian. Micah was supposed to breach tonight. We've lost contact with him, and we're hearing reports of FBI and SWAT presence in the vicinity of the Fermilab campus."

"Shit." He couldn't think of what else to say.

"Son, you have to kill the Lock." Larkin paused. "I'll contact you when I get a better idea of when your backup will be there, but don't wait. We can't wait. Identify the Lock and eliminate him, no matter how messy it is. After, get clear if you can; but we have the resources to extricate you no matter how bad it is."

"I won't let you down, sir," he said.

"You're not doing this for me, son. You're doing this for the whole world." Larkin's call disconnected.

"No pressure." He said to the empty air.

Deb spotted Leo chatting with one of the uniformed officers that were maintaining the perimeter as she was giving her boss Mike Reynolds a rundown of what she and the forensics team had found in their preliminary inspection of the corpse in the alleyway. No animal prints were identified in the alleyway, and no indication of vehicles entering or leaving the alleyway for the past several hours. That eliminated the two likely causes for the kind of trauma that had been inflicted on the victim.

The remains had already been collected and were on their way to the morgue for autopsy. Whoever he was, he was an operator and probably an experienced one. They had found a wide variety of lethal and non-lethal weapons in a backpack and on his remains. A suppressed low-caliber semi-automatic pistol with subsonic rounds. Four grenades: smoke, teargas, flashbang, and a good old-fashioned fragmentation. Two sophisticated pipe bombs with variable delay timers. A hand-held taser. An old-fashioned self-defense baton. Last but not least, four knives of various sizes and uses. The ID they found on him said that his name was James Frank and that he was from Sheboygan. However, they'd also found a pack of gum with English, French, German, and Dutch writing on it. Not something you would commonly find in the upper Midwest.

A bus had come and gone, taking all of the 'rioters' to a police holding facility. FBI agents would be there to meet them and begin the booking and interview process. Luckily, she was free of that duty. Interrogation wasn't exactly her forte.

The five that she had identified as being of particular interest had been separated, and we're going to get special attention. They had been equipped similarly to the victim in the alleyway, and none had been carrying ID. Everyone else had been identified, and most of them were Nadir rejects. They had only been given cans of spray paint and firecrackers. It was apparent there were two separate agendas: one of general mischief and the other of serious mayhem.

"Good work tonight, Kazdin. Get some sleep tonight, and we can start going through the interview transcripts tomorrow." Reynolds replied after she had given her status report.

"Thanks, boss. You get some rest yourself. You're not exactly a spring chicken." She jabbed.

Special Agent Mike Reynolds, her temporary boss of about three weeks, gave her a look that could melt steel. Her whole body tensed. She was tired; she didn't know him well enough to be that informal. Maybe he was sensitive about his age. Suddenly he burst out laughing. "Gotcha." Then turned and walked away.

She must be tired because she giggled like a nervous little girl and her whole body melted in relief. I must have passed some internal test because he'd never been that casual with her. She headed toward the police line to chat with Leo. She had to resist the urge to speed up when she spotted him visibly holding a very large coffee over the police line at her.

"You're a lifesaver." She said as she accepted the drink from him and took a delicate sip. "Mocha? How did you know?"

Leo shrugged. "I thought I caught a whiff of chocolate from your coffee the last time we met. Besides, chocolate makes everything better."

He'd been here for a while, waiting for her to come over, so it was only a little warm. It didn't matter; she closed her eyes and took a deep drink of heaven.

"Hey, I'm glad you're ok. When you told me to come here." He waved at all the assembled emergency vehicles. "I was not expecting such a large production. There's lots of speculation going on out here, but unsurprisingly no one on the tape line is talking. Is there anything you can share?" He prodded.

She nodded and ducked under the tape. "Let's take a walk." They strolled away from the commotion of the press and rubberneckers that lined the police line. "It was a group of people assembled to assault Fermilab."

"Holy shit. Please tell me it wasn't Nadir." Leo said.

She shook her head. "I can't be certain, but my gut says no. I'm not going to take them off the table, but I suspect this was someone else deliberately recruiting Nadir rejects."

"I saw them wheel a body out to the meat wagon. Was there a casualty during the breach?" Leo asked.

"I can't talk about the details of that body, but it was not a result of us." She took a deep drink of mocha and let it roll down her throat. She sighed and then whispered. "But it was weird as shit."

Leo's eyebrows rose. "Well, when you can talk about it, you better fill me in on all the juicy details."

She gave him a half-assed salute. "Maybe over wine. Lots of wine."

"Hey, if you're almost done here, I have a proposition for you." He laughed when she raised one eyebrow in suspicion. "You have a dirty mind. No, I have some friends that live maybe half a mile from here as the crow flies. If you're not too tired, I'd love it if you met them. They'll ply you with liquor and make sure you get home safe and at a reasonable hour. I imagine you have a long day ahead of you."

"Normally, I would have to say no. But we're almost wrapped up here, and I've been pardoned from having to participate in the interviews." She looked around. "Let me do one last lap of the scene to make sure everyone is packing up. I'll need to give Phil Baxter a call. After that, I'm definitely going to need a drink so let's do it."

"I'll be here interrogating that Batavia PD officer over there." Leo nodded vaguely at an officer manning the police line.

She looked at the officer in question. "I'm pretty sure he's more my type than yours, but good luck." She pulled out her phone and stared at the mobile number for Phil Baxter. Another deep drink of Mocha, and then she hit send as she walked back toward the alleyway.

Phil Baxter's arrogant sarcasm oozed out of the phone, although she had difficulty hearing him over a loud thrumming sound in the background of his call. "Agent Kazdin, how lovely to finally hear from you."

"Mr. Baxter, I'm calling to give you an update. A large group of potential aggressors has been apprehended approximately three blocks from the campus. Some of them were armed." She sped on to keep him from interrupting. "The FBI and a combination of Batavia and Chicago PD were involved in the operation. I'm calling to update you on the situation, but we're asking that you keep your teams on alert in case there is a backup crew. We're also sending some Batavia PD to checkpoint the campus vehicular entrances as an extra precaution."

The thrumming continued from her phone when Phil spoke again; his voice was almost pleasant. "The reinforcements are welcome. I'll inform the perimeter stations to be on the lookout for them." His sarcasm suddenly re-engaged. "Thank you for telling me how to do my job. We have no intention of coming off alert. According to the eggheads, they're about fifteen minutes from their first full-power collision. Now, if you'll excuse me, I have to finish clearing the maintenance huts before that happens. I'll talk to you tomorrow, Kazdin." And the call disconnected.

Her disgust at talking to Phil was overridden by a strong desire to call Hank Lee and find out how in the hell they could be doing a full power test. As she finished her lap of the scene, she gave in and tried calling him. Unsurprisingly he didn't answer. If they were about to do a full-scale HERBERT test, he wouldn't bother to answer his phone. She sent herself a note to follow up with him tomorrow. Very strange; they must have started powering up the ring at least three or four days ago to be at full power tonight.

She found Leo and listened to him natter on about the hot cop whose number he didn't get as they walked to his car. Before she could circle to the passenger side, he stopped her and pulled her in for a strong embrace. She leaned her head on his shoulder and closed her eyes. She didn't return the hug; she just felt content to be squeezed. At last, she nodded her head and stepped back. "Thank you."

Leo said nothing; he just nodded and unlocked the car.

Brian had circled the residential subdivision twice. It lay just South of the Fermilab campus, and he now knew approximately where in that maze the Lock was at. His best chance for a clean getaway was to approach through the large forest preserve that backed up to the houses. He left his car in the parking lot of a large church that also backed up against the preserve.

He grabbed Excalibur's case and hoofed it through the trees. He estimated it was about a Kilometer from his car to the cluster of homes he believed the Lock was holed up in. It should take him about ten minutes to get back to his car once his mission is complete.

Based on the large police presence he had seen in the commercial district to the West of Fermilab, he suspected they had other fish to fry.

Chapter 46

Brian crouched next to a tree. He leaned against it so anyone glancing in his direction couldn't distinguish his outline from the trees. In the fading light of dusk and with the sun in front of him, it should make it nearly impossible for his prey to spot him. He peered through the woods and underbrush between him and the back yard of a large suburban home. The yard was ringed with decorative flowers and shrubs. A large jungle gym loomed over a pit of sand, and an old-growth oak tree dominated one edge of the yard. A tall skinny man in his late thirties or early forties sat on the back steps, and a young boy around nine or ten amused himself on the playground.

With a pistol in his right hand at the ready, he opened the hard metal carrying case that lay open at his feet. He picked up Excalibur with no small amount of reverence. He aimed the blade in the direction of the house. His wrist flicked it slightly from left to right several times. Eventually, he looked down at the hunk of metal in his hands with a bemused expression, and his emotions flashed through frustration, anger and settled on disgust.

"Lancer to Legion over."

"Lancer, Legion Actual, what's your status?"

"Lancer to Legion. I'm in position."

Brian was prone on a rocky outcrop with a small ledge over him. The lens of his laser designator poked through a dried-out shrub. For the last four days, he had peered through the optics at the squat building in the valley below. He had seen armed men in trucks bringing artillery shells to this building, and every time they left, they took with them bundles of what he knew were a type of Improvised Explosive Device that had been showing up in Kandahar. The building was on the edge of a sizable village, and he was marking it for a precision bomb drop.

"Roger Lancer, you are cleared to deliver the package."

"Roger Legion, target is lit."

"Lancer, strike is inbound. ETA two minutes."

Jeff McIntyre

"Roger Legion."

One of the delivery trucks was parked in its usual spot when the door to the building flew open, and a man came out with a couple of the IEDs in his arms. He could barely make out movement inside the building, but its interior was dark, making it difficult to discern what was going on. Figures seemed to be setting things on the floor just inside the entrance.

"Legion, what was the previous designation of the target?"

"Intel designates it as a bomb making facility."

"No sh… ah, does intel show what it was before that?"

"Notes say it used to be a school."

"Fuck" exploded out of Brian's mouth. He swiftly swung his designator up into the hills above the village, hoping to either abort the drop or put it off course, but it was too late. The laser-guided bomb struck the building on the side opposite from where the soldier was loading the truck. The bomb exploded and gutted the building blowing out windows on all sides. A secondary explosion from the materials inside caused a gout of flame to erupt from the door and envelope the truck and its driver. A small figure stumbled out of the doorway covered in flame and collapsed to the ground.

He was over a kilometer away, so the only sound was the whump of the shockwave caused by the initial explosion. His mind had filled in the screams and the smell of burning flesh in his nightmares ever since.

The sword distinctly vibrated in his hands as he pointed it at the house, but neither fit the profile. He kept hoping that some other man, maybe inside the house, would walk out and join these two, but his gut told him the truth.

The muffled sounds of someone quietly creeping through the forest came from behind him. He turned slowly and aimed his pistol in the direction and waited.

Katrin crept slowly out of the gloom, a pistol in her hands aimed casually near him but not at him. "Don't shoot. I'd hate to have to kill you." The humor evident in her voice.

Brian lowered his pistol. "Of course, they sent YOU to babysit me. I should have known."

She smiled, "You are the new guy, and this is as important as it gets. Just think of me as sexy backup."

"How did you find me here?" he asked.

Katrin shook her head slowly and smiled. "Aw, sweetie, I've been on your tail since you got out of your car."

Brian leaned Excalibur against the tree, pulled out the short black barrel of a suppressor, and began to screw it onto the barrel.

"Why do you need that? Can't you just do it from here?"

"That was the plan. Random gun violence in the suburbs would be to blame, but I can't tell which one is the Lock from here. Boy is too young; the man is too old. I can only guess that there's someone in between still in the house, so I'm going to get closer to confirm." He finished attaching the suppressor, slid the receiver back, and chambered a round. "Here, hold this and see if you can tell." He held out Excalibur to Katrin.

Katrin stared at Excalibur as if entranced. She shook her head to wake herself and then crept through the underbrush toward him. "I've studied it many times, but I've never actually held it." She slipped her pistol into a shoulder holster and then, with both hands, gingerly took the sword from him. She turned toward the house and pointed the blade toward it.

Two sharp cracks sounded as Brian fired into her ribs. She staggered to the side, and Excalibur slipped from her grasp. She tried to reach for her pistol, but Brian plowed into her, knocking her to the ground. He knelt, his knee on her shooting arm, and placed the end of his suppressor against her forehead.

He looked sadly into her eyes and whispered hoarsely. "I'm sorry, but I can't kill any more kids. I don't care what the cost is." The pistol cracked once more.

Brian stood up and looked towards the house. The man and boy were walking casually toward the back door, seemingly unaware of the events that had just transpired. The last light of day had faded away. He picked up Excalibur, idly twirling the artifact by its hilt, trying to decide what to do next.

His gaze shifted from the house to the sword and back. He nodded to himself, the decision made, then placed the blade back in its case and snapped it shut. He quickly kicked dead underbrush and leaves over Katrin's body. It was a poor attempt to hide her, but it would make her difficult to notice unless someone got within ten feet or so. He would have to come back and do something more permanent later. He picked up the case and, with one last look at the mound of leaves, took a deep breath and strode toward the house.

Chapter 47

Deb was standing behind Leo when the door opened and revealed a tall skinny man with sandy blond hair and bright blue eyes in his late thirties dressed in a button-down long-sleeve blue shirt and khakis. "Leo! Not that I don't love surprises, but you usually call first."

"Hey, Daniel. Sorry to drop in unannounced, but I was in the area with a new friend that I wanted you to meet." Leo stepped to the side and gestured in a lame ta daa kind of way. "This is Agent Deb Kazdin of the FBI. She and I have been collaborating for the past few weeks. Deb, this is 'Professor' Daniel Fitzroy. He's one of my oldest friends."

"Geez, Leo. Did you have to air quote the professor part? You didn't air quote Agent." Daniel griped. Then with a laugh, he stepped aside. "Pleasure to meet you, Deb. Come on in."

Daniel shouted, "Babe, we've got company." he led them down the hallway past a dining room and family room on opposite sides and into a large kitchen and dinette where a short, attractive woman with her long dark hair braided into a ponytail sat staring intently at a laptop with a frown of concentration on her face.

When the woman looked up and saw her, Deb could see her eyes widen and then flick to Leo with a concerned expression.

Leo spoke up. "Hey Soph, this is my friend Deb. Deb Kazdin. She's the agent with the FBI that I've been working with the last few weeks."

The woman nodded and then smiled, the concern mostly disappearing from her face as she stood up and extended her hand. "I'm Sophia. Nice to meet you, Deb. Leo's been telling me about you. It's nice to put a face to the name."

She smiled and shook the proffered hand. "Should I be worried about what you've been telling them, Leo?"

"Wha…t? No?" Leo turned back to Daniel. "Hey, where's Big T?"

Daniel pointed a thumb up the stairway to the second floor. "He's not feeling very well, so I tucked him in early."

"I guess we shouldn't get too rowdy then." Leo walked over to a set of cabinets. "I don't want to impose if you guys have had a rough day, but Deb's had one for the books. We were in the area, and I wanted you all to meet, and I thought I could offer her a stiff one from your well-stocked liquor cabinet."

Jeff McIntyre

Daniel shrugged and sat down next to his wife. He pointed to Deb and then pointed sharply to one of the chairs opposite them. "Sit. Leo, I think we could all use one. You know what I like."

Leo smiled as he opened the cabinets and began pulling glasses and bottles out.

Daniel smiled and shook his head at Leo's back before turning his attention back to her. "So, Deb. You've had a crap ass day, and you work for the FBI. Anything you're at liberty to talk about?"

She shook her head. "Not really. Let's just say there was 'nearly' an incident at Fermilab, but we managed to stop it. I'm sure you'll hear more about it in the news over the next few days."

"Oh my. I'm glad you stopped it, whatever 'it' is. I know it's just my subconscious messing with me, but I'm always on the lookout for extra eyes or limbs on Tony." Sophia laughed. "Most of the time, I just accept my husband's assurances that we're safe. But I sometimes tell him I think he's getting shorter."

Leo spoke over his shoulder. "Maybe you're just getting taller."

She laughed at the playful banter; the day's tension started to leave her. She was turned in her seat to half face the Fitzroys sitting side by side and half face Leo at the other end of the kitchen. She heard the door behind her left shoulder open with some force, and all four turned swiftly as a man stepped into the kitchen from the back yard.

Her training kicked in. The suspect was a white male, approximately six foot two, two hundred

342

and ten pounds. He has black, slightly graying hair with one to two days of stubble. He appears to be in his late thirties or early forties. He was last seen wearing a black jacket over a dark gray V-neck t-shirt and blue jeans. He is considered armed and extremely dangerous.

He had an athletic build and stood in a stance of readiness that indicated some form of combat training. He was holding a suppressed pistol in his right hand, which he used to broadly cover everyone at the table. In his left hand was what appeared to be a single-capacity hard-sided rifle carrying case. She could tell as he scanned the four of them that he was not expecting this many people to be here. He also noticed her sizing him up, and a hard smile came across his face.

"You." He gestured his pistol at Leo. "Hands up. Come here and sit down." Leo did as he was told and slowly crossed the kitchen and sat beside her. "All of you put your hands face down on the table. Now."

When they obliged, he placed the case on his end of the table with the clasps facing toward them. She kept her eyes mainly on the intruder so she couldn't see how Leo was doing, but Daniel looked like he was going to be sick. Sophia had a surprisingly hard look on her face. Leo had told her she was a project manager at IFI. If she had any kind of law enforcement or military training, he had never mentioned it.

Jeff McIntyre

The man lowered the pistol, so it did not directly threaten any of them. She was kicking herself for putting her sidearm in the lock box in her car before coming here with Leo. All she had on her was a hold-out pistol in an ankle holster, and there was no chance she could get the drop on him unless he turned around. Even if she could, she wasn't sure she wanted to get into a shootout with this man with these civilians here.

"This isn't going to put any of you at ease, but I'm not here to hurt anyone. I'm holding you hostage because I need you to listen to what I have to tell you and know I am being dead serious." He looked pointedly at her and Leo. "I was not expecting to have an audience, but I suppose the more people who hear this, the better."

He reached forward and flicked the clasps on the rifle case open. He gestured to her with the pistol. "Flip that lid open for me, please."

She was startled by the matter-of-fact request but reached over with one hand and flipped the lid open. Resting on a bed of black velvet sat not a rifle or shotgun but a sword. She had taken a class on historic weaponry while at the academy. They mostly covered firearms, but there had been a chapter on types of cutting and piercing weapons. Her OCD had led her down a rabbit hole of medieval and iron age weaponry. This looked like a Gladius, but she could tell by the length of its blade and hilt that it was a weapon called a Spatha. Still Roman but had come into favor as the Empire began to decline.

"No interruptions, please. This will be hard to swallow, but I'm going to talk, and you're going to listen." When he saw that she was studying the sword, he tapped the table. "Up here, sweetheart. I need you to pay attention to what I'm about to tell you."

She drug her eyes away from the sword and locked eyes with him.

"Good. Up until about ten minutes ago, I was a member of a secret organization dedicated to preventing the return of magic to the world." His voice was flat, matter of fact. Like he'd just told them it might rain later.

Her heart sank. This man is a lunatic. A well-trained lunatic, to be sure. This situation couldn't be any worse. There was no telling where this could go. She might have to risk going for her hold-out. She scanned Daniel and Sophia but was startled by their reactions. Sophia's face had gotten even harder, and Daniel seemed to have relaxed. He no longer looked stressed; his expression looked… sad. She couldn't help but twist to look at Leo, and to her surprise, he did not look surprised, scared maybe, but not surprised.

"What in the hell… "She started.

The pistol thumped on the table, and she snapped her head back, and the gun was pointed back at her. "Quiet. I see that three of you know that something unusual has been going on, but you seem to be new to this party." He waved the pistol at her. "Who are you?"

345

"Deb Kazdin. I work for the FBI," she said.

"Well, that's just lovely. If you're going to burn bridges, you may as well burn them all." He took a long slow breath. "Agent Kazdin, could you please stand up and carefully remove any weapons you may have on your person."

She hesitated. Her training said she should look for an opening, but it also told her there was no opening to be had. Not without multiple people getting shot. Her gut was also telling her that this man showed no signs of being unstable. She slowly stood up and peeled off her jacket, carefully showing him that there were no weapons there or around her midsection. She lifted her right leg and placed her foot on her chair, revealing the holster and making sure he could see it.

"Allow me." He said, waving his pistol up and down. She placed her hands on top of her head obligingly. He reached down, pulled the gun out of her holster, and slipped it into his jacket pocket. He gestured with his pistol, and she sat back down. "Anyone else have any weapons they want to share?" He didn't wait for an answer; he just pointed the pistol at Daniel. "I know you're the father." He pointed at Sophia. "I'm assuming that you're the mother." He then pointed the pistol at Leo. "Who are you?"

Leo swallowed. "I'm Leo Schafer. I'm a reporter for the Chicago Tribune."

The man started laughing. "A reporter and a fed." He gestured at Daniel and Sophia. "That means you two must be a priest and a wizard." Daniel started to open his mouth, but the man waved him down. "I know who you are, Daniel and Sophia Fitzroy. Luckily no one else does." He leaned over the table and took a couple of deep breaths.

"Allow me to continue. The organization I worked for sent me to kill your son. They believe that he is the vessel that will bring the return of Merlin and magic with him."

Deb looked at the other three and again saw no real signs of surprise, only concern.

"This sword is attuned to him." He reached down and touched the hilt of the sword. At his touch, it began to glow softly. "I know that he is upstairs." He picked up the sword and aimed the point in a direction just above and behind her head. As he did so, the blade's glow intensified, and he wiggled the tip until the brightness reached its peak intensity. "Right about there."

The man replaced the sword in its case and then slumped in the chair. There were dark rings under his eyes and a slight pallor to his skin. He methodically removed the suppressor from the pistol and placed it in his pocket; then, he slipped the gun into an underarm holster under his jacket.

"Now that I've got your attention. There is a secret multinational organization with deep pockets, and a long reach called the Knights of the Stone. Don't bother trying to find anything about them; they're buried under countless layers of obscurity." He spun the case around until the sword was closest

347

to him. "I know this sounds insane, but you have to believe me. The organization was founded fifteen hundred years ago by Gawain of round table fame and this." He pointed at the sword. "Is the sword Excalibur. Your son is Merlin reborn, or soon will be. And when he is awakened, magic will return." He stopped speaking and just sat there staring at each of them in turn. Perhaps trying to find a sign that they at least partially believed him. He flipped the lid shut without closing the clasps. As if he didn't want to look at it anymore.

Sophia took a long hard look at her. Then she looked at Leo and shook her head in annoyance. "We've been recently made aware that Tony is the key to magic. We did NOT know that there was an organization whose sole purpose for existence was to kill him."

Deb jabbed Leo in the ribs. "What in the hell have you gotten me into?"

"This wasn't my intent. I just wanted you to meet my friends." Leo said sheepishly.

Daniel seemed distracted. It looked like he was peering past the newcomer. As if he expected someone else to come in from the back yard.

"Can we get back to the task at hand?" The man asked. "This sword is the only way the Knights have of tracking your son. And I'm giving it to you so you can keep him safe."

"I don't think I'll ever feel safe again," Sophia said softly.

The Garden Gnome

Her butt felt numb. No, not numb. Her chair was subtly vibrating. They all came to the realization simultaneously as they looked down at their seats in unison. The vibration was steadily increasing, and it was affecting the table as well. Soon the sword's case began making noise as it vibrated out of harmony with the table and began to dance across the surface. Plates and glasses clattered in the cabinets. They quickly stood up and looked around. From the stairwell to the upstairs, light began pouring into the kitchen. As if a switch had been flipped, the vibration and light disappeared, and the five of them just stood there staring at one another.

The front door opened, and down the hallway walked Rebecca Drake.

Chapter 48

Sophia looked at Rebecca with a mixture of shock and fascination. Those emotions quickly turned into almost panicked laughter. "A CEO, an assassin, and an FBI agent walked into a bar."

Rebecca walked up and patted her on the shoulder. "It's ok, Sophia. Everything is going to be all right."

The intruder, whose name she still didn't know, spoke up. "Jesus. You're the CEO of IFI." He looked around the table in bewilderment. "Who is going to walk in next? The President and maybe Tom Cruise for an encore?"

Rebecca ignored him. "Good evening, Daniel; it's a pleasure to finally meet you. And you must be Leo; I don't believe we've met." She extended her hand to him.

Leo, with a dazed expression on his face, took her hand. "I've uh, heard a lot about you, ma'am."

"I'm sure you have." Rebecca smiled and turned to Deb. "Agent Kazdin, nice to see you. Although I'm curious as to how you came to be here tonight."

Deb shrugged. "I'm friends with Leo. Leo is friends with them. This is my first time meeting them."

Rebecca leaned forward and rested her fists on the surface of the table, facing off against the intruder. Her eyes narrowed as she glared at him. "And last but not least." Her voice changed from casual conversation to forceful interrogation mid-breath. "What is your name?"

Sophia resisted the urge to answer even though the question wasn't aimed at her. She saw Leo open his mouth and then snap it shut as he struggled with the same problem.

"Brian Cooke. US Army Special Forces. Mustered out, ma'am." The man replied. The look of surprise on his face made it clear that he had not intended to answer.

"Well, Brian. I can't say it's a pleasure to meet you. Why are you here." Rebecca's voice maintained that same hard line.

"I was sent here to kill the Lock, but I couldn't bring myself to murder another kid." The bewilderment on Brian's face was obvious. He looked like he wanted to vomit.

"The Lock. That's an interesting term for him. Who sent you?" Rebecca's voice almost hummed with intensity.

"The Knights of the Stone. Ma'am." Perspiration was starting to appear on Brian's forehead.

"Are you a Knight then, dear boy?" Her voice had lowered to a dangerous whisper.

"I was up until twenty minutes ago. I tendered my resignation when I murdered the other Knight sent to make sure I killed the Lock." Brian's entire body was tense, and he was panting.

"Hmmph." Was all Rebecca said as she straightened. Brian practically collapsed back into his chair in suddenly released tension.

Sophia finally came to her senses. "Rebecca… Ms. Drake. What are you doing here?"

Rebecca nodded. "Yes, my dear. To business. I'm here for Tony. He's awakened, and you can no longer protect him." She said it as she had just told her she had to work on Saturday. Rebecca pivoted and walked to the base of the stairs. She yelled up the stairs, her voice reverting to the same tone she had used against Brian. "Tony, come here. It's time for us to go."

Sophia panics, she has no plan, but she knows that Rebecca is going to take her son. She rushes Rebecca. To push her away, to plead with her, to save Tony.

With incredible grace, Rebecca Drake pivots and shoves Sophia right through the pantry door.

"Sophia!" Daniel calls out and runs at Rebecca. This time there is no grace, only power. Rebecca is easily a foot shorter and eighty pounds lighter than Daniel. She extends both arms, shoving her hands into his chest, and he flies across the kitchen and slams into the table, causing Leo and Deb to leap back. Still stunned, Brian gets slammed in the chest by the table and knocked over backward, still in the chair. The sword case slides off the table and clatters onto the floor.

Tony appears, walking down the stairs, still wearing his pajamas. His body is rigid, and his eyes are closed. His skin is pale, and his hair is wet with sweat. He steps off the stairs and stands next to Rebecca.

"It's time to go, my dear," Rebecca says to him.

Leo's eyes go wide, and he charges at Rebecca. She takes a step back, her arms wide, waiting for him, but instead, he lunges for Tony, grabbing him by the waist and rolling across the floor away from Rebecca.

A loud explosion reverberates through the kitchen, and Rebecca staggers forward. Her jacket is ripped completely off, and her blouse is in shreds. Sophia stands with one foot still in the wreckage of the pantry door holding her father's double-barrel shotgun. Smoke rolls from both barrels.

Deb had reflexively raised her hands to her face to protect it. She peeks through her hands. "There's no blood. Why isn't there any blood?"

Jeff McIntyre

Rebecca slowly straightens. "Fine." And her body begins to change. Her clothes, already in tatters, completely disintegrate and fall to the floor as she grows. In an instant, the short middle-aged woman is replaced with a seven-foot-tall creature.

Deb stares in fascination at the creature that Rebecca becomes. It is completely covered in dull black scales. Not the smooth scales of a snake or the uneven scales of a crocodile, but the heavy, evenly spaced, overlapping scales found on some lizards. It has a long sinuous tail, and its feet are equipped with eagle-like talons, three toes forward and one backward. Its hands have shorter but no less frightening claws, but instead of a backward toe, the fourth is an opposable thumb. Despite the bird-like feet, its legs remind her of a large cat. Powerful muscles rippled below the scales. Its upper torso strongly reminds her of a lion or tiger if that creature were covered in scales rather than fur. Broad chest tapering to a slender waist with powerful hips and slim muscular legs. Its neck was slender but proportionate to its head. The head again reminded her of a scale-covered feline. It was vaguely triangular in shape, but instead of the cute triangular nose of a cat, it tapers almost to a beak with very reptile-like nose slits near the side. Protected hearing slits instead of ears and two sharp horns swept out the back of its skull made the head streamlined as if for speed. The eyes were neither feline nor reptilian. They were a warm hazel color and looked disturbingly human. Despite all the animal features, it still had a distinctly feminine air. Everything about it seemed familiar but taken as a whole, it was disturbingly alien.

Taking advantage of their stunned inaction, the creature swiftly swats Leo away from Tony and gently scoops him up, cradling him in its arms.

"I'm taking him, and there's nothing you can do to stop me. Don't make me hurt you." The voice was Rebecca's, but it was more powerful and resonant. And the creature's mouth didn't move. The voice sounded like it was emanating from its chest.

Brian lurches to his feet, still disoriented. He staggers as he struggles to free himself from his tangled jacket and kicks the sword case causing the lid to flip open. Excalibur tumbles out of the case; he sweeps it up and points it at Rebecca. The blade becomes enveloped in a blue, heatless flame as soon as he touches it.

Rebecca pauses, transfixed by the sword. "So, that's how they've been finding him." Her eyes move from the sword and into the closed eyes of the boy in her arms. For a long moment, she stares at him. Her eyes eventually raise to Sophia with pity apparent in her eyes. "If you ever want to see Tony again, come to the lake house. All five of you and no one else. And bring that." Her tail flicks, and points at the glowing sword. "Joe will be expecting you."

With swift, powerful strides, Rebecca pushes past Deb and Brian and kicks open the back door. She steps out into the yard and then unfolds membranous bat-like wings that had been camouflaged against her back. She launches into the air with a powerful leap and quickly disappears from view.

Sophia dropped the shotgun and ran out into the yard, quickly followed by the rest. Scanning the night sky, there was no sign of Rebecca or Tony.

Chapter 49

Sophia stared up into the night sky. When she was a little girl, she had been obsessed with stories of unicorns and magic. She still had a worn and faded copy of The Last Unicorn that her mother had given her. She'd grown up on Tolkien and LeGuin. Her love of fantasy had been what attracted her to Daniel. His passion had been mythology, where history and fantasy merged. The ancient stories of fantastical creatures, powerful gods, and wondrous heroes had brought them together.

The little girl had wanted magic to be real. The beauty of doing the impossible with spells and force of will had filled her dreams. The teenager dreamed of magic breaking her out of high school life and maybe helping her find her true love. The woman that got married and had a son; she knew that magic didn't exist. Not like in the books. But she knew the magic of love in her husband's eyes. She knew the magic of hearing her unborn baby's heart at her Ob-gyn. And she knew the magic of her love reflected in Tony's eyes every day. She never expected that magic would take him away from her.

She felt sadness that her childhood dreams had been betrayed. Magic was supposed to be… magical. Not screams and tears. Her anger rose and swept out the sadness and the past. Tony had been taken by a dragon. "A fucking dragon has taken my son." She whirled and pointed at Brian, although she had intended to point at Brian and Deb, but the FBI agent was nowhere in sight. "You're coming with us."

Brian shook his head. "I should really be going. I need to put as many miles between me and Chicago as I can before the Knights can muster a response. Besides, you don't need me. This is about your son, and it's between you and that thing."

"Dragon." Sophia insisted.

"Whatever," Brian said.

Leo let out a sad laugh. "Rebecca Drake is a dragon. She must think that's hilarious."

Deb appeared at the door to the kitchen with two pistols in her hands and had them both aimed at Brian. "I believe the… dragon, if that's what she is, instructed all of us to come. That includes you, Knight."

Brian sighed. "I suppose it wouldn't be very noble of me to sacrifice my entire life and career to save your son only to let him get eaten by a dragon. Relax, Agent Kazdin; I'll come peacefully. Honestly, she'll probably kill us; but I think that may be preferable to being on the run from the Knights for the rest of my life."

"Daniel, Sophia, you don't know me, but I'm going to do whatever I can to help you get your son back," Deb said as she pocketed Brian's larger pistol but kept her smaller one at the ready.

"Thank you, Agent Kazdin. I'm not sure what we've got waiting for us, but I appreciate you playing your part." Daniel scanned the yard. "I wonder what happened to Bob. I'm not sure what he could have done, but Tony needed him."

Leo patted his friend on the shoulder. "I suspect Rebecca is the 'Ancient' that Bob was telling us about. The one who bound him and fed him. I doubt there's much he could have done against her. Hey Deb, do you think there's any way we could get some backup?"

"You are a funny man. What would I tell them? Hey, come help me repatriate a young boy who's been kidnapped by one of the most powerful CEOs in the US; and oh, by the way, she's a dragon and flew off with him. If we are going to get killed, let's just keep it to ourselves." Deb walked over to Leo and punched him square in the chest.

"OWW! What in the hell was that… never mind. I deserve that. Look, by your same argument, it's not like I could have told you, 'Hey, hope you don't mind my friend's son is magical.' I only half believed it myself."

"Come on; we should get a move on." Sophia began herding them back into the house. "Rebecca's plane is based out of Midway, so we've got a decent drive and a long flight ahead of us."

As they shuffled into the house, Brian asked. "Who's Bob?"

Sophia left the cabin and stepped into the co-pilot's seat next to Joe. She left the other four discussing all the events that had transpired over the last few weeks. Daniel and Leo had explained to Brian and Deb about Bob. Brian, who thought he would be the knowledgeable one on magic, seemed dumbstruck that a magical creature was wandering around when there wasn't supposed to be any magic.

Brian had given them all a quick overview of the Knights of the Stone. Their origins, how they'd found Tony, their suspicions about the HERBERT experiment, and most worryingly, their resources and power.

Sophia despaired over how they would ever hide from such an organization. Brian, for his part, tried to reassure her that the Knights only had one way to track Tony, which was in the case next to him. All they know is that he's somewhere in the greater Chicago area south of Fermilab. That was millions of people and hundreds of square miles. The organization's ignorance of Bob and Rebecca gave her some small reassurance that they weren't all-powerful.

Deb, Leo, and Daniel had been discussing why the heavily shielded Fermilab experiment would suddenly cause Tony to activate. A Key event is what Brian called it. They were grasping in the dark, but she wanted to get some answers.

She put on the headset that would allow her to talk to Joe and was surprised when Seasons in the Sun by The Byrds came flowing out.

Joe switched off the music and nodded to her but said nothing.

She remained silent as she gathered her thoughts. Finally, she asked, "Joe. Did Rebecca tell you why you're taking us out to the island?"

"No, ma'am, she didn't." He looked at her sheepishly out of the corner of his eye. "She did tell me not to talk to you any more than necessary."

"I'm sorry, Joe, but I don't care if you get in trouble. Rebecca came to our house and took Tony."

Joe's head whipped to look her in the eyes. "No. She wouldn't do that. Not my Rebecca."

"It's true." She said sadly. "She demanded all of us come to the house if we ever wanted to see him again."

Joe shook his head. "Ma'am. I've known Rebecca for close to thirty years. I've seen the good side, the bad side, every side."

"Not every side," Sophia murmured.

He kept speaking as if she hadn't said anything. "That woman is one of the most honorable and thoughtful people I've ever known. I'd take a bullet for her. I don't know what's going on between you, and I probably don't want to know. But Rebecca Drake does everything with purpose, and she always has a plan."

"Why do you trust her so much?" Sophia asked. "She's a powerful woman with a mysterious past. She has to have secrets. Maybe you don't know her as well as you think you do."

"I've been with her through some ugly things, and she's been with me through some uglier things. For that, she has my undying devotion." He said seriously. Then with a smirk. "I also like to think I'm a good judge of character. I knew the Fitzroy family were good people the moment I met you."

Sophia patted him on the arm. "Joe, you're a wonderful human being, but maybe you trust too much."

"Maybe… maybe." Joe nodded. "When we get there, try to keep an open heart."

"Don't you mean open mind?" She asked.

"Nope," he said. "Meant what I said. Rebecca has been through some things. She has scars that run deeper than you can imagine. Besides, if she meant you ill will, I don't think she would have sent her private plane with a registered flight plan to come get you at a public airport."

Sophia sat back and chewed on that for a minute. "Can you turn the music back on, Joe?"

Chapter 50

The five of them left Joe and the plane behind and began walking the long path that led to the house. There was no Takashi and no golf cart to greet them this time.

Daniel had been awestruck by the solitude and tranquility the last time they arrived. He had been excited to spend quality time with his family in such a beautiful and exclusive place. They had made some fantastic new friends. He had never seen Tony have so much fun, and they had left here joyful.

Now, they walked quietly through the night with only the stars to show the path. Tony had been kidnapped; they had been assaulted; they had been manipulated and lied to. He couldn't imagine a darker time in his life. Sophia seethed with a cold rage.

He wanted to comfort her, but how could he? Everything was going to be all right. We've been through tougher times. Things could always be worse. We'll work through this; we always do. Hollow platitudes that held no context in a world where your son is the source of magic, and there's an ancient secret organization bent on murdering him. And oh yeah, your wife's boss is a dragon and has kidnapped him.

The professor part of his brain, which was filled with myths and legends, pointed out that drake might be more accurate. After all, she hadn't breathed fire. Oh god, what if she does breathe fire?

"Do we have a plan?" Leo asked.

"I think we listen to what Rebecca has to say," Deb said. "She's holding all the cards, and we don't know what she wants."

"I unfortunately agree," Sophia said. Her voice was a mix of anger and resentment. "I wish I could say there was some elegant or sneaky way through this, but we're way out of our league. Joe had some interesting advice. He said to keep an open heart; I'm going to try; but so help me, if she's hurt one hair on his head, I'm going to… I don't know what I'll do."

As they rounded a bend in the path and cleared the forest line, they could see Rebecca in human form waiting for them in the distance. She was wearing a simple evening robe and standing in a wide stance with her arms akimbo. Her eyes were closed, and her face was almost meditatively calm.

When they got within thirty feet, she opened her eyes and said. "That's close enough." She held up her hands to reinforce the point.

"We're all here. We brought the sword. So, what do you want, Rebecca?" Sophia asked.

"Sophia and Daniel. You've now gotten a glimpse of what's in play here." Rebecca's tone was gentle. "Even still, you've only seen a fraction of what's at stake. Can you really say that Tony would be safe with you?"

"Ms. Drake." Sophia's voice dripped with sarcasm. "Tony's safety is our biggest priority. Like keeping him safe from you."

Rebecca shook her head. "You're not being honest with yourself, Sophia. Tony isn't yours anymore; he's too precious and too important. Let me keep him here. I can protect him."

"What kind of twisted harpy are you that you think keeping him from his parents is what's best for Tony" Sophia countered.

Rebecca laughed, but her voice was becoming strained. "I'm no harpy. What I am is the one person in the world who cares more about your son than you do."

Sophia took a step closer to Rebecca, her voice raised and her hands clenched in fists. "So, you're delusional. Have you gone crazy?!"

"ENOUGH!" Rebecca roared. "If you won't see reason, then I'll have to show you fear." In a single motion, she stepped out of her robe and transformed into the form she had at their house. Only this time, she kept getting bigger, much bigger.

Daniel marveled at the form. When she stopped growing, she was larger than a T-Rex. He'd seen Sue at the Field's Museum often enough that he was pretty sure she was nearly twice the size. The palpable fear in his belly couldn't stop his mind from being amazed by what he saw. Even at that size, he got the impression that she was capable of enormous speed. She was bent over in a way that implied she could run on two legs or four. She spread out her massive wings. He doubted they could bear her weight, but he supposed magic played a part in that. Then came the cherry on top. Rebecca lifted her head to the sky and opened her mouth; a massive gout of orange and white flame burst a hundred feet in the air.

"Definitely a dragon." Slipped out of his mouth. He looked around at his friends embarrassingly. Sophia looked at him bewildered but just shook her head before returning her attention to the dragon.

The flame tapered out, and Rebecca returned her attention to them and took a menacing step forward. Her voice boomed from her chest. "THIS. THIS IS WHAT YOU HAVE TO CONTEND WITH. HOW WILL YOU PROTECT HIM FROM A WORLD WITH NIGHTMARES SUCH AS THIS?"

Leo scrambled back so suddenly that he fell. Sophia wrapped her arms around him tightly, closing her eyes as if she knew this was their end. Brian and Deb stood, their faces slack with shock. Despite their training, they were both paralyzed in fear or indecision. Daniel could only stare in fascination at the magnificent creature before him. He should be afraid. For his wife, for his son, for himself. And there was fear. A fear that shook him to his core. But at the bottom of that fear was an almost profane joy. The joy that he would die at the hands of a dragon.

The earth began to rumble and shake. This wasn't the tight vibration they had felt at the house; this was an earthquake.

Rebecca even looked around in confusion. The shaking caused her to lower one of her arms to balance.

All five of them were knocked off their feet as the earth erupted to the right of Rebecca. It looked like an explosion of soil and rock slammed into the dragon's side. It hit her with so much force that she flew a hundred feet and crashed into the tree line.

They had watched her hurtle through the air, and then all five heads turned as one and beheld… something. It was a roughly spherical shape about as wide as a school bus was long. It was perched on two stumpy pillar-like legs. The whole thing was formed of mostly dirt and gravel, but large stones and a few small boulders poked out in various places, and there were a few massive tree roots weaved into its form. A large swathe of Rebecca's lawn covered its upper surface but at its top was a massive flat slab of what looked like bedrock canted slightly off center.

They all scrambled to their feet and took several steps back from whatever this new threat was. From the tree line, they could hear crashing as Rebecca struggled back to her feet. When she emerged again, she paused when she saw the orb of earth and stone. "HOW DARE YOU!" She screamed. "YOU MADE AN OATH TO ME, GNOME. HOW DARE YOU BETRAY THAT OATH."

And a familiar, deep, and gravelly voice, amplified tenfold from what Daniel was used to, emanated from the creature. "*I BETRAY NOTHING. I SWORE TO PROTECT ANTHONY FITZROY FROM ALL THREATS TO HIS SAFETY. AND THAT INCLUDES YOU. YOU BETRAY YOURSELF BY ACTING THE FOOL.*"

Rebecca screamed incoherently and charged across the field at the creature with her claws extended. In a swift, sudden move, the creature's legs disappeared. As it began to fall, pseudopod-like arms of earth extended from its sides and grabbed Rebecca, using her momentum to hurl her a hundred and fifty feet to the opposite side of the clearing, where she again crashed into the trees and disappeared.

The creature's legs had reappeared, lifting its body back up, and the 'arms' morphed back into the dome.

Daniel cupped his hands together and yelled, "Bob, is that you?"

The creature turned as if suddenly realizing they were there. A crack emerged in the side facing them that couldn't be mistaken for anything but a thirty-foot-wide smile. A pseudopod appeared and swept the massive slab of stone off its head like a jaunty hat, and the whole form bowed at them. "*DANIEL! SOPHIA! LEO! NEW FOLKS!*" The gnome's voice boomed cheerily. He then grew somber as he replaced his 'hat' on top of his dome. "*I MUST APOLOGIZE, MY LADY, FOR NOT BEING THERE FOR TONY EARLIER, BUT THAT INFERNAL CREATURE,*" and an earthy limb gestured in the way Rebecca had flown "*TOOK ALL OF HER MAGIC BACK AND PUT ME TO SLEEP.*"

A roar emanated from the forest where Rebecca had disappeared. A black streak burst through the canopy flying straight up. It hovered a few hundred feet above the tree and roared again.

"Why don't we all go inside and let the two of them settle this? It would be safer for you." A male voice behind them said.

They all whirled as a Native American man in a worn blue shirt and jeans with a wide-brimmed hat appeared behind them. Standing there calmly with his hands in his pockets, he seemed unfazed by the excitement.

"Who the hell are you?" Leo asked.

"*LOKI!*" Bob exclaimed. A large pseudopod happily waved at the newcomer.

The man laughed and waved back at the mound of earth and stone. "You can just call me Carl." He said to them, "I'm a friend of the family, so to speak. We really should get you inside where it's safe."

"How in the hell is being in the house going to protect us from these two going at it?" Deb asked.

Jeff McIntyre

The front door opened, and Takashi and Elektra were frantically waving at them to come inside.

"Trust me. Tony is inside, and despite her rage, Rebecca will not risk harming him." He gestured frantically for them to move away from Bob as Rebecca began to swoop towards them.

This time she was taking a more tactical approach as she flew fifty feet above him, hovered, and began breathing fire on the gnome's head. The grass withered to nothing, and some of the exposed roots burst into flame. The large boulder on his head darkened from the heat and smoke.

Despite the spectacle, they all hurriedly followed Carl as he skirted the fight and ran into the house. The last thing Daniel saw before Takashi slammed the door shut was Bob hurling a boulder at Rebecca with enough force to spin her and cause her to career into the ground with an enormous thump they felt through the floor.

Chapter 51

When they ran into the house, Brian had brought up the rear and almost plowed into the largest Asian man he had ever seen as he was throwing the door shut. The fellow smiled and bowed his head at him before wandering over to a window to keep an eye on the events outside.

Brian resisted the urge to watch what must be an epic fight between a dragon and a pile of dirt. The home was impressive and beautiful with understated extravagance, and on any other day, he'd be tempted to explore, but for the moment, he was concerned about the people in this room.

The large elderly Asian man and the small elderly Mediterranean woman were apparently this place's caretakers and Rebecca's servants. Sophia had called the woman Elektra and had given her a stiff hug before the woman, despite all the excitement, wandered back into the kitchen and began balling out cookie dough onto sheet pans. A man in his mid-twenties with movie star good looks wearing gym clothes sat in a chair at one end of the room, oblivious to the commotion and the newcomers. Brian studied him closely to confirm that he was, in fact, breathing, calmly sitting there staring straight ahead.

And lastly, the man who called himself Carl, but whom the earth monstrosity named 'Bob' had called Loki. He didn't regret not killing the kid. But he most definitely regretted not running for his life when he had the chance.

"Should we be worried about what's going on outside?" Leo asked.

Carl shook his head. "I wouldn't be. They can't hurt each other. Rebecca is releasing a lot of pent-up frustration and rage on one of the few creatures that can take it. If she really wanted to hurt him, claws and fire would not be how she would do it. For his part, Burbalobonomicus is just trying to wear her out. Physically and emotionally."

"Why did Bob call you Loki?" Daniel asked. "That seems like a strange name for someone who appears to be of Native American descent."

Carl had walked over to the kitchen and didn't immediately answer. He took his hat off and then leaned over and tried to swipe a bite of cookie dough, but Elektra swatted his hand away. "You should tell them." Elektra admonished him.

Carl plopped down on one of the stools and spoke. "You should all have a seat."

As they took a step toward the kitchen stools, they all paused when there was another thump that reverberated through the floor. Takashi quickly turned and gave a thumbs up and a smile before returning his attention to the fight.

They each continued their walk and, one by one sat down at the stools around Elektra's island.

He, in turn, looked them each in the eye as he spoke. "Bob knows me as Loki, Elektra calls me Dolos, the indigenous people called me Coyote, among other things. In North Africa, they called me Set, but in West Africa, I was Anansi. I have many names."

"You're a GOD?" Daniel asked incredulously.

"It may surprise you, but I do not consider myself such. It is true I have been worshiped, revered, and feared as such. But I am a magical immortal creature like Rebecca and like Bob." He paused briefly before continuing. "Ancient magical creatures can seem like gods. We can do miraculous things, but we have no control or knowledge of an afterlife. Neither I nor any creature I have encountered is the caretaker of a heaven or a hell, nor do we have any sway over people's souls."

"What are you to Rebecca, and why do you care about what is going on here?" Sophia asked.

"Rebecca asked me to help defend Tony in the event that the Knights of the Stone attempted to launch an assault on the island to get to him." He pointed at Brian. "I'm guessing by your presence here and the way she's reacting that that scenario may no longer be in the cards. As to why I care, that's a very complicated question."

Elektra chucked a ball of cookie dough at the back of his head. "No, it's not. He's your grandson."

Sophia and Daniel both squeaked out a "WHAT?" as Coyote peeled the squished ball of cookie dough off the counter where it landed and popped it in his mouth.

"That was kind of blunt." He finally said after he finished swallowing. "Did the gnome tell you about Tony's soul being reborn?"

Daniel answered. "Yes, he said that the rebirth of his soul was tied to the return of magic."

Coyote nodded. "That it is, but it might surprise you to know that his soul has been in a cycle of birth and rebirth for over fifteen thousand years."

"Holy…" Brian started.

"Indeed," Coyote replied. "I am, to my knowledge, the youngest of Tony's many children, and I was born about thirteen thousand years ago. As such, in a strange way, I am your grandson."

Sophia wasn't convinced. "That doesn't feel true to me. I mean, is Tony even our son? What will this awakened man in a child's body even be?"

"You'll soon find out. But I have known him for thousands of years. If you were to ask him, all of his hundreds of parents were every bit a part of his family as I am." Coyote stood up and put a hand on Sophia's arm. "Each time he awakens, he is a reflection of the family that raised him, but with the knowledge of all those times before. It will be disconcerting, but that little boy loves you no less today than he did yesterday."

"What is Rebecca in all this? Is she just power mad?" Daniel asked. "Kidnapping our son to protect him is extreme, even for what we've seen."

"Hold that thought," Coyote said." As Takashi clapped his hands to get their attention and then pointed outside. "I think the fight might be over. I haven't heard any thumping or roaring for a little while."

Coyote stood up and walked towards the front door, and the rest of them followed him. When he opened the door, they could see the bulk of Bob 'sitting' just ten feet from the door. On the ground in front of them lay the human form of Rebecca. She was naked, covered in sweat, and unconscious. He stepped out, gently scooped her up in his arms, and walked back into the house. As the small crowd moved out of his way, he walked over to the couch opposite Jason's unmoving form and laid her gently down on it. Elektra handed him a blanket which he gently draped over her and then sat down at her feet.

Daniel and Sophia took the seats next to Jason while Brian, Deb, and Leo stood behind them, hoping Coyote would continue his tale.

Coyote nodded to them. "Before you judge her too harshly, let me tell you the tale of Anki and Minussa."

Chapter 52

Thousands of years ago, in the time before there was such a thing as civilization. A boy was born into a tribe of hunter-gatherers in the land of the Tigris and Euphrates. He was beloved by his mother and father, and they named him Anki. Before long, Anki had a sister, and the two of them grew up in a time when the survival of the tribe was a daily battle.

Anki's sister, although younger, was helpful to their mother and the other women of the tribe. Anki, however, was very different from the other young boys. He became easily distracted. He would not make eye contact with other members of the tribe. He would scream if anyone attempted to embrace him, which was a ritual greeting among the tribe members. He often would not respond when called by his name and would occasionally repeat nonsense words. Sometimes strange things would happen around him.

The elders believed he was damaged or possessed and frequently argued that he should be left in the wilds to die. His father believed he could be forced into being a valuable member of the tribe, so he beat him mercilessly for any indiscretion. This, of course, made things worse.

Despite these challenges, his mother and his sister clung to him. They knew he was a sweet boy who just didn't see the world in the same way that others did. He could be extraordinarily insightful and exceptionally kind in a culture that had little of either. So, they worked harder on his behalf and hid his difficulties when they could.

This went on for many years until it was time for him to undergo a rite of manhood. He had been trained to hunt, and although not particularly good at hunting, his father had instilled him with enough knowledge that he should have been able to succeed at bringing down an antelope or deer by himself. However, when it was explained that the animal would not be eaten but only its blood spilled and its entrails spread as a sign to the spirits that he was worthy of joining the tribe, he simply walked out into the grass and slept.

In the morning, he returned with no antelope. He did not understand the disappointment in his father's eyes. The rage that the elders hurled at him. But he did understand the fear in his mother's and sister's eyes as they pleaded with the elders not to exile him. This was the last straw. No one in the tribe would stand up for him, and he was cast out.

Jeff McIntyre

Now a teenager, he wandered alone for many months. He avoided other tribes for fear they would kill him. Every day a struggle for survival. At night he dreamed. He dreamed of returning to his tribe, not for them, but for his mother and sister. Over time, the dreams became more vivid, and he thought about them in the daytime as he foraged for food and water. At his age, his hormones were raging, and he began to think about the things that teenage boys dreamt of.

As the months went by, he had several narrow escapes. He was nearly killed by a crocodile and then was wounded by a leopard. He was caught by another tribe and beaten but set free. His dreams began to coalesce. The same dream over and over, in the night and the day, until one night he woke up from his dream. He stirred his fire back to life to beat back the cold, and out of the darkness stepped a woman. She had no clothes and could not speak. But she didn't need to, for she was a product of his mind and magic, and she was everything he needed and desired.

He called her Minussa. At first, she played games with him and gathered food as his sister had. Then she helped make clothes for the both of them and cooked food like his mother. Eventually, as he got older, she became something more. His mixed-up mind did not really have a concept of sexuality, but eventually, his body's hunger led the way, and she fulfilled those too.

The Garden Gnome

With her by his side, he flourished. She was tireless and devoted to him. Her mind was simple at first, but it began to grow and challenge him. As he learned things, so too did she. Without having to struggle to survive, he began to explore his intellect. In their wandering, they discovered a box canyon with a small stream that ran through it. There were fruit-bearing trees, and not far from the canyon were grass whose seeds could be harvested and eaten. For an entire tribe, it would have been a few weeks' worth of food, something to harvest and move on. But for the two of them, it was paradise. It was in this valley that he saw the seeds of their discarded fruit grow into trees that he knew would grow more. He began to plant and harvest fruits and grains to sustain them. He began to cultivate the land so they would not have to leave their valley.

All paradises must end. Eventually, an aggressive tribe discovered their home. They found Anki peacefully tending his field. The tribe's leader struck Anki with a club. At that moment, Minussa became the final thing that Anki's mind had created out of need. A protector. She transformed into a beast that was an amalgamation of his dreams and his nightmares. The hard scales of the desert lizards to protect her. The fierce talons of eagles to rend their enemies. The strength and speed of the great cats. Mighty wings, because what child doesn't want to fly? And lastly, fire. The primal energy that all peoples of the grasslands fear. She laid waste to Anki's attackers before returning to tend to him.

Jeff McIntyre

Anki lived for a time, but eventually, he succumbed to his wounds and passed on. Minussa mourned in a way that you cannot fathom. She had been created by him, for him. What purpose could she have? She lay by his body and cried for a month. Eventually, she left his side, unable to bear the sight of him rotting away. She wandered the lands seeking a purpose but finding none.

Sometime after his passing, she felt the magic that had sustained her bleed away. She could no longer fly or breathe fire; even turning into that form was difficult. She became hungry. Luckily, he had taught her everything she would need to survive, and survive she did but little else.

Tales of the wandering woman spread from tribe to tribe. It became bad luck to harass or assail a solitary woman should a tribe stumble across her. For forty years, she wandered alone. One day she felt a yearning in her. South, she went seeking what it was that pulled her. Soon she realized she could take flight again, so fly she did. Swiftly she went out of the fertile crescent and into a land of sand and dunes. There she found among tribes that had learned to pull fish from the sea, a young man with darker skin and darker eyes who ran to her and embraced her. He had returned, and so had magic. He had a different name and a different upbringing, but she knew it was him.

She lived her life with him, frolicking in the ocean and learning with him until, at the ripe old age of thirty-nine, he became sick and died. And again, she mourned.

Time and again, he dies, is reborn, and they are reunited. For thirteen and a half thousand years, this cycle repeated itself. In time, he learned to master magic and science. He would be known by many names. Marduk was one, Prometheus another, his last known to us was Merlin, and she was known as Morgan.

Through all this, she was his constant companion. Mother, sister, friend, lover, wife, and sometimes rival. As she grew in knowledge, she became more independent. They sometimes disagreed, and those disagreements could be epic in scale, as you might imagine.

But they always returned to each other. That is until fifteen hundred years ago when the Knights of the Stone, out of a misguided belief that Merlin and magic were an evil that needed to be suppressed began their cycle of finding and murdering Anki before he could awaken.

Coyote's vision had drifted into the past as he told his tale. With his story finished, he looked up and saw tears in the eyes of the people around him.

"So now that you've heard my story," Rebecca said wearily, her eyes still closed. "What do you want to do?"

Chapter 53

Rebecca slowly sat up and then opened her eyes. She wrapped the blanket tightly about her as if she wanted an embrace. "Despite all the theatrics of tonight, you have a decision to make. All of you." She slipped off the couch and fell to her knees, her head lowered. Her voice was not the fearless CEO but the woman who fears she has lost everything. "Sophia, Daniel. I must apologize for my actions. I should not have taken Tony from you, but my impatience and fear got the better of me. He is asleep upstairs, unharmed. If you want to take him and go, I won't stop you. But I beg you, don't cut me out of his life."

Daniel spoke first, a weary sadness in his voice. "I'm not sure he's our Tony anymore. Isn't he awakened? If he has all those memories, shouldn't he just make his own decision?"

Rebecca shook her head. "I didn't realize until I got him here. Magic has returned, but Tony is still just your beautiful little boy. This has never happened before, but he's never been awakened this young before."

"Then why the scare tactics? Why did you do this to us?" Sophia demanded. Her hands clenched in fists.

Rebecca kept her head bowed. "Partly out of anger and frustration that he isn't awakened." She lifted her and looked into Sophia's eyes. Her eyes glistened but shed no tears. "But mostly, I wanted you to understand what your future holds. Magic has returned, and Tony is at the heart of it. If you let me, I can help protect him…" Rebecca's voice trailed off to a whisper. "If you let me."

Sophia stood up quickly. "Daniel and I have some things to discuss. We're going to go check on Tony."

Rebecca nodded. "Of course. He's in the room he stayed in before."

Sophia and Daniel disappeared into the stairwell.

"The three of you need to sit." Rebecca gestured to the chairs across from her as she got up and sat back on the couch.

Leo sat in the chair Sophia had recently vacated while Deb took a seat in Daniel's. Brian looked at the somewhat disturbing presence of Jason and decided to sit on the armrest of Deb's chair.

Jeff McIntyre

"All three of you have a decision to make. Perhaps the most important decision you'll ever make. You can choose to keep your mouths shut about everything that happened here and everything you know about Tony." She paused to let them consider that. "Or I can make you disappear."

Leo looked shocked. Deb only nodded sadly. Brian had a thoughtful look on his face.

"Elektra, can we get some of those cookies?" Rebecca called towards the kitchen. She turned back to them. "One shouldn't be hungry when making life-changing decisions."

Elektra suddenly appeared with a large plate heaping of warm chocolate chip and caramel nut cookies that she offered to them. Leo and Deb each took one, Brian one of each. Takashi soon arrived with a platter filled with glasses of milk.

Coyote grabbed a couple of cookies and a glass of milk and then walked out the front door. They sat quietly contemplating her question as they ate, the indistinct voices of Coyote and Bob carried back to them.

"Now. Mr. Schafer, you're a reporter whose business is information. What say you?" Rebecca finally asked.

Leo was somber when he replied. "I will never betray my family. Daniel, Sophia, and Tony are my family, and so weirdly, by extension, are you. I never thought in a million years that I would say that to Rebecca Drake, let alone a dragon. But there it is."

He suddenly laughed. "It's not like anyone would believe me anyway. But no, I'll keep these secrets."

Rebecca turned to Deb. "And you, Agent Kazdin? You've taken solemn oaths to the federal government to report criminal acts and apprehend those responsible. Tonight, you've witnessed a kidnapping and assault, and I will confess that earlier this evening, I murdered a Knight of the Stone in cold blood. What is your decision?"

"Micah… " escaped Brian's lips before Deb could respond. "You murdered Micah."

"I didn't know the man's name, but I killed him to keep him from leading an assault on Fermilab," Rebecca confessed. There was no remorse in her admission.

Deb wanted to believe that she was torn about her loyalties, but she had already made up her mind. Maybe it was the little girl in her that wanted to believe in magic. Or perhaps it was her dormant OCD wanting to bring order to a world that could no longer make sense. All she knew was that she wanted to be a part of this. "I'll keep your secrets. No one, and I mean no one, would believe even the slightest part of this even if I tried. They'd lock me up. But mark my words, Ms. Drake. I'll be keeping an eye on you. I am probably the only person in law enforcement in the world that knows what is coming, and I want to be prepared."

Rebecca nodded her understanding. "I understand your desire and accept your word." A wry smile cracked her face. "But believe me, you have no idea what's coming."

"Maybe you can help me with that." Deb countered.

"We shall see." Rebecca turned to Brian. "Well, Brian Cooke, former Knight of the Stone. Can you keep this a secret?" Rebecca leaned back and studied him while she waited for him to respond.

"I suspect you'll make me disappear no matter what I say." Brian shrugged. "I'm not sure what I could tell you that would convince you that I have no interest in returning to the Knights."

Rebecca leaned forward. "Show me the palms of your hands."

Brian looked at her oddly before slowly extending his hands toward her. "Is this some sort of weird dragon palm reading?"

The look on Rebecca's face gave off the disapproving teacher vibe. She reached out and flipped one of his hands over and inspected it. "Where is Caledfwlch?"

"Gesundheit?" Leo exclaimed.

Brian laughed out loud. "It's sad that I know this, but the Knight's records are very thorough. That's the original Welsh name for Excalibur." He reached behind Deb's chair, pulled up the case, and sat it on the floor in front of Rebecca. "You should probably keep that. It's the only way the Knights have of tracking the boy."

"Take it out," Rebecca commanded.

Her voice was so forceful that Brian bent down and opened the case without even thinking about it. The hilt was shockingly warm, but not uncomfortably so. It was like shaking the hand of an old friend. As he picked it up, the blade again burst into a dim blue flame. Not quite as brilliant as it had been at the Fitzroy house.

Deb gasped. "Your hand!"

Brian looked down in concern at his hand, now enveloped by the flames. He studied the effect with fascination. During the confrontation in the kitchen, he hadn't noticed that the fire had gone past the guard before. There was no discomfort, so he hadn't paid attention.

"That is why I believe you will not betray Tony." Rebecca seemed to be satisfied. "It is a long-held misconception that Caledfwlch, aka Excalibur, was the sword of Arthur. It was Merlin's sword, and he let Arthur use it. The whole sword in the stone thing was equally humorous. Merlin 'drew' the sword from the stone. He forged it from a lump of meteoric iron for some purpose only he knows. History has a way of hitting the high points and mucking up the real story."

"I'm not sure why that helps you trust me," Brian said.

"Because, my dear boy. The sword of Merlin does not bear the touch of those who would do him harm." She gestured at the flames. "If you had any intention of harming Tony, directly or indirectly, it would charbroil you."

Jeff McIntyre

Brian replaced the sword in its case, and the flames extinguished. "You know it's weird. Even when I'm not touching it, I can sense that he's right about there." He pointed at a spot in the ceiling that was above and to the right of Leo's head.

Rebecca gave him an approving nod, then leaned over, secured the case, and set it on her lap. "I will keep this sword safe, Ser Knight. But you should know that it has chosen you. Should you need it, you need only ask."

"Uh, sure," Brian said with a dubious expression. "Not sure when I would ever need a sword. I still think you should make me disappear."

"And disappear you I shall." She said with a mischievous look as Brian reacted with a start. "I'm going to have Joe fly you into Canada. He knows a few grass airstrips in rural areas where you can disappear. Before you leave, I'll get you some cash and a way to reach me should you need anything. I'll also work on getting you a new identity. That, combined with your own skills, should make it nearly impossible for them to find you."

"One thing you should be aware of. I left a body in the woods behind the Fitzroy's house. Another Knight that was sent to back me up." Brian looked at his hands uncomfortably. "If I didn't kill her, she would have just killed the boy."

"Tony," Deb said quietly. "His name is Tony Fitzroy, and you saved his life at great personal cost. He's no longer 'the Lock'; he's not just 'the boy.' He's living and breathing, thanks to you. Setting aside all the mystical implications of him. You saved Tony's life, and that's enough."

Coyote had quietly returned and was watching from the entryway. He strode over and put a hand on Brian's shoulder. "Burbalobonomicus has taken care of her body. He assures me that he treated her with respect, but no one will ever find her."

Brian nodded sadly. "That's good to know. I'll have to thank him before I leave."

"Rebecca, what's going on with your assistant? He's been sitting here unmoving and unresponsive to anything going on around him." Deb asked. "I had to double-check that he was even breathing."

"Jason, you may act as my assistant again," Rebecca said.

Jason swiftly stood up and smiled. "Ms. Drake, is there anything I can do for you?"

"Yes, please. If you could go upstairs to my room and pack a couple of changes of clothing for me and then leave one travel outfit on the bed, I would appreciate it." Rebecca replied.

"Of course, ma'am." Jason flashed that winning smile at Deb, "Pleasure to see you again, Agent Kazdin." Then he turned and strode out of the room and into the stairwell.

"Jason was one of Tony's greatest gifts to me." Rebecca began after Jason's footsteps had faded. "He's a magical machine indistinguishable from a human being. He's meant to keep me company and, if necessary, protect me in the times when magic is gone."

"How's that possible? If he's magical, how does he keep going when magic is gone?" Brian asked.

"Because he isn't powered directly by magic," Rebecca said with a smile. "He's powered by dragon fire. I bring him out here so I can recharge him discreetly. He's also pretty frightening in a fight, and I thought he might be useful if the Knights came for Tony."

Deb stared in the direction that Jason had gone. "I'm more than a little terrified of something that you describe as frightening."

Leo's curiosity got the best of him. "Uh, Rebecca? Can I ask you a potentially indelicate question about your family?"

Rebecca's face was inscrutable as she considered the reporter's question. Leo squirmed a bit before she finally answered. "You can ask. I may not answer."

"Fair enough." Leo exhaled in relief. "Coyote mentioned that he was the youngest of Tony's many children. How many children do you have…?" he looked a little nervously at Coyote, "and are they all… uh… immortal gods?"

Rebecca smiled at Leo's obvious discomfort. "It's not indelicate, but it is complicated. I'm not human. No matter how badly I wanted, Anki and I could not have children naturally. I bore and birthed all thirteen of them in my body as a mortal woman would, but that couldn't have happened without Tony's magic." Coyote shifted uncomfortably behind Rebecca as she said this, but Leo left it alone for now. "And yes, they are all immortal and have been worshiped as gods throughout history."

"The thirteen of us call ourselves The Kin, but that's a story for another time," Coyote interjected.

Rebecca looked side-eyed at her son before continuing. "Tony has many more children than the ones he had with me, but most of them weren't immortal per se. He became more interested in creating self-sustaining magical races over time."

"I have so many questions I think my brain might burst," Leo said.

Footsteps sounded from the stairwell behind Deb. Rebecca held up a finger. "That will have to wait."

Chapter 54

Daniel and Sophia reappeared in the stairwell. They both looked physically and emotionally exhausted. Instinctively Brian and Deb stood up to let them have the chairs directly across from Rebecca. Daniel shook his head. "No, we should all step outside. This involves Bob too."

Magically, Takashi and Elektra appeared. Takashi held up a robe for Rebecca to slip into instead of the blanket she was currently using to cover herself. As she slipped into it, Elektra placed a warm blanket around Sophia's shoulders and gave her a quick squeeze as she did so. Sophia nodded her thanks to Elektra but remained silent.

The entire household stepped outside, and the massive earthen form of Bob had been replaced with a new version. He had shrunk down to his original size but was in a more anthropomorphic form. He had distinctive arms, legs, and head. With a bit of a pot belly and warmly familiar eyes, nose, and mouth, but it was all constructed of soil and stone. He even had a grassy beard and a small sharp stone perched on his head like a hat. He gave his now familiar hat-sweeping bow to Sophia as she walked up and kneeled in front of him.

"Thank you for protecting Tony," Sophia said with sad seriousness.

Bob's earthen face was somber. "It was my pleasure. Magic has returned, the Dawning has arrived, and he is safe. Is he awakened?"

"No, he is still just Tony," Sophia said.

"Good! He deserves to be a little boy." Bob replied with a glare at Rebecca. A rough smile appeared on his face as Sophia patted him on the rock.

Sophia stood and walked to Daniel's side, but her eyes punched daggers through Rebecca as he spoke. "Tony is exhausted, but he seems fine. We woke him up briefly to let him know we were here. He hugged us, asked how Bob was, and then went back to sleep."

Rebecca was stiff with tension as she waited for him to continue.

Daniel leveled a steely glare at Rebecca. "We are still torn about what to do about you. On the one hand, you are the worst thing that has ever happened to our life. On the other, Tony is now a part of something bigger than we can handle. It's difficult to grasp how much our life has changed in such a short time. If it were just us, the decision would have been easy, but we're trying to do what's best for Tony."

Rebecca said nothing, simply waiting for the guillotine to fall.

"Tony deserves to live as normal a life as possible. We will do what we can to prepare him for what's to come. But we won't spoil his childhood." Daniel said.

Sophia cut in. "Things are going back to the way they were for him, for all of us. I won't quit my job, but I also won't be giving you status updates on how he's doing." She said bitterly.

Rebecca nodded sadly, her eyes moist.

Daniel continued. "You are to have no direct contact with him. He needs the opportunity to be a kid. We'll love and protect him the way we always have. And I'm sorry, Elektra and Takashi, but we won't be coming back to the island for quite some time."

Elektra simply nodded in understanding, but Takashi's reaction startled all of them. He sank to his knees with his eyes closed. Tears streamed down his face, and his shoulders heaved with silent sobs. Elektra wrapped her arm around the large man's head. "He'll be all right. He's very fond of Tony; he just gets like this sometimes."

Daniel paused, obviously struggling to deal with his own emotions. He finally cleared his throat and continued. "You'll be allowed to earn our trust back by staying away from us."

Rebecca's voice was strained. "Please… please don't."

"I'm not done." Daniel continued, his voice firmer. "Bob will be allowed to stay. We'll probably have to make some accommodations so that he and Tony can interact without anyone seeing, but he has proven that he will do whatever it takes to protect him." He turned to Deb. "Agent Kazdin, you barely know us, but you're a part of this now. I think we'll have to depend on you to tell us what, if anything, the government discovers about all of this."

Deb nodded. "I've already given my word to Rebecca that I will keep this secret. As long as it isn't classified, I'll keep my ear to the ground and let you know if anything comes through the system."

"Thank you, and I'm so sorry Leo drug you into this," Sophia said.

"I'm never going to hear the end of this," Leo murmured.

"No, you're not," Daniel said. "Lastly, Rebecca, we will allow you to continue all the surveillance you've undoubtedly been using to keep tabs on us. I doubt we could stop you, but you have our permission to use your resources in any way you deem suitable to protect Tony, as long as you personally keep your distance. Someday, we will introduce you into his life. But it's going to be a while, and you're going to have to prove yourself."

Rebecca collapsed to her knees. Her body shuddered as she sobbed. No one moved to console her. At long last, a hoarse whisper escaped her. It was too soft to make out. Sophia stepped forward and sank to her knees to hear what Rebecca was saying. "Thank you, thank you, thank you."

Sophia stood up and said to the top of Rebecca's head. "Don't thank us yet. I want a raise."

Rebecca's whisper turned raucous. "HA!" She slowly lifted her head and looked into Sophia's eyes. Anger, pity, sadness, and understanding looked back at her. Sophia reached down and helped her to her feet.

"All right, I think it's time for breakfast. No one should travel on an empty stomach." Elektra said. She slapped the back of Takashi's head. "Enough blubbering; we have guests to attend to."

Daniel and Sophia stood side by side outside the front door of Rebecca's home. A tired Tony, still in his pajamas, was standing in front of Sophia. Her hands wrapped around him, lending him some support.

They were going to let him sleep, but the smell of eggs and bacon had lured him downstairs. True to her word, Rebecca had disappeared into her chambers upstairs as soon as he blearily stumbled out of the stairwell.

Leo had introduced Deb and Brian as friends of his to the sleepy boy. Brian had shaken Tony's hand with a serious look on his face. Deb spontaneously called him sport, and Tony had been thrilled by that.

The Garden Gnome

Elektra had introduced 'Carl' to Tony as an old friend of hers. He and Tony became instant friends when Coyote gave him a kid-sized version of his own feather and bone necklace.

After they finished breakfast, Takashi reappeared with a small duffel bag for Brian, which he took without comment.

Awkward goodbyes were said between the adults as they all contemplated the strange future that lay before them. Tony gave sleepy hugs all around. Daniel, Sophia, and Tony would stay on the island until after Joe had returned to give Tony a little more rest and some time to say goodbye to Elektra and Takashi. Deb and Leo were returning to the city, but Joe was taking Brian to a small Ontario town on the edge of Lake Superior, so it would be a while.

They all stood there waving as Takashi's golf cart headed toward the airstrip. Leo and Deb waved back as they disappeared into the trees.

Coyote walked out and joined them. He rustled Tony's hair but said nothing.

"Mom? Can I have some more bacon?" Tony said, his voice starting to perk up a bit.

"Sure thing, kiddo," Sophia said. She leaned in and hugged Daniel before she and Tony walked back into the house. Tony mischievously closed the door behind them with a smirk at his dad.

Daniel shook his head and smiled before turning to Coyote. "I have so many questions. You've seen so much, and I want to know it all. This family, your history. The 'Kin' Leo said you called them?"

Jeff McIntyre

Coyote smiled and put a hand on Daniel's shoulder. "Relax, professor. There will be plenty of time to talk about the past. Right now, you need to be with your son." He looked off into the forest. "For now, I need to be moving on. The return of magic is going to have some dangerous ripples, and I need to keep an eye on those. I promise, when the time is right, we'll talk about history as much as you'd like." He clasped Daniel's hand and squeezed it tight, then turned and walked toward the closest trees and disappeared.

Daniel took a long deep breath, stretched his arms over his head, and let out a big yawn. The sun was coming up, casting long shadows through the trees. As he turned to head back into the house, he marveled at the way the dappled light struck the carvings in Rebecca's front doors. For the first time, he stopped to take in the design. The carvings were intricate swirls and swoops with jagged perpendicular lines at irregular intervals that separated different sections of the swirls. But if you followed them to their conclusion, there were highly stylized heads with horns, and if you squinted, the perpendicular lines could be claws, and the swoops were wings. He shook his head as he pulled the doors open. That was when he spotted a faint inscription carved into the top of the door frame facing down, where it would be hidden when the doors were closed. 'Hic sunt dracones'... Here be dragons.

Tony spun on his stool to face the front doors. "Mom? What's dad laughing at?"

Epilogue

$$E=MC^2$$

"Hey, boss man." Yuri Stepanov said as he walked into Hank Lee's office. "I've got something I want to talk to you about."

Hank looked up from his computer screen and resisted the urge to roll his eyes. "Is this about that residue your team found in the target room?"

Yuri nodded. "Yah, boss. I want to assign a team of students to run a series of tests on it."

"Yuri, it's probably just some tungsten that ablated off of the target that mixed with some carbon," Hank said disapprovingly. "You know that the focus in the target room was a little off. We let Material Science look at it, and they didn't think anything of it. I don't think it's worth the resources."

"Yah yah boss. I know all that." Yuri agreed. "But I also know that Materials is preoccupied with other stuff, so I had a couple of my students run some experiments against samples I took of the substance."

"I suppose what you do with your students is up to you," Hank said. He suddenly eyed Yuri suspiciously. "Did they find something unusual that Materials didn't?"

"Yah, boss. You could say that." Yuri said with a big smile on his face. "But you won't believe me unless I can reproduce it, and that's going to take some effort."

Hank considered Yuri's request. "Is this going to be one of those blind faith kind of requests?"

"Oh, definitely. But it won't take too long. I have a couple of people in mind that are critical to this. No one you can't spare." Yuri assured him. "It will take a couple of months to write up and run through the test scenarios I have in mind. If it works out the way I think it will, there's someone at UC Berkeley I want to collaborate with to help replicate the results."

"Oh? Doctor Peters? I think he's still in charge of their particle physics department." Hank said.

"No, boss. Doctor Abramovich." Yuri replied. "He's the head of their Behavioral Neuroscience research department."

'What? What the hell do you need to work with them for?" Hank asked.

Yuri smiled. "Like I said, you wouldn't believe me if I told you."

Jeff McIntyre was introduced to science fiction and fantasy with a three-book collection of A Wrinkle In Time, Charlie and the Chocolate Factory, and The Lion The Witch and The Wardrobe when he was eight, but his love of the genres took off in high school when he was introduced to The Foundation and The Hobbit. He has been an avid gamer his entire life. Video games, role-playing games, and table-top wargaming. The list of games he's played is very, very long. His day job is working in Telecommunications, and The Garden Gnome is his first novel.

He currently resides in Omaha, Nebraska, with his lovely wife Deb and 185 pounds of fuzzy dork named Magni and Zeus. They're Hovawarts… Look it up.

jeff-mcintyre.com

Made in the USA
Monee, IL
18 October 2022

16117032R00236